LAURA CARTER

The *Kitchen*

First published in the United Kingdom in 2021 by

Canelo
Unit 9, 5th Floor
Cargo Works, 1–2 Hatfields
London, SE1 9PG
United Kingdom

A CIP catalogue record for this book is available from the British Library.

Print ISBN 978 1 80032 583 8
Ebook ISBN 978 1 80032 174 8

This book is a work of fiction. Names, characters, businesses, organizations,
places and events are either the product of the author's imagination or are
used fictitiously. Any resemblance to actual persons, living or dead, events
or locales is entirely coincidental.

Look for more great books at www.canelo.co

Printed and bound in Great Britain by Clays Ltd, Elcograf S.p.A.

1

The Kitchen

Laura Carter writes women's fiction with a romantic slant. Exploring everyday relationships and getting under the skin of her characters is her passion. She takes inspiration from everything she overhears in cafes, so be wary of that strange woman 'listening' to music next time you're chatting over coffee. Laura lives with her family in Jersey, Channel Islands.

Rep'd by Tanera Simons of Darley Anderson Literary, TV & Film Agency.

Learn more about Laura and her books here: www.lauracarterauthor.com.

Connect with Laura through Facebook (https://www.facebook.com/lauracarterauthor), Twitter (@LCarterAuthor) and Instagram (@lauracarterauthor).

Also by Laura Carter

Girlfriends
The Kitchen

For my baby

Chapter One

Maggie

'One foie gras, one escargot, one langoustine, one Saint Jacques,' Jean-Sébastien called out from the pass as he read the handwritten check from a waiter.

Resounding replies of 'Chef' and 'Yes, Chef' came from those allocated to cooking the various elements of the starter dishes.

'Main course,' Jean-Sébastien continued. 'One Dover sole, one canard, two poulet.'

'Chef.'

'Yes, Chef.'

'Oui, Chef.'

Amongst those replying was Maggie, sous chef de cuisine to Jean-Sébastien, who served as both executive chef and head chef in his eponymous restaurant, within the Grande Parisienne Hotel, Upper East Side Manhattan.

The kitchen of the classic French restaurant was as large as the dining room, but where the dining room reflected an old-money, jackets-only, fine-dining ambience, the kitchen was slick and modern in its design. Bright and airy, it held immaculately clean rows of stainless steel work surfaces and state of the art appliances, worthy of the three Michelin stars Jean-Sébastien's had held for more than a decade.

It took fifteen chefs, working Tuesday to Saturday, with training on every other Monday, to maintain the standards required by Jean-Sébastien and the reputation of the hotel.

As soon as Jean-Sébastien called for service in his native French accent and three perfectly dressed plates of food had been carefully whisked away by a suited waiter, Maggie anticipated his next request.

'The duck jus,' she said, as Jean-Sébastien called out for a portion of foie gras – a signature dish of the restaurant.

As her boss and mentor dipped a teaspoon into her jus, she held her breath, waiting for his response.

'Exquisite,' he said, kissing the air, his fingers forming a gesture that said *perfection*.

Maggie exhaled, beaming internally and giving one curt nod externally. She strived for perfection, as Jean-Sébastien had taught her. Outwardly, she had merely done her job – she was sous chef and in control of all sauces. Inwardly, she delighted in every flawless sauce and every word of praise she received. She craved Jean-Sébastien's approval, his acknowledgement that he thought she was good enough. She was also too aware that the kitchen was a man's world and if she wanted to be seen as the best, she had to work that much harder than her male peers.

Service was starting to get into swing. With eighty covers in the restaurant spread at thirty-minute intervals from seven thirty p.m., Saturday nights peaked around nine o'clock. That was the time the shouting started at the pass, service was slower due to the unanticipated requests of guests, chefs' efforts were thrown back at them or into the trash because they had been overcooked by mere seconds. It was important for every chef to know that their components – whether they be a jus, fish, meat or vegetables – were on point before the rush began.

As Maggie moved back to her station to prepare the lemon and caper butter for the first serving of Dover sole for the evening, she received an order from Jean-Sébastien.

'Chef take the pass.'

It wasn't an uncommon request. Maggie was his second in command and would often take the pass if he had other business to attend to, such as a request to meet an important guest, or if he needed a bathroom break. Unlike many fine-dining restaurants that had an executive chef – who acted predominantly as a kitchen manager – and a head chef – who took the lead on cooking and service – Jean-Sébastien took on both roles himself, never wanting to be solely managerial. She sometimes wondered if he was also unable to relinquish control.

But what was different about this request was the pained look on Jean-Sébastien's face as he held a fist to his chest and headed unsteadily in the direction of the back door onto East 63rd Street.

'Are you okay?' she asked subtly as he walked past her.

'Just say "Yes, Chef",' he said, continuing to move.

'Yes, Chef,' Maggie said. Then she turned to a colleague and said, 'Jack, take my station.'

Jack was an apprentice chef, alternatively known in Jean-Sébastien's as a floater or sweeper. He did the running for chefs who needed ingredients or utensils, he took dirty dishes from a chef's station to the pot-wash station, and he manned a chef's station in the event of a call of nature or otherwise.

After plating up four main course dishes for table eight, Maggie glanced to the back door and found no sign of Jean-Sébastien returning. At that stage, she wasn't so much concerned, as interested in her boss seeing how beautiful the food looked on service. She had pressed the duck with her fingertips to make sure it was tender inside, tasted the jus from a teaspoon before delicately pouring it around her dish, and she had forked the texture of purée to ensure it was perfectly smooth.

From the pass, she called out for service, then proceeded to shout out the starter dishes for table nineteen, the component elements of which, for the most part, descended on her within seconds.

'Where is the pickled cabbage?' she called out, mid-plating up.

'Sorry, Chef. Here, Chef,' Lucas, a commis chef, said as he rushed to her side.

Maggie sent the three finished plates to the dining room and glanced at the large clock on the wall. Jean-Sébastien had been gone for eleven minutes. Something didn't feel right. She was about to untie her apron when a waiter carrying dirty but empty plates backed through the doors into the kitchen.

'Table ten main course, please, Chef.'

'Two Dover sole, one poulet,' Maggie read out from the white piece of paper that was tucked into the steel rim of the pass and marked as table ten's order.

By the time she had plated the poulet, she was still waiting for the Dover sole.

'Where is the sole?' she snapped into the room.

'I had to put it back on, Chef,' replied Josh, the chef de partie who was running the fish station.

'How long?' Maggie asked, her heart starting to race.

'Two minutes, Chef,' Josh told her.

Before Maggie could process the dilemma, Jean-Sébastien appeared at her side. Picking up the perfectly finished plate of poulet from the pass, he threw the plate and its entire contents into the trash and hollered, 'Do it again! Everything again!'

He turned to Maggie, his face flushed, and silenced her enquiry after his health with a glare. 'Back to your station, Chef,' he told her.

She nodded, doing exactly as she had been instructed, because like everyone else, she knew her place in the hierarchy and it was beneath Jean-Sébastien.

-

Midnight after a Saturday shift was Maggie's favourite time of the week. The chaos, though she thrived on it, was over. The kitchen surfaces were clean. Happy, full diners had left compliments for the chefs and made their way home or to their luxury rooms at the hotel for those staying.

'Here we are.' Charles, the head sommelier, made his way into the kitchen holding a tray of full wine glasses. Behind him, another member of the bar staff carried a tray of beers.

They set the full trays down on the pass and the kitchen staff descended to pick up their chosen drink, all leaning back on the work surfaces to enjoy their first mouthful of hard-earned reward at the end of a busy week.

'For you, Maggie, something new,' Charles said, handing her a glass of white wine, chilled enough to have caused a thin cloud of condensation on the glass.

Maggie held it up to the light. She knew from the pale golden colour that it would be full-bodied but crisp. Refreshing after a hot night in the kitchen. She brought the glass under her nose and inhaled citrus.

Smiling, she told Charles, 'The new Sancerre.'

'Exactly right. You liked it at the tasting, I think.'

Maggie took a sip and closed her eyes as she let the flavours of the wine explode on her palate. 'You are the best thing about my week, Charles,' she said.

He beamed in a way that made the lines at the edges of his eyes crease further. While Charles frequently bemoaned the signs of ageing (as if his shock of white hair wasn't indicative enough), Maggie loved the physical proof on Charles' face of his characteristic warmth and humour – always to be found, even after a long and gruelling shift.

'So many people have expressed similar sentiments this evening, my dear.'

As Maggie laughed, Charles straightened his tie, then the jacket of his suit, and he came to rest against the pass between Maggie and Jean-Sébastien, each of the men holding onto a glass of Burgundy. Despite being close in age, where Charles wore his sixty-odd years with the charm of receding height, darkening sun-kissed skin and a rotund tummy, Jean-Sébastien was tall and lean and had retained freshness in his skin and colour in his hair – an impressive feat after years of stress in the kitchen.

'Good service tonight, everyone. Thank you for your efforts,' Jean-Sébastien announced, raising his glass.

As usual, the chefs started to banter amongst themselves, throwing jibes around the room, though rarely aimed at Maggie, the only female in the kitchen. She hoped it was her more senior position and not that after six years working in the kitchen they still didn't see her as one of them.

'Excellent work tonight, Maggie, as always,' Jean-Sébastien said, leaning into Maggie's ear as he placed his almost full glass of red wine on the pass beside her. 'I'm going to head home a little early tonight.'

'Is everything okay?'

He seemed to force a smile, nodding as he pressed a hand to Maggie's shoulder. Then, uncommonly early, he was gone.

'You know, I'm going to take off too,' Maggie said, receiving acknowledgement only from Charles, who kissed her cheeks and, with the French lilt he had retained despite more than two decades of living in New York, told her, 'Goodnight, ma chérie.'

In the back of a hotel cab – free to staff – Maggie took off her white hat and released her long brown hair from the tight chignon it had been held in for more than twelve hours. Her neck clicked as she rolled her head from side to side.

It was a short ride to her one-bedroom apartment at this time in the morning but there was no shortage of cabs, tourists and weekend party-goers on the streets of New York City. It was one of the things she loved and loved to hate about New York – the city truly never slept. And right now, that was all she wanted to do, without noise from the streets beneath her bedroom window. But late August was still bringing some muggy nights, the stuffy heat of summer not yet cooling off and she couldn't sleep with the window closed.

She traipsed up the three flights of stairs in the old building with heavy legs. Inside her apartment, she was welcomed home by Livvy, her beautiful, silver-grey Egyptian Mau.

'Hi girl,' she said, setting her handbag and keys down on the kitchen counter as she picked up the cat. 'What have you been up to, huh?'

Livvy was a rescue that Maggie had taken into her care two years ago, as a twenty-eighth birthday present to herself. A house cat, Livvy was generally quite happy in her own company but sometimes she needed a snuggle on the sofa – just like Maggie. They were a perfect match.

Navigating the kitchen with one hand as she held Livvy in the other, Maggie poured herself a glass of home-infused mint and cucumber water from the refrigerator and crossed the open-plan living area to unwind on her sofa with an old episode of *Friends*. As exhausted as she felt after a long shift, she was also too wired to go right to bed. Her mind ran through every dish she had made and everything, no matter how miniscule, she could have improved in her never-ending bid for flawlessness.

She heard her mom's words: *dreamer, fantasist*. Words that Maggie had been told over and over as a girl. Words that gave Maggie as big a reason as any to prove her worth in a kitchen like Jean-Sébastien's.

At some point, sleep must have got the better of her because she woke on the sofa with a start just after three a.m. as her phone rang, vibrating loudly against the glass-topped coffee table.

Netflix had paused – *continue watching?* – and Livvy was nowhere to be seen. Rubbing her eyes, Maggie reached for her phone.

Who on earth would call at this time?

When she saw the name Isabella dancing on her screen, Maggie accepted the call, her heart racing without her truly knowing why. All she did know was that Jean-Sébastien's wife didn't often call, and she had never called Maggie in the middle of the night.

'Isabella? Is everything okay?'

'Maggie… it's… it's Jean-Sébastien. He's… he's dead.'

Chapter Two

Emily

Emily groaned as she rolled over in bed, coming out of her alcohol-induced coma with the kind of headache that made her think she'd been hit by a truck. In actual fact, she'd been hit by the inevitable consequences of a pre-dinner cocktail, an eight-course tasting menu paired with wine, and one, no two, possibly three digestifs in the form of a very nice fortified wine. For the record, the digestifs did not aid her digestion but resulted in her head hanging over a porcelain pot as soon as she arrived home.

Would she ever learn?

Through the ringing in her ears, she could hear the familiar slide and clink of Oliver's rowing machine as he carried out his Sunday morning regime in the other room. The sound told her it was not even nine a.m., despite the fact that Oliver was fully aware that she hadn't got to bed until the early hours after dinner last night. Oliver was one of those people who just couldn't lie in, no matter how pig-selfish he was being.

It wasn't as if she had just had a night out on cocktails with the girls, she had been working. It didn't sound much like work, as Oliver liked to remind her, but she was the lead restaurant critic for the *New York Times* and that meant she had to spend her evenings eating indigestion-inducing rich food paired with copious amounts of alcohol.

Okay, so it was a job with perks. But as she staggered from her bed, pulling on her robe from the back of the bedroom door, her mouth so dry the skin of her lips was peeling, knowing she had to write a twelve-hundred-word review by Monday lunchtime, she didn't feel so perky.

She and Oliver had been together for two years. A combination of Oliver's Wall Street salary and her salary from *NYT* had recently allowed them to purchase a bright, open apartment in Brooklyn Heights, with a waterfront view and, traffic dependent, relatively quick access to the city across Brooklyn Bridge. She popped a pod into the coffee machine in the kitchen and switched it on. Then she sliced in half four Jaffa oranges and put them into the presser because pressed is best.

Armed with a glass of fresh orange and a black coffee laced with a hangover helping of sugar, she made her way through the lounge to the Juliet balcony window and watched the sun dance across the East River.

'Emily, would you call your mother? She's left five missed calls on my phone in the last hour,' Oliver said, appearing from the second bedroom, shirtless and sweating. 'Each time it cut out my workout music.'

'My mom? Oliver, why didn't you answer? She never calls.'

He shrugged as he flung a towel around his shoulders and moved into the kitchen.

Emily couldn't remember when she last had her phone. Looking around the lounge, she saw her handbag on the floor next to the sofa.

'Eleven missed calls. What does she want?' Emily asked aloud, coming to sit on the sofa.

'How about call and ask her?' Oliver said in his mocking, childish tone, which drove Emily up the wall whenever he did it.

Scowling at his back as he left the room with a large glass full of iced water, Emily dialled her mom's landline, but it wasn't her mom who answered.

'Emily, it's Maggie. Thank you for calling.'

'I called my mom. Why are you answering the phone in her house?' Emily snapped.

After her father, Maggie was second in line for the people Emily least wanted to talk to, ever.

'Your mom is sleeping, and she's only just managed to go off.'

'Fine. Tell her to call me—'

'Emily, it's your dad. He… he had a heart attack.'

Despite herself, Emily sat up straighter and asked, 'How is he?'

'I'm so, so sorry, Emily. He didn't make it.'

Emily's heart started pounding in her chest. 'What do you mean he didn't make it?'

'He's… He died.'

—

'I don't understand why you're rushing off. You don't speak to your dad. Or, you know, didn't,' Oliver said, now dressed in a button-down shirt and lounge pants after his shower.

Emily paused mid-pulling a sweater over her head. 'I have to go see mom.' Slipping the garment into place and tucking it into her jeans, she said, 'Plus, *Maggie* is already there.'

'Maggie? Fine. So, are we still going to lunch with the Sandersons?'

Emily glared at him. 'Clearly not, Olly.'

'Well, what should I tell them?'

'Tell them my dad died! God, Olly. They're friends, they'll understand.'

He turned, leaving the room, muttering as he went, 'He's a client not just a friend, and a damn lucrative one.'

She probably wasn't sober enough to be driving but Emily took the chance, heading to her parents' house in record time, thanks to the limited Sunday traffic.

When knocking lightly on the door didn't receive a response, Emily decided to use her old key, hoping the locks hadn't been changed in the six years since she had last felt welcome enough to let herself into her parents' home.

She hadn't been to the house at all for five, maybe six months, since her mother's birthday, but nothing had changed. Nothing ever changed. The wood floor of the hallway. The oil pictures in gold frames on the walls. The vintage banister of the staircase. There was no noise in the house, so Emily made her way through to the large, well-stocked kitchen and filled the water pot in the oversized, ex-restaurant owned coffee machine her parents kept on their breakfast bar, leaving it to heat as she went in search of her mother.

In the dining room, the old walnut table was set as it always was, with plate placers, glasses and a candelabra. In the lounge, she found the outline of a person curled up and sleeping under a blanket on one of the sofas. But it wasn't her mother. The long dark hair and tall, slender frame was Maggie's.

With a sudden burst of rage, Emily pulled the lounge door shut as loudly as she could without causing the picture frames to fall from the walls.

Maggie's limbs jerked as she instantly came awake. Beautiful, talented, perfect freakin' Maggie.

'I'm here now, you can go,' Emily said.

Maggie moved up to sit and pushed the blanket from her lap to one side.

'Emily, I'm so, so sorry about your dad. He was—'

'Is mom still sleeping?'

Maggie nodded, and the women fell into an awkward silence, their eyes locked until Maggie stood and folding the discarded blanket, said, 'Okay, Emily, I'll go. But if you or Isabella need anything, you know how to contact me.'

Emily watched her old friend in silence as she placed the folded blanket on a nearby foot stool, grabbed her phone and keys from the coffee table and made to leave. In times gone by, Maggie would have stayed over in Emily's bed or in the spare bedroom that had been considered her own. It struck Emily as an odd but not unwelcome sight that Maggie had felt more comfortable on the sofa.

'I suppose it's a good career break for you, huh?' Emily called out, knowing it was a hateful statement but unable to stop the venom leaving her. 'I guess you'll finally be able to fill his shoes. The mentee becomes the head chef. Congrats.'

Maggie turned quickly. 'If you think there's any part of me that even remotely sees a silver lining in this, you're even more messed up than I give you credit for.' Then she sighed and added, 'Make peace with him, Emily. For your sake and your mom's.'

Emily watched Maggie leave, preferring not to acknowledge her red-rimmed and puffy eyes or that she should be looking as drained as Maggie did from being up all night comforting her mom. Instead, she set about making two cups of coffee and headed upstairs in search of her mom.

The carpet was softer under her feet than she remembered, and she wondered if they had replaced the old carpet with a new, identical one – which would be just like her parents, stuck in their ways.

As she walked, Emily ignored the family pictures that lined the staircase in chronological order. She didn't need to watch herself grow. She didn't need to see the smiling faces of the happy family they had once been.

But she did stop in front of one framed picture at the top of the landing. The image came alive as if she was standing behind the camera lens in real time, snapping the memory of her father in front of a Michelin banner, his smile almost jaw-breaking, and his arm draped around the shoulders of his sous chef, Maggie. The apple of his eye.

She wasn't sure how long she had been staring at the picture before she remembered she was on the landing of her parents' home, holding two hot mugs of coffee.

Pushing open the door to her parents' bedroom gently, she saw the petite frame of her mother lying on top of the covers, fully clothed. Emily's first instinct was to watch for the rise and fall of her chest.

Rather than wake her, Emily placed one mug of coffee gently on the bedside table. Then she slipped the black and white photograph of her parents on their wedding day out of Isabella's hand and folded the duvet from the empty side of the bed across her mother.

Being careful not to make a sound, Emily made her way back downstairs with her own coffee, took her laptop from the weekend bag she had brought with her and set herself up to work on the kitchen table.

After two mugs of coffee, her hangover was manageable, and her words were beginning to flow.

> …the succulent meat of the pork belly oozed with flavour beneath crackling crisped to perfection… the sharp apple finish of the wine was a finely matched accompaniment to the splendid fifth course.

And although the food had been truly wonderful, as she recalled the tastes and aromas from last night, her stomach churned. Barely making it to the downstairs loo, Emily threw up the contents of her near-empty stomach.

Chapter Three

Nayomi

'Roshan, let's go, we'll be late,' Nayomi called along the hallway of her two-bedroom apartment in Queens. Her youngest son, Nuwan, was already waiting by the front door with his backpack on, ready to go.

Nuwan was seven and loved nothing more than running around the school yard with his friends. Roshan, by contrast, was ten-going-on-eighteen and currently found everything in life to be *so uncool*.

'Roshan,' she called again.

'I can't find my shin pads for soccer,' Roshan snapped back.

'Do you really need them?'

In response to her question, Roshan stepped out of the boys' bedroom into the hallway, his shirt unbuttoned, his trousers unfastened, his hair not yet combed, and asked, 'Have you ever been kicked in the shins?'

This seemed a fair point and so Nayomi headed to the boys' room, telling Roshan, 'Finish getting dressed, quickly. I'll find—' Picking up Roshan's duvet from the floor, Nayomi spotted the shin pads.

'Right, let's go, you can button up as we walk.'

Outside on the street, Roshan trudged huffily beside Nayomi. Nuwan happily held onto her hand, waving at familiar faces they passed each day on the walk to school.

'Why are we in such a rush today, anyway?' Roshan asked, kicking a mouldy lemon that had fallen from a trash bag on the street.

'We're in no more of a rush than any other day, Roshan, but today I have a job interview and I can't be late. I don't want to make a bad first impression.'

'You already have a job,' he muttered in that way pre-adolescents do, too lazy to enunciate.

She did already have a job, working locally as a seam-stress. Her boss was flexible in letting Nayomi start after she had dropped the boys at school and finish in time to pick them up. Sometimes she would sew on her own machine at home, if they happened to have a spike in demand, which often coincided with the start of a new school year and seasonally for Christmas parties.

But flexibility came at a cost. Nayomi was paid peanuts. She and the boys lived on the breadline and had done for two years, since her husband had lost his battle with cancer. She was fortunate to have a job at all, having never worked before Shan's death and lacking any meaningful skills or education. Every week she worried that it might be a week her employer just couldn't afford to pay her, or she might lose her job. Then what? The only thing she could be thankful for was that her apartment, small and cramped though it might be, was paid for.

Now, Roshan was getting to an age where his school trips were costing money and while he never pressed her about it, she didn't ever want her boys to miss out. It was bad enough that she couldn't afford the latest sneakers and branded backpacks for them. Roshan's soccer kit was a fake Inter Milan kit that had cost twenty bucks from a friend of a friend. Roshan hadn't asked questions when he opened the birthday gift and as far as Nayomi could tell, it was a good replica. But that same week, Nayomi had been forced to ask a neighbour if she could spare butter so she could bake a small birthday cake.

'I know I have a job, but this one would be extra work, in the evenings, after you guys are home from school.'

'Who would look after us? I'm not looking after him.' Roshan's expression was one of such utter disdain that it made Nayomi laugh.

'I have a plan, don't worry. Anyway, I might not get the job.'

When they reached the school gates, Nayomi crouched down and kissed Nuwan on the temple. 'Have a good day. Have fun. Learn lots. Do what your teacher tells you.'

Nuwan give her the shortest hug and told her, 'You too, Mom,' leaving her smiling after him.

She stood, knowing that she mustn't baby Roshan in front of his school friends – a discussion, or argument, they had had numerous times – and held up a hand in a subtle wave. 'Have a good day, Roshy.'

To her surprise, after a quick glance around, Roshan stepped towards her, gave her a nano-second hug and said, 'Good luck. I love you.'

Nayomi watched her boys walk into school, swallowing the lump that had formed in her throat. Then she checked her watch and rushed to the subway station to get to her interview.

Chapter Four

Maggie

Tuesdays were the first day of the working week for Maggie. The restaurant had been closed for over two weeks, as a mark of respect. Now the funeral had passed and life, it seemed, was supposed to just get back to 'normal'. *How could life be normal at Jean-Sébastien's without Jean-Sébastien?*

Maggie took a steeling breath then stepped through the back door to the restaurant. Usually, she and Jean-Sébastien were the first people in the kitchen but this morning, when she flicked on the lights, it was empty. The countertops were gleaming under the fluorescence of the lights. There were no pots or pans on the benches. No ingredients or other signs that Jean-Sébastien was trying a new dish or making himself breakfast.

The space felt… empty.

Had it not been for the faint smell of toast filtering through from the buffet breakfast in the main dining room of the hotel, Maggie could have imagined she had walked into the end of the world.

'It's strange, isn't it?' Charles spoke in his usual calming voice but still managed to startle Maggie when he stepped into the kitchen from the restaurant dining room. 'Nothing looks different, yet everything has changed.'

They hadn't seen each other since the funeral a week earlier. Maggie crossed the room to embrace Charles. It felt nice to be in someone's arms and cold when she stepped back from him.

'How about I rustle us up some crêpes – ham, egg and cheese, just how you like them?' Maggie asked, trying to sound upbeat but unsure if she achieved it.

Charles gave her what was barely a smile. 'My cuisine princess. That would be *merveilleux*. I'll do drinks. Mimosa or Bloody Mary?'.

'How about a Virgin Mary?'

With a nod, Charles left the kitchen. Maggie nipped to the staff changing room where she took her laundered white jacket and black trousers from the chef closet and quickly swapped them for her skinny jeans and sweater, braiding her hair in the mirror.

In the kitchen, Maggie took her ingredients from the commercial refrigerator, which was more of a giant cupboard. The food orders she had placed two days ago in anticipation of the kitchen reopening would be arriving over the course of the morning. Food ordering would typically have fallen to Jean-Sébastien, and Maggie had struggled to stay focused during the task.

She warmed the crêpe pan that lived in the pâtissier station and set about whisking her light batter in a bowl. With the mixture poured thinly over the rounded pan, she carved thin slices of cured ham from a joint and cut fine chunks of Gruyère cheese. She cracked an egg into the middle of the almost-cooked crêpe, then added the ham, cheese and some light seasoning to the top.

Perfectly timed as she plated the first crêpe, Charles came back into the kitchen carrying a tray aloft with two Virgin Mary mocktails. He flicked his hand in a way that usually accompanied him saying 'voilà!' but this morning, he was silent.

By the time he had brought two bar stools into the kitchen, Maggie had set out two mouthwatering crêpes. As she took her first forkful of the dish, she realised it was one of the first proper meals that she had eaten over the last couple of weeks. Barring the bread or cakes she baked as a distraction, the only savoury food she had made since Jean-Sébastien died had been for Isabella and Emily. She longed to be invited to share the meals with them but with Emily's scowl ever-present, Maggie had managed only brief chats with Isabella, each along the lines of *How are you holding up? If there's anything I can do, anything at all...*

'Maggie, this is delicious. Just how I like it.'

Maggie smiled. One of her favourite things in the world was to see people enjoy her cooking. Praise wasn't just something she liked but something she needed, after an entire childhood starved of support or encouragement. 'Would you like another?'

'Oh, no, no, no.' Charles patted his round stomach beneath his shirt. 'I don't have the metabolism I used to. My wife tells me, "No more treats, Charles". And do you know what I tell her?'

'What?'

'I tell her, "Maggie makes me do it."'

They shared a short laugh as she finished the remnants of her food and set about clearing their plates.

Charles replaced his tailored suit jacket which he had slipped off to eat and dabbed the sides of his lips with a napkin. 'So, circumstances aside, how does it feel to be the head of your own kitchen?'

Maggie looked at him through narrowed eyes. 'How do you mean?'

'You were second in command, Maggie. Without Jean-Sébastien, you're the head chef, no?'

Leaning back against the sink, Maggie flicked her chef towel over her shoulder and folded her arms. 'I guess. I've tried not to think about it, to be honest. I mean, I knew I would have to step up until we find our new normal, I suppose, but I haven't had a conversation with William yet, or Alexander.'

William Boucher, whom everyone loved, was the now semi-retired proprietor of the restaurant and good friend of Jean-Sébastien's. The pair had been in the business together since the beginning. Latterly, William had been turning over the reins to his son, Alexander. Maggie wasn't sure who the conversation would be with but she knew it was inevitable because, while she hated it, change had arrived at their doorstep in the form of tragedy.

Now, she thought about the prospect of being head chef of her own Michelin-starred kitchen. It was never how she would have wanted to come into the role but she couldn't deny the flutter in her stomach as she realised she was on the cusp of her dreams coming true. Years of hard work, sacrifice and painful lessons – both physical and metaphorical – might finally pay off. Years of being mocked by her parents for being a 'dreamer' and a 'fantasist' and finally she would have the last laugh.

'But do you think they'll appoint me? Don't you think they'll look for someone else, someone with more experience? I mean, head chef maybe, at a push, but executive chef?'

Charles took hold of her face in his palms like a father might to a child. 'More experience than being trained by the best? More experience than being sous chef to the best? Maggie, Maggie, Maggie, the job will be yours and you have earned it. You deserve it.'

She took a long deep breath as Charles released his hold on her and all she could think to say was, 'Oh boy.'

'Oh boy, oh boy, oh boy,' Charles said, wafting a hand and chuckling as he left Maggie alone… in her very own kitchen.

Her own kitchen. *Wow. Just, wow.*

She hadn't had time to process the idea when Alexander, the restaurant manager and in-grooming son of the proprietor, came into the kitchen. Though his father hadn't relinquished full control to Alexander, as yet, Alexander seemed to think he owned the place already and apparently, that that gave him reason to act like an entitled—

'Good, you're here,' he said. 'We need to discuss things. I know it's still early days…' He fiddled with the cufflinks attached to his too-tight fitted navy shirt as he spoke. 'I'm sure you're sad.'

Sad? Understatement of the century. He was such a jerk.

Jean-Sébastien had not cared one bit for Alexander. But as long as Alexander kept his nose out of the kitchen, Jean-Sébastien had tolerated him, no doubt out of respect for his friend and business partner.

Nevertheless, rolling her shoulders back, Maggie thought she'd best take a leaf out of her mentor's book. 'Sure, I understand. I'm free now?'

'Right. Now's as good a time as any.' He dragged a hand through his fancily groomed dark hair and raised eyes completely devoid of empathy, to look at her. 'The running of the kitchen…'

Maggie braced herself. This was it. The moment she became head chef. It was a shame it was Alexander telling her but still…

'Go on,' she encouraged.

But before Alexander could finish his sentence, the kitchen phone rang. Maggie moved to answer but Alexander beat her to it.

'Alexander speaking. Yeah. Damn it, I'd forgotten about that. Can she come back another day, like when we haven't just reopened? She only came from Queens, it's not like she's travelled for days… Fine, bring her to the dining room in Jean-Sébastien's.'

He hung up the phone as Maggie resisted the temptation to rest her hands on her hips in annoyance.

'We'll talk later,' he said, turning to Maggie. 'We've got to do an interview.'

'An interview?'

'Yes, Jean-Sébastien and I were interviewing for a new pot wash to replace the other one. What's his name? Doesn't matter. She'll be here in a minute, do you want to tidy yourself up?'

Maggie felt her eyes go wide as Alexander slithered out of the kitchen. She hadn't felt the need to *tidy herself up* but now she would have to do a quick check in the ladies' room.

With her uniform straightened, Maggie headed into the restaurant dining room to see a petite woman with long, thick black hair, braided like her own, and rare golden eyes that shone against her brown skin. Despite the slightly grungy nature of the job, the woman had clearly made an effort for the interview, wearing a smart blouse beneath a leather jacket, tucked into the waistband of her indigo chinos. Though she wore practical sneakers, they were royal blue in colour and decorated sparingly with small studs to give them a smarter look.

The woman was shaking Alexander's hand. 'It's a pleasure to meet you. I'm Nayomi.'

Maggie smiled as she approached the pair and held out her hand. 'Hi there, I'm Maggie.'

'The sous chef,' Nayomi said. 'So nice to meet you.'

She had done her homework. No one had ever done their homework for the role of a kitchen porter, Maggie thought.

'Shall we sit?' Alexander instructed more than asked.

As they tucked into a table – Maggie and Alexander on one side, Nayomi on the other – Nayomi twisted her fingers in her lap, obviously nervous. 'I just want to say, before we start, that I'm sorry about Jean-Sébastien. I read about it on your website. And thank you for not cancelling my interview, when I know you've been closed.'

The words caught Maggie off guard and perhaps due to their obvious sincerity, she felt tears threaten her eyes. 'Would you like a drink, Nayomi? Tea, coffee, water? If you have a hot drink I'm sure we could find some petit fours.'

With a soft smile, Nayomi thanked Maggie and accepted the offer. Charles, who had been pottering in the restaurant situating wine buckets at table sides according to the evening's seating plan, offered to arrange the drinks.

'Since you brought it up, Nayomi, now isn't the best day for us,' Alexander said. 'We need to regroup and, to be honest, I just forgot to cancel the interview.'

As the woman across from them visibly sank in her seat, Maggie wanted to kick him under the table.

'Yes,' she interrupted, 'that's true. But you are here now and we're glad that you are. Our regrouping doesn't mean that we don't need a new kitchen porter.'

Nayomi's head shot up and Maggie saw something in her eyes that made her want to hire the woman on the spot. Was it hope? Desperation?

No one dreamed of being a kitchen porter. This was a job a woman was willing to travel from Queens each day to do. It was a job she needed.

'Do you have any kitchen experience?' Alexander asked too sharply to hide his annoyance with Maggie.

'Not specifically. Not in a commercial kitchen, anyway, but I cook and clean at home.'

Maggie didn't need to look to know that Alexander would be doing something akin to rolling his eyes.

Just then, Charles cut the tension by delivering three coffees and a plate of homemade petit fours.

'Try the white chocolate and mango one,' Maggie said.

Nayomi did, taking a moment to appreciate the treat. 'Oh my goodness, I'm sorry, it's just so good.'

Maggie chuckled. She liked Nayomi. There was just something about her, not least that Maggie would like to have another woman in the kitchen. But Alexander was a tough audience, rudely checking his watch.

'So, you have no experience?' he asked.

Nayomi took a breath and seemed to grow taller and stronger in her seat. 'I'm an incredibly hard worker. I'm reliable. Always on time. And I know these kinds of jobs aren't passion work for people. I know they're hard to keep staffed. Well, not me. I have two boys who are fully dependent on the money I bring into our home. If you hire me, I'll be here every day, I'll do exactly as you ask, and I won't up and leave three months from now.' Nayomi paused and Maggie couldn't resist giving her a small nod of encouragement. 'My current employer said he'll give me a reference and, just so you know, he has no problem with me taking on a second job.'

'You already have a job?' Alexander asked.

'Er, yes, I'm a seamstress but it won't affect my work here, I promise. I get off work to pick up my boys from school. I'll get them home then catch the subway here in time for my shift.'

'How old are your boys?' Maggie asked, trying to relieve some pressure from Nayomi.

'Ten and seven. They're really good boys and I have childcare sorted already.'

They were interrupted by the bleeping of Alexander's pager. He stood, ignoring Nayomi, and told Maggie, 'I have business to deal with. Can I trust you to wrap this up?'

Trust her? Dick.

He eyed her in a way that told her exactly how he wanted the interview to end; with Nayomi making the trek back to Queens without a job offer.

Once he was out of earshot, Maggie told Nayomi, 'It would be five nights a week, Tuesday to Saturday. You would have to stay as late as we needed, unless you could work something out with Bill, the other porter. Generally, service finishes around eleven, a little later on Friday and Saturday nights. The hotel cabs will take you home for free and you'll be paid weekly in arrears. How does that sound?'

Nayomi pressed her lips together, as if she was trying to contain her excitement, then she said, with a slight tremor in her voice, 'It sounds perfect.'

'How soon can you start? Is next week feasible?'

Nayomi nodded vigorously. 'Next week is perfect. Thank you so much, Maggie. I mean, Chef.'

Maggie smiled. 'I'm Chef when we're in the kitchen. Otherwise, you can call me Maggie.'

'Thank you, Maggie. Thank you so much.'

Just like that, Maggie had taken her first executive decision as stand-in head chef. And she had taken her first step towards ticking off Alexander the Great Big Jackass.

—

Maggie looked around the kitchen, taking in the chatter passing between the chefs, the smell of stocks and sauces that had been prepared throughout the afternoon. Leaning back against the pass, waiting for the first order of her first service as acting head chef, she thought everything looked right. But it didn't feel right. There was a huge presence missing. A hole the size of Jean-Sébastien.

'Okay, everyone, let's gather around for a minute,' she said to the kitchen generally.

The chefs who could leave their stations unattended moved closer to Maggie.

She stood up straighter and smoothed her white jacket. 'I just want to say, I appreciate that everything feels strange and tonight's service is going to be tough. In losing Jean-Sébastien, I've lost much more than a head chef and colleague. I've lost a mentor and a friend. I know that's the same for you all, too.'

Maggie inhaled a sharp breath, her hands shaking.

'There will only ever be one Jean-Sébastien and I'm not trying to stand in his shoes. There's no part of me that would have wished to become head chef in this way. I hope you already know that.'

She swallowed deeply and when that didn't clear her throat, she coughed gently, until she felt composed.

'I think the best way to honour Jean-Sébastien, and what he would want, is for us to put on a great service tonight. One that he could be proud of. One that maintains his high quality and standards. Tonight, and for every service after. So, let's get our heads down and let's make our best dishes. No mistakes, no slips. The best. The way Jean-Sébastien has always been. Are you with me?'

She dared to look around the space, feeling empowered more than sad, ready to make Jean-Sébastien proud. To prove she had what it took to head up his kitchen, albeit she hadn't yet been formally appointed.

A resounding chorus of 'Yes, Chef' followed, just as a waiter came into the kitchen with the first check of the night.

This was it. Time to step up. 'Check on,' Maggie called. 'One foie gras. Two Saint Jacques to start. Followed by one duck, two sole.'

When Maggie received only one 'Yes, Chef' in response she asked, 'Did you hear me?' Only then did she receive a full cohort of responses.

Did she need to be louder?

It was ridiculous that she should be so nervous. It wasn't as if she had never stood in for Jean-Sébastien but tonight felt different. She felt like all eyes were on her, watching her, waiting for her to be flawed, deficient, wanting by comparison to her predecessor. She felt exposed and under pressure. The heat of the kitchen, which never usually bothered her, tonight felt too hot and irritating against her skin. She was aware of her jacket collar pressing around her neck and the way her hat rubbed against her ears.

It wasn't until she had called for service on her third table of the evening that her nerves settled, her pounding heart calmed and the tremble in her fingers as she tried to delicately finish her plates dissipated.

Then came words that she really hadn't wanted to hear tonight of all nights. The head waiter appeared at the pass. 'Chef, we have a last-minute special guest on table two. Alexander sent me to tell you.'

Though inwardly Maggie's chest felt like someone had stuck a fish knife in it and let all the air out, she asked with a deceptive calm, 'Who is it?'

'Erm, crap, I've forgotten. Wait, I read it. A chef. Erm—'

Charles appeared at the pass, as smart as ever in his suit and tie and said, 'It's Ethan James.'

'Ethan James,' said the waiter, clicking his fingers. 'That's right. Sorry.'

'Ethan James?' Maggie asked, unable to stop herself rounding the pass and poking her head out of the kitchen door to look into the restaurant.

Sure enough, there was Ethan James, sitting at table two and looking as handsome and dapper as always. His admittedly extreme good looks were ruined by the fact he knew just how attractive he was – and that his beauty was only skin deep. Alexander was sitting opposite him and they both appeared to be drinking an apéritif. On colour alone, Maggie would have surmised whisky. Scottish. Single malt. Ethan James's drink of celebration.

'What is he doing here?' she asked herself, only to receive a reply from Charles, who was also now peering into the dining room across Maggie's shoulder. 'Your guess is as good as mine.'

'And so, the vultures descend. Knowing Ethan James, he'll have come to see me mess up, then gloat about it to his Michelin-star groupies.' She stepped back into the kitchen, her arms folded across her chest, a scowl planted on her face.

'Just don't give him a reason to gloat,' Charles said, rubbing her arm in reassurance.

The check soon came in for Ethan James's order and Maggie read out his choice of foie gras, followed by poulet. 'This order is for Ethan James, guys, let's not give him a reason to say that we aren't up to scratch, okay?'

When it came time to serve Ethan's starter, Maggie was meticulous in checking that the dish was faultlessly cooked and precisely presented.

Polishing the edge of the white plate with her chef's towel, she muttered for her own benefit, 'Why would Ethan James, of all people, have to come tonight, of all nights?'

Except the words must have been louder than she thought because Josh, who was lingering by the pass and reviewing the orders of fish he had on, flipped his towel across his shoulder and replied, 'Because he's a dick, Chef. What do you expect when he's a friend of Alexander's?'

And as Maggie allowed Ethan's starter plate to be carried away, she couldn't help but smirk. Ethan had been an arrogant, self-important ass at chef's school and the few times their paths had crossed since then, his behaviour had only cemented Maggie's opinion of him as an entitled, elitist jerk.

Well, that plate of foie gras had been no less than perfect, *so up yours, Ethan James, you hateful vulture.*

Chapter Five

Emily

It was a beautiful morning. The sun shone between the high rises and cast an orange sheen along 42nd Street. Emily had decided to take the subway to the Bryant Park and have a pre-work stroll around one of her favourite green spots in the city with her preferred morning companion – a coconut milk latte carefully heated to the precisely right temperature.

Given that her job consisted primarily of eating out five to seven days per week and writing one weekly publishable review, there wasn't much need for her to work from the office but she preferred the background noise to the solitary silence of working from home.

Fuelled by her caffeine hit and suitably energised by people-watching in the park, Emily made her way to her office on 8th Avenue.

In the *New York Times* building, she stepped into the elevator with four other journalists. Right before the elevator doors closed, a hand pushed bravely against one door and the body that followed the hand belonged to Emily's friend and fellow food section reporter, Janey.

'Oh my God, it's so sticky out there this morning,' Janey said, fanning her face with a copy of *Marie Claire*. She lifted her sunglasses to the top of her head, pushing the ends of her caramel bob behind her ears. As she fussed with her bangs, she asked Emily, 'Do I have panda eyes?'

Emily checked. 'You're good.' Feeling obliged, she added, 'Do I?'

'Nope. Fully hot. Fully immaculate, as always.'

'What do you want?' Emily asked in good humour.

'What every person who pays a woman a compliment wants…'

'A blow job?'

Janey snorted. 'I'll settle for a Thai lunch.' The elevator pinged to announce its arrival at their floor. 'One o'clock at that cheap place I like on 9th Avenue?'

They turned a corner and walked nearly the length of the office to get to their desks, which were happily right next to each other. Emily liked the background noise of the open-plan office but she wasn't a huge fan of the staff, Janey aside. As Janey had told her on more than one occasion, it didn't much matter because Emily was one of those people others either loved or hated and, in the office, people mostly hated her.

Almost as soon as Emily's computer came to life, her IMs pinged with a new message:

Archer Turnbull (Food Section Editor)
I'd like to see you in my office.

'Urgh, Archer wants to see me. I'm going to need another coffee. Do you want one?'

When Janey replied that she was full to her limit on caffeine, Emily made her own instant coffee, then made her way to her boss's office, gently tapping on the closed door.

'Come in!'

'Hi. You wanted to see me?'

'Great, come in, Emily. Sit down.'

As Archer went to sip coffee from his take-out cup, somehow missing his foghorn mouth and dripping the drink down the front of his shirt, Emily pretended not to look, instead lifting a messy pile of papers from the chair in front of his desk and placing it on the floor to befriend many other similar piles.

Emily wondered if she should wave the white flag now and confess that she knew last week's article had been below par but that she had written it under the circumstances of one, a major hangover, and two, looking after her grieving mother. *Or were they just the latest excuses she was making for her general lack of enthusiasm for the job?*

Rubbing his shirt pointlessly with a tissue, Archer finally met Emily's eyes. 'I want you to know you don't have to be here.'

Her eyes narrowed. 'Come again?'

'I know about your dad dying and I'm very sorry to hear the news. You don't have to be here. Take some time. The paper reported that he died suddenly. A heart attack, was it?'

'Oh, ah…'

'You look surprised. Have I said the wrong thing?'

She had never seen Archer quite so flustered. Angry, bothered, irritated, crabby. Yep, all of those she had known, but never flustered.

'I thought you were going to say my critique hadn't been up to par last week.'

'Actually, I thought your article last week was top drawer.'

'Oh…'

'Now you look even more surprised.'

A smirk tugged on Emily's lips. 'Archer, you ask to see me in your office around four times a year. Only one in four of those times do you compliment me or my work and that one time is usually during the Christmas party season, when I'm fairly certain you're drunk. So, forgive me for looking a little surprised.'

Archer stopped fussing with his shirt and shook his head. 'All right, I admit, you seem your usual, pain-in-the-ass self, but don't be a martyr, that's all I'm saying. If you need time—'

She held up a hand to stop him. 'Archer, my dad died more than two weeks ago now and, in any event, we weren't close. I'm sad for my mom but otherwise, I'm fine.'

As she spoke those words, her throat tightened for no obvious reason. Nothing that couldn't be soothed by a sip of her warm drink.

'Right. I just thought, what with him being a chef and you being a food critic...'

'That we'd have something in common?'

Smiling meekly, she rose from her chair, keen to be out of the conversation and Archer's office. 'I'm a food critic in spite of my dad. And I've been working for the last two weeks from home. So, if that's everything...?'

Archer nodded and gave her a look of sympathy which she didn't care for.

'Okay, then,' she said, her back already turned as she returned to the sanctity of her desk.

—

As she sat in the window of Janey's much-loved Thai cafe on 9th Avenue, staring at everything and focusing on nothing, Emily wondered if Archer had been right. Should she be grieving? Surely not. She had barely spoken to her dad in six years. Any communication they'd had was limited solely to the topic of her mom, and only when strictly necessary.

But was she a hard-faced, cold-hearted—

'One medium veggie massaman curry for you. A spicy king prawn pad see ew for me. And two chilled green teas.' Janey set the dishes on the bench in front of Emily, since it had been her turn to order.

Emily took two sets of chopsticks from a pot on the bench and handed one to Janey. 'Thanks for this.'

'Anything to provoke a reaction this afternoon. You've been MIA today.'

'I've been sitting right next to you.'

Janey nodded as she filled her mouth with noodles. 'Staring into space,' she managed around her half-masticated food.

It was true. Since her meeting with Archer this morning, Emily had felt entirely out of sorts. Deflated, maybe? Bored? Maybe even hormonal. She wasn't sure.

Janey dabbed her mouth with a paper napkin. 'Ems, don't get tetchy when I ask you this but *are* you okay to be in the office? I mean, are you *okay*?'

Emily rolled her eyes and pushed her curry around her bowl. 'I'm fine.'

Holding her hands up in surrender, Janey said, 'I told you not to get tetchy. If you say you're good, I'm good. But…'

'If I need to talk, I know where you are?' Emily softened, turning her lips up at one side. 'I know. But I'm good. Really. You know my dad and I didn't get along.'

She looked back to the street, not feeling hungry for her lunch at all. There was something bothering her. There were *things* bothering her. She just wasn't sure what or why.

'Janey, are you happy?'

Janey's eyes went wide, perhaps at the breadth of the question, maybe because Emily had caused her to swallow too much food in one go.

'That's a pretty big question.'

But Emily needed the answer. She set her chopsticks aside and eyed Janey, waiting.

'Right now, eating this, with my friend, I'm happy. I'm happy with my husband and kids.'

'Like, all of the time?'

Janey paused, as if she were thinking. 'Yes, always. Don't get me wrong, they drive me crazy sometimes. The mess, the noise, the weekend mayhem of classes and clubs. But they're my favourite people in the world. They're the people I want around me always, even when they're driving me nuts.'

Emily sighed without meaning to.

'Are you and Oliver okay?'

'Yeah. Course,' she responded too quickly to sound convincing, even to herself. 'What about work?' she asked, shifting the emphasis from her relationship. 'Do you like your job? Does it make you… happy?'

Janey seemed to ponder the question. Emily willed her friend to respond, to give her an answer that might help her work out what was wrong with *her* right now.

'The job itself, sitting at my desk, writing the same thing over and over, it doesn't make me *un*happy but it doesn't bring me happiness, as such. But the people…' She inclined her head playfully to Emily. 'Being in the office with the city on the doorstep for food, shopping. The confidence and security I get from having a life that's my own and making money with mouths to feed at home, those things make me feel fulfilled. Yeah, fulfilled is probably the right word.'

Emily recognised the sentiments. She had felt them once. But she was struggling with whether she felt them still.

'Aren't you happy, Ems?'

'Sure. Sure, I'm happy,' she lied. 'Maybe I'm just a little bored.'

Janey chewed another mouthful of noodles then pointed her chopsticks at Emily. 'Do you know what you need? A new swanky restaurant with amazing cocktails and a shopping trip to dress for the occasion.'

'You're dead right.' Emily hoped so because she was stuck in a rut, not certain how she felt about anything.

Chapter Six

Nayomi

Nayomi inhaled the richness of spices as she spooned squash curry from the pan where it had been simmering into two small bowls. She set the bowls amongst the others already laid out on the dining table, squishing them together to make sure there was space for a side plate for each of the boys, her neighbour Farah, and herself.

Cooking was both relaxing and thrilling to Nayomi. She loved pleasing people with tastes and full tummies, playing with flavours and combinations of spices. She was possibly her happiest when she was cooking for her boys.

The boys had been born in America and loved everything their friends loved – burgers, hot dogs, fries, wings, waffles – but Nayomi had always wanted them to understand that they had Sri Lankan heritage. That their father, though he had been born in America to first generation American parents, had been brought up to understand the pleasures of Sri Lankan cooking. That Nayomi had spent the first eighteen years of her life in Kandy. That she had come from a village where she had spoken Sinhala and been taught by her parents to cook with the fruits of their island.

She didn't have the money for airfare to take regular trips to Sri Lanka but she could bring Sri Lanka to them.

And tonight, to celebrate her new job at one of the city's best restaurants starting tomorrow, she had cooked an array of dishes from the cuisine she loved.

Beetroot fried in cinnamon. Squash curry with the aromas of dill seeds and coriander. Chicken curry, using every part of the chicken, even the bits that western families tended to consider scraps but which actually brought the biggest flavours. Cashew curry, with the nuttiness of the main ingredient enhancing the creaminess of coconut milk. And, of course, no Sri Lankan buffet would be complete without shredded poppadum, boiled rice and spicy coconut sambol.

One of the things Nayomi had had to get used to when she moved to New York twelve years ago had been eating with cutlery, rather than with her hands. It had seemed bizarre, an unnecessary faff that led only to more washing-up, but her boys had always eaten with cutlery and so, she laid four knives, four forks, and spoons for serving in the middle of the table.

Then she poked her head around the kitchen wall and called for the boys and Farah in the lounge. 'Dinner's ready.'

It was past eight by the time they sat down to eat. She had given the boys snacks of pineapple and masala nuts after school, knowing they would otherwise be too hungry to enjoy the meal by the time she had cooked. Things would change from now on. The boys would eat at a regular time, and Nayomi would prepare the week's evening meals in advance on Sundays.

Farah had been helping the boys with their homework and now brought her glass of wine into the kitchen. 'This looks great,' she said, taking her seat and tucking her square of kitchen towel into the neck of her sweatshirt.

Farah had a typically petite Malaysian frame and as a nursery nurse, she was constantly on her feet in her day job, so no matter what she ate and drank, she seemed to stay slim.

She tied up her long hair and comically flexed her fingers in front of her then creaked her neck as if she were a boxing champ gearing up for a big fight. 'I've got my stretchy pants on especially for this.'

Nayomi chuckled as she took a seat opposite Farah, the boys on either side of the women, and she took the first sip from her own glass of wine. She didn't drink much and she didn't want to run out too soon of the one celebratory bottle she had bought for dinner, so she would pace herself and make sure Farah was topped up. She had no idea if it was good wine or bad wine but it had been wine she could afford for less than five dollars and Farah seemed happy enough with the choice.

As Roshan reached out for one of the bowls of chicken curry, Nayomi placed a hand on his wrist, and said, 'Not so fast. Before we start, let's say thank you to Farah, please. Mom couldn't have taken this job if Farah hadn't agreed to sit for you guys in the evenings.' Nayomi figured that, as a single woman in her early thirties, there were probably a thousand other places Farah would rather be in the evenings.

Roshan retracted his hand to his lap. 'Thank you, Farah.'

Nuwan got off his chair and wrapped his arms around Farah's waist. 'Thank you, Farah-Bara.'

Farah hugged him back, pressing her lips to his hair, then smiled at Nayomi. 'You're welcome. Just make sure you bring me some fancy leftovers every now and again.'

'I'm not sure how many perks a kitchen porter gets but if I can lay my hands on leftovers, they have your name on them. I really do appreciate the help, Farah.'

'You'll help me out one day when I have my own little terrors.'

Nayomi nodded. 'Always.'

—

'Hose 'em, stack 'em, steam 'em.'

There were five components to Nayomi's new job and Bill, her fellow kitchen porter and the other half of their two-person team, was relaying three of them to her for the zillionth time. Nayomi may not have six college degrees or a Nobel prize but she was pretty sure she could work a fancy dishwasher.

Still, she smiled politely and told him, 'That's great. I think I've got it. Thanks for showing me the ropes, Bill.'

She was rewarded with a proud grin and flushed cheeks she'd expect to see on a five-year-old rather than a man in his late fifties or sixties. Bill adjusted his navy hat and his thick-rimmed glasses and waved a hand bashfully before getting back to hosing, stacking and steaming the crockery used in the pre-service prep.

The other two elements of her job were to collect dirty dishes from the kitchen – pots, pans, utensils, the items that the waiting staff wouldn't bring directly to the 'pot-wash station', as they called it – and to be invisible at all times. Alexander had made clear that Nayomi wasn't to speak to the chefs when they were working and she was absolutely, definitely, never to get under their feet. Despite being given a uniform of navy pants, a maroon polo shirt, a navy pinstripe apron and industry issue kitchen safety shoes that could apparently fend off boiling water and sharp knives, she was not to create a situation where her protective uniform had to be relied upon.

'When the machine's cycle is finished, you can put those pots in their rightful home, then take five minutes to yourself before service gets started. It can end up hot in the kitchen,' Bill told her.

Nayomi could already feel the heat from the lights and ovens in the main kitchen from where she and Bill were tucked around a corner with their deep-cleaning machines bellowing out steam every time they were opened.

Taking her five minutes, Nayomi slipped out of the kitchen unnoticed, or at least not acknowledged, and rested back against the cool bricks of the hotel wall. Outside, three chefs were standing around, one smoking, two there for the ride, it seemed.

'Do you think the rumours are true?' one chef asked the others.

'I don't know. It doesn't seem right but I can't see Alexander letting Maggie stay in post,' one replied.

'Alexander asking a woman for advice, to be his equal? Not going to happen,' the third said. He stubbed out his cigarette on the ground. 'Ultimately, it's a business. We have to be the best. And we can't stay as Jean-Sébastien's forever. Change is coming, and the question is, is Maggie as good as Jean-Sébastien was? Is she good enough?'

As the chefs turned to make their way back into the kitchen, they finally clocked Nayomi. They didn't speak to her or even smile but she noticed their eyes flick in her direction. *Invisible.* She didn't care so long as she was getting paid, she supposed.

She closed her eyes and let the cooler air wash over her. Then she heard the soft brush of the vinyl strip curtain that hung over the open door to the kitchen, followed by the shuffle of more feet coming outside and turned to see the head chef. Maggie creaked her neck on one side, then the other, interlacing her fingers and stretching her arms out behind her back.

'Oh, hey, Nayomi,' Maggie said. 'How's your first shift going?'

Taken by surprise that Maggie would remember her name or even speak to her, Nayomi forgot to smile back but replied, 'Great, it's going great. Bill has shown me the ropes.'

Maggie giggled. 'Bill's a real stickler for process but he's a nice guy. He cares. He's been with the restaurant as long as I have and we've never failed a health and safety check.'

Nayomi nodded. 'How long have you worked here?'

'About eight years. I was good friends with Jean-Sébastien's daughter, Emily.' It seemed the mention of Jean-Sébastien deflated Maggie and Nayomi knew from that small movement that Maggie had truly cared about her old boss. 'Emily used to work here. She was destined to take over and carry on her dad's name, I guess. She introduced me to Jean-Sébastien and got me a job as an apprentice chef in the kitchen while I went to chef school. Then, a couple of years later, Emily left.'

Though she was happy for the conversation, Nayomi wondered why Maggie had decided to share Emily's story. Perhaps there was something more to the relationship, she wondered. 'That must have been a blow for her dad?'

'Oh, it was. He was devastated. Jean-Sébastien's father and grandfather had been restauranteurs in France. It was

44

in the family and Jean-Sébastien assumed Emily would follow suit.'

'Where does she work now?'

'She's a food critic now for the *New York Times*. A very influential one, at that. But it's a shame. She was a great cook.'

Nayomi sensed the history went deeper than that but she didn't want to overstep and simply replied, 'They're funny things, families.' She knew too well how true that was. 'You have all the plans in the world...'

'...then life throws you a curve ball,' Maggie finished.

A curve ball. Exactly. Nayomi had been thrown a curve ball when her husband's family had come to Sri Lanka to choose him a traditional wife. She had been surprised when that wife-to-be was her and even more surprised when she found out her marriage had already been agreed and that she would be moving to America immediately after her wedding to a man she had met twice. It hadn't been a union of love but she had cared for Shan and knew that he had her best interests at heart, too. They were, after all, parents to their gorgeous boys together, and the devastation she had felt when he died was real.

'Well, I'd best get back,' Nayomi said, not wanting to outstay her welcome or seem to be slacking and not wanting to drift into the dangerous melancholy she knew lingered in her mind and surfaced whenever she thought of her broken family.

Maggie nodded but lingered outside alone. And Nayomi wished she had known what those three chefs had been talking about earlier because whatever it was, she felt like Maggie could do with a heads-up.

An hour into service and Nayomi was mesmerised. She had never really considered the workings of a commercial kitchen, especially a fancy one like Jean-Sébastien's. Nayomi had always cooked alone or amongst family, quiet or pleasantly jovial.

Here, dirty plates of all different shapes and sizes were constantly being dropped off at the station by waiting staff. Every ten minutes, or if 'pot wash' was yelled from the kitchen, she would do a round, collecting crockery, pans and cutlery from the chefs' stations and weaving in and out of moving bodies and hot hazards.

The smells were torture in the best possible way. Her mouth watered and her stomach rumbled as she worked. It was easy to get distracted but Nayomi was determined to do a good job and not give Alexander any excuse to let her go.

When she heard 'porter' called by a female voice, she knew, by process of very quick elimination, that it could have only come from Maggie. Nayomi walked quickly – but very, very safely, for the benefit of Bill's nerves more than her own protection – to the pass and found Maggie adding the finishing touches to a main course dish. Nayomi was transfixed as Maggie smudged some kind of green purée on a plate, as if she were creating an oil painting. Then she slid neatly rectangular-shaped white fish onto the plate and used tweezers to delicately place flowers on top of the meat.

It was a work of art, truly. If Nayomi could have taken a picture and hung it up in her apartment, it would be the finest decoration she had ever owned.

'It's beautiful,' she said to herself.

But she must have said the words aloud because Maggie looked up from the pass and said, 'Thank you.'

Invisible. She was supposed to be invisible. 'Sorry,' she said, collecting dirty trays from the pass and hurrying back to her station.

She hosed, stacked and steamed dishes, wondering what it must be like to be as talented as Maggie and the other chefs. To create such magnificent art from food. She lost herself in a daydream, imagining guests in fancy clothes, drinking fancy champagne, not considering the price tag first, coming to eat *her* food and give compliments to *her*.

As the dishwasher beeped, it brought her back to the reality of her situation and she scoffed at her own thoughts. She was a pot wash and a seamstress, as far from swanky clothes and bottles of fizz as she could get.

But it was the first time she could remember ever imagining herself with more, *being* more than just a widow and a mom.

Chapter Seven

Emily

Without checking with her, Oliver had rearranged their cancelled lunch with the Sandersons to Friday night dinner. Emily didn't want to eat out, she just didn't feel like it tonight. More than that, she didn't want to be zipping herself into a tight-fitting cocktail dress, hot from blow-drying curls into the ends of her long hair.

What she really wanted to do was put on yoga pants and an oversized sweater and eat copious amounts of ice cream while watching the kind of romantic comedies she used to watch in her early twenties. *When did being thirty-one start to feel so old?*

She looked over her finished ensemble in the free-standing bedroom mirror. She looked like a woman in her thirties who was ready to go to one of the finest restaurants in Manhattan then for after-dinner cocktails. She felt like a woman in her seventies who had been forced into doing something she really could not muster the energy to do.

Defeated, she slumped onto the edge of the super king-sized bed and stared at her own reflection. She imagined herself eight years younger, getting dressed in her bedroom at her parents' house, Beyoncé playing loudly, her and Maggie sharing a bottle of wine before heading into the city to dance the night away – carefree.

'Babe? Are you ready? The car's downstairs,' Oliver shouted from the lounge, where he would have been enjoying a pre-dinner glass of single malt in one of his weekend suits – much like his week-day Wall Street suits except a bluer shade of blue.

With a grumble, she stood up on her high-heeled strappy sandals, pasted on her smile, and went to Oliver, linking her arm through his as they headed out.

On the drive into the city, Emily umm'd and ahh'd, making interested noises as Oliver talked about securities trades and stock markets. And while it would usually be a source for irritation, she was relieved when he answered a call to one of 'the guys' and between overzealous chortles, made arrangements for a poker night at their apartment. Naturally, he went ahead without checking what Emily's plans were and whether the apartment would actually be free. On a normal day, they would end up rowing once he hung up the phone – Emily would yell her annoyance at his selfishness and Oliver would say something like, 'Are you really the kind of girlfriend who makes her guy ask for permission to do things?'

Tonight, though, she looked out of the window and watched rain drops bounce off the sidewalk as their driver worked through traffic into the city. In her body, she felt lethargic, yet her mind was distracted, unable to settle her thoughts or focus on any particular one but without knowing why.

Was she still reeling from Oliver arranging the evening's plans without consulting her? Was it that she just wanted to be left alone, in her own headspace tonight? Neither of those things accounted for the heavy feeling in her chest.

As they drew up to the restaurant, Emily's door was opened by a member of staff. He held a large black umbrella over her head, shielding her from the undesirable weather. As she swung her legs, knees together, onto the sidewalk, she looked up to the metal spokes of the umbrella and her breath was stolen by a vivid image of herself getting out of the black limousine that had followed her father's hearse barely more than two weeks ago.

She must have seemed unsteady as both the staff and Oliver, who had appeared at her side, reached out to her arms.

'Woah, there,' Oliver said. 'New shoes?'

Emily shook her head, bringing herself back to Downton Manhattan from the memory of her father's graveside. She laughed bashfully, rolling her eyes at the restaurant staff. 'Freakin' Dolce, they never take practicality into consideration, do they?'

And as well-trained as he ought to be, the man holding the umbrella smiled politely and told her, 'Worth the price to look as beautiful as you do this evening.'

It was a good line and worthy of an extra five bucks in tip.

Inside, the dapper maître d' welcomed Emily and Oliver in a way that seemed just a little nervous, suggesting the staff were fully aware of who Emily was and for whom she worked. She wanted to say, *I'm here socially, relax*. But the polite way to do this, she had found, was to let Oliver take the lead on small talk.

'You are first to arrive. Would you care to take a drink in the bar while you wait for your guests?' the maître d' asked.

Though she wanted to let Oliver take the lead, she wasn't risking him saying no. 'Yes. Yes, please,' Emily said quickly.

Not only did she love the cellar bar here – luxe interiors and extravagant chandeliers against the red brick walls – but she really wanted a drink. Something sour. The more bitter, the better.

Sitting on a royal blue suede sofa that made Oliver blend into the furniture and look like a floating head and hands, Emily and Oliver were halfway through their cocktails when Cassandra and William Sanderson arrived.

'Hello, hello!' Cassandra said, toddling ahead of William in her silver heels, looking like she was struggling against the tight wrapping of her pencil skirt around her knees.

'You look as stunning as ever,' Emily said, rising to kiss her friend on the cheek, while trying not to mess Cassandra's impeccably styled blonde bob. 'You too, obviously,' she told William, jovially winking as she greeted him. Her whisky sour had started to lighten her mood... marginally.

A bartender was on top of them as soon as they had positioned themselves as a foursome, the ladies seated together on the sofa as the men each took up a high-back chair.

'Would you like to see the cocktail menu or perhaps the wine list?' he asked, holding leather bound copies of both in his hands.

'I'll take a Vesper,' William said, not needing to peruse the menu.

'And *I*...' Cassandra almost sang the word *I*, holding the note like a ballad, 'will take a virgin passion mojito.'

Emily shot a glance to her friend. 'Are you...?'

Cassandra nodded, beaming as she reached out to take William's hand. 'We're having a baby.'

Cassandra and Will? Just a month ago Cassandra was crying into her lunch and telling Emily she wanted a divorce. Now they were having a baby?

'That's, wow, that's lovely, lovely news,' Emily said, knowing she had to do better. 'I mean fantastic news. The best news *ever.*' And now she was overdoing it.

They hugged and shook hands and Emily gushed and asked all the right questions – *When are you due? Will you find out the gender? Are your families ecstatic?*

But inside, her mood grew even darker and she just didn't know why. She had drained her whisky sour, ordered a second despite the fact Oliver was still drinking his first, and she was almost finished with that too. The good news was, two whisky sours on an empty stomach was making her head feel floaty, like she was drifting in clouds, weightless, numb. And numb was much more pleasant than unexplainably miserable.

'Hey, what's up with you?' Oliver asked, holding her back by the elbow as the maître d' led their foursome upstairs to their table.

'What do you mean, what's up with me?'

'You're behaving erratically, Ems. Slow down on the drinks, huh?'

She scowled in a way she imagined made her look like a petulant teenager and told him, 'I'm a grown woman, Olly, I'll decide when I've had enough.'

'I'm not saying stop, I'm saying slow down and drink some water. Eat something before you tuck into the wine, all right? You'll thank me tomorrow.'

She snatched her elbow back. 'Right, and now he cares about me all of a sudden.'

'What the hell is that supposed to mean?' he whisper-shouted.

'Exactly what I said.' She turned on her heels, having to admit to herself that she felt less than steady, and stomped to the dining table, feeling like she could roast her octopus starter on her temperament alone.

And just because she felt like it, when the bottle of champagne that Oliver had discreetly ordered as a surprise to toast their friends' news arrived, Emily was the first to take a large mouthful, eyeing her fiancé as she did so.

She hated it when Oliver told her what to do; she hated it even more when she knew he was right. By the time the waiter brought around a tray of bread and explained the various infused flavours, Emily regretted polishing off her champagne so quickly, feeling ravenous, woozy and a little bit sick.

She ate her roasted tomato and olive square of focaccia in one bite and was grateful when Oliver subtly nudged his own bread plate towards her and she ate his bite-sized piece too.

With her appetiser lining her stomach, she was beginning to feel sober enough to start on the wine Oliver had chosen for the table. It was a bone of contention in their relationship that, despite her being a professional critic of wine and food pairings, Oliver felt that his investments in various vineyards – which were done via a broker – meant he was more qualified than Emily to choose wine. He was just another man in her life who thought his judgement in the culinary world was *always* better than hers. In reality, Oliver associated the price tag with the best. And since he had declared he was paying for dinner tonight in celebration of Cassandra's pregnancy, he was certainly going to show off with a high price tag.

As Cassandra spoke about the importance of family and how idyllic her own upbringing had been, Emily found she didn't care whether the wine was a perfect match for her main course of halibut or not. She was simply happy for the smooth slide of alcohol down her throat, leaving a vanilla finish on her palate and a care-less attitude in her mind.

They never made it to after-dinner cocktails on account of Cassandra being tired, but she suspected Oliver had subtly declared that Emily's night was over in William's ear.

Oh, whatever. Couldn't she just have a blowout every now and then?

Seemingly not. Oliver strode into their apartment building, leaving Emily trailing behind. She was sober enough to recognise that she would never make it to their front door upright in her heels and sat on the sofa in the vestibule to unhook her sandals and carry them to the elevator, the cool floor tiles very welcome on her hot, bare feet.

Oliver was banging cupboards in the kitchen and pouring himself a nightcap when Emily walked in, stumbling into the wall as she tried to kick the apartment door closed behind her.

'What was that, Emily? We were celebrating our friends' good news and you can barely string a sentence together.'

She rolled her eyes before turning away from him and moving to the lounge, where she slumped onto the sofa.

But she wasn't escaping Oliver and there was no hiding from him as her loud, painful hiccups led him to where she was sitting.

Armed with a glass of iced water, he followed her into the lounge, handed her the glass and sat opposite her on a foot stool.

'Is it jealousy? Is this because Cassandra is pregnant? I didn't think we were there yet. You've said so.'

Emily scoffed. 'No, it's not about a *baby*.' She didn't know what it was about though, and she didn't want to dwell on that. 'Olly, I got drunk. Do I have a go at you every time you get drunk? No. I don't. So get lost.'

He did. Shaking his head and untucking his shirt as he walked, Oliver left the lounge.

He left her alone.

She was alone.

From nowhere, tears filled her eyes and trickled down her cheeks. It was the booze, she knew, but she couldn't stop the water from falling. She pressed a hand across her mouth to stop any noise escaping as her body began to chug under the weight of silly tears, too much alcohol and a stomach full of food she was desperate to throw up.

'I need to be out of it,' she mumbled as she tried to stand, fumbling with her too-tight dress, unable to get the zipper herself. 'I just need. To. Be. Out. Of. It.'

Then the material was releasing as Oliver drew down the zipper, freeing her from everything that was causing her so much discomfort.

She wouldn't say thank you – she was mad at him. And he clearly didn't want thanks because he was gone before she turned around to look at him, mumbling as he went, 'I'm so sick of fighting with you.'

She was, too. *When had they started fighting so much? Why?*

Sniffing and stumbling, she made her way to the main bathroom, where she fell to her knees and threw up three hundred dollars of food and alcohol, over and over.

She pulled a warm towel down from the hot rail and lay on top of it. Before she fell asleep, she thought to herself,

They didn't ask how I am. Not one of them. Not her fiancé, her close friend, nor William. No one asked about her dad or whether she was sad that he was gone, that she never got a chance to say goodbye. Or how she felt knowing that the last words she had spoken to him six years ago had been poison.

No one asked.

No one asked because she had told them she didn't care.

She *didn't* care.

At least, she wouldn't care tomorrow morning, when her stomach and her head and her heart had stopped aching.

As she closed her eyes, too weary to stop her mind from wandering places she didn't want it to go, she imagined Maggie sitting next to her on the bathroom floor, stroking her hair and telling her gently, 'You'll feel better in the morning.'

Chapter Eight

Maggie

Maggie knocked on Isabella's front door then let herself inside the house, the way she had been told to do many times before, carrying a large wicker basket of bread in with her.

'Isabella? It's Maggie,' she called out, setting down her basket in the hallway and unzipping her ankle boots.

In her socks, she made her way towards the faint voice that seemed to be coming from the kitchen.

Isabella was tying the top of a bin bag, wearing a pair of marigolds, her paisley shirt rolled up to her elbows and the hem of her beige pants rolled up to her calves.

'What a lovely surprise,' she said, giving Maggie that wonderful smile that she had missed seeing on her friend during recent visits. 'Goodness, how long have I been cleaning?'

Reflexively, they both turned to look at the large clock on the wall.

'Oh, not long at all,' Isabella said.

'I'm sorry it's so early, especially on a Saturday. I wanted to stop by before I go to the restaurant. I've made bread.' Maggie raised the basket from her wrist and placed it on the old wooden kitchen table, lifting back the checked cloth that had been covering one sourdough, two brown bloomers, a white bloomer and a baguette. 'I don't know why I made so much. I've not been sleeping well and kneading is the best therapy I know.'

Isabella let out the shortest, sweetest laugh – a sound Maggie was delighted to hear. 'He used to say the same thing.'

They each knew that *he* didn't require any further explanation.

'I was hoping you'd help me work through some of this.'

'Take a seat and I'll put on some coffee. I could make some eggs, or would you rather have jam and butter?'

'I'll make eggs,' Maggie offered.

'Nonsense, you've got a long day of cooking ahead of you. It's time I started cooking more, anyway.' Isabella paused part-way through taking plates from her display unit. 'It just seems so pointless for one.'

Then she set three plates, forks and knives down on the table top. 'Your timing is excellent. I'm expecting Emily any minute now. She's coming over for breakfast and now breakfast will be much tastier.'

'Oh.' Maggie's stomach felt like it fell three feet from her abdomen. 'I don't want to interrupt your breakfast. I have lots I could be getting on with anyway and I'm sure you'd like to have some quality time with Emily.'

But as she made to stand, Isabella placed her hand on Maggie's shoulder, gently encouraging her back into her seat. 'Let's see if we can't have a nice meal, the three of us. I would love nothing more than to see you and Emily get along again, the way you used to.' As she busied herself again with the coffee machine, Isabella said quietly, 'I think she could use an honest friend.'

Excellent, Maggie thought. Her plans for a nice hour with Isabella had become an inevitably awkward as heck breakfast with the woman who used to be her best friend. The woman who could barely tolerate being in the same room as her.

'Where are the eggs?' she asked, moving to the cooker. If anything could bring her comfort, it was cooking.

With a full mug of coffee steaming on the countertop beside her and the scent of fresh bread as Isabella cut slices of bloomer on the table, Maggie's nose started to twitch with joy and her empty stomach sang a loud baritone tune. She mixed eggs, milk, full cream and real butter together in a bowl, sprinkling in salt, pepper and finely chopped chives from Jean-Sébastien's home herb garden. Then she made a bain-marie on the oven top and set her eggs above the steam to slowly cook.

As her eggs began to thicken, there was a knock on the front door.

'Come in!' Isabella called out. But the door didn't open.

Maggie pretended not to see Isabella's exasperated expression before she headed to the front door to let her daughter into the house. Instead, Maggie braced herself for Emily's whiplash.

'What are you doing here?' were Emily's first words.

Despite the years of separation between them, it still hurt that Emily didn't want her there.

'Hey, Emily. Look, I didn't mean to step on any toes, I just had some spare bread—'

'Five loaves?' Emily quipped, looking at the partially carved bloomer in the middle of the table and the four other breads still in the basket.

'I haven't been sleeping well. You know what I'm like when I can't sleep.'

'And, what, did you have spare eggs too?' Emily jibed with a scowl.

She looked like hell, Maggie noticed. Either she also hadn't been sleeping, or she was displaying the telltale signs of a nasty morning-after-the-night-before.

Maggie had spent many nights on the bathroom floor with Emily, stroking her hair as she threw up the contents of her stomach. Emily could always take or leave alcohol but one drink had most often led to too many – a trait common amongst chefs.

Maggie would always say, 'You'll feel better in the morning,' knowing they would spend the entire next day lounging around watching romcoms and eating every form of carb they could get their hands on. While Maggie had always preferred the next day to the night before, for Emily, it had usually been tough.

Now, Maggie wasn't even welcome for an hour or two, let alone a full day.

'Your mom thought it would be okay if I stayed for breakfast but, look, you two had plans. Why don't I finish up making the eggs and then leave you to it?' Maggie offered, not wanting to be there just as much as Emily clearly didn't want her there.

Emily glared at Maggie. 'I know how to make freakin' eggs, *Maggie*.'

'That wasn't what I was—'

'You look like you would appreciate a coffee, darling,' Isabella said, planting a mug of coffee on the kitchen table and encouraging Emily to take a seat. 'Did you do something nice last night or were you working?'

It took long seconds before Emily released Maggie from her cold glare and took a seat. 'I was out to dinner and cocktails with friends.'

'That's lovely,' Isabella said, as she sat down next to her daughter. 'It's good that you're getting out.'

'Why wouldn't I be getting out?'

Why are you such a bitch? Maggie wanted to ask as she saw Isabella flinch in response, but she held her tongue and finished fluffing her light scrambled eggs.

Isabella and Emily chatted as Maggie set three plates with scrambled eggs, grated a small amount of parmesan on top, then laid three strands of chive across each for garnish.

Maggie wondered if she might even prefer eating with misogynistic Alexander over breakfast in the ice chamber she was currently sitting in.

She buttered her bread in silence and tried not to purr when the scrambled eggs hit her palate.

'Oh, Maggie, these eggs are delicious,' Isabella said.

''Course they are, Mom, *Maggie* made them,' Emily said sarcastically.

Maggie forced herself not to react.

As they ate, the atmosphere seemed to soften, thanks mostly to Isabella's relentless efforts at conversation (or mediation). Maggie was relaxed enough to miss the presence of Jean-Sébastien at the table. She wondered if Isabella and Emily were feeling it too. Years ago, she had enjoyed many meals at this very table as Emily's guest, feeling more welcome with Emily's parents than she had even with her own parents growing up.

Maggie missed those simpler times. She missed the feeling of being in their warm home. She missed Jean-Sébastien and she missed the Emily of old. As Isabella cleared the empty breakfast plates, nostalgia made Maggie feel comfortable enough to ask Emily, 'How are you doing? I mean, I know things were… difficult between you and your dad but he was still your dad.'

Maggie regretted the question as soon as she saw Emily's jaw clench.

She was likely saved from Emily's wrath by Isabella returning to the table with another round of coffee. 'Emily, Maggie is head chef now at the restaurant. Isn't that wonderful? Who better to carry on your father's wo—'

Her words were cut off as Emily brought her palm down on the table and pushed out her chair, scraping the legs against the slate tiled floor. 'Didn't that work out just perfectly for you!'

Stunned, Maggie opened her mouth to speak, without knowing what she wanted to say. *It's temporary? It hasn't been confirmed yet? I'm sorry?*

She didn't have time to think of the most appropriate response before Emily had grabbed her handbag and stormed out of the house.

–

The buzz before Saturday night service was missing for Maggie tonight. Even as she had chatted with the other chefs during food prep throughout the day, her head and heart hadn't been in the kitchen.

Breakfast with Emily and Isabella had been awful. She hadn't ever done anything to deserve Emily's hatred. And it was hate. She was vile to Maggie. But more than that, Maggie was saddened by seeing just how broken Emily was. Her eyes were dull and sunken and her skin looked dry and gaunt – more than the result of a single hangover. She had looked like a fragile girl in her hooded sweater and leggings.

All Maggie kept thinking was that Emily was hurting and, she suspected, regretful. She remembered clearly the night of the falling-out between Emily and Jean-Sébastien, right here in the very kitchen where Maggie was about to begin service.

Emily and her dad came to blows often, usually because Emily wanted to introduce a new dish to the menu or because Jean-Sébastien had been hyper-critical of Emily's work in the kitchen. Although she didn't ever want to speak ill of Jean-Sébastien, Maggie had to admit that his perfectionism and criticism was worse than ever when it came to Emily's food. This particular row, the night Emily stormed out of the kitchen, had been building like a volcano waiting to erupt for months, years maybe. At the time, Maggie had hoped that it was just another row that they would work through, but she found herself unable to believe they would.

Six years later, they had never resolved the fight. Now, they never would and that *had* to be hurting Emily. She wasn't as hard and vicious as she would have people believe; at least, she never used to be. She'd certainly always been tough – Maggie remembered when a chef had made a snide comment about her background as a baker, and Emily had leapt to her defence, cutting the man down to size with a few sharp words.

Her lips twitched at the memory of Emily fiercely brandishing a whisk like she was about to club him.

Maggie wished at times that she had backbone like that. And maybe... maybe she should have spoken out for Emily once or twice when Jean-Sébastien had been on her case. *Would that have changed how things had worked out?*

'Maggie, do you have a minute?'

She was snapped out of her trance by Alexander. 'Now? Service is about to start.'

'Someone can cover the pass,' he said, already walking towards the back door.

Outside, Alexander sent two chefs back into the kitchen and pulled the door closed after them. Though Alexander had occasionally asked Jean-Sébastien to step outside for a discussion of some sort – rarely either of them returning in a good mood – this was a first for Maggie. She found herself anxious without knowing why.

'What's up?' she asked, hoping she had managed to sound casual.

'I just want to give you an update on the situation.' He brought one arm across his body and rested his opposite elbow on top, pinching his chin between his forefinger and thumb as if he were considering the response to a conundrum, all the while looking smarmy and bull-headed.

'Situation?'

'Jean-Sébastien's replacement.'

Oh.

'I'm very happy to tell you that Ethan James has agreed to come over to the restaurant. Actually, it was agreed a couple of weeks ago but there hasn't been a good time for you and I to catch up, has there?'

What?

'He's agreed that you can retain your position as sous chef, so long as the pair of you work well together.'

Her mouth fell open but no words came out. *Ethan James. Head Chef. Her, sous chef to his head chef. What the actual…?*

'He has a sous chef now who he's worked with for a year or so. My advice to you would be, don't mess it up. Don't give him a reason to want to bring in his own guy.'

'W-what? When?'

'Three months. Well, less two weeks. They need to find a replacement at his current post, so you'll stay as stand-in until then.'

'W—I—He—' She swallowed and licked her dry lips. 'Alexander, Ethan James is a jerk. He'll change this restaurant completely. His style… It's not—'

'It's not traditional French fine dining, I know. He's experimental. He's innovative. That's why he has two stars behind him, Maggie. And that's why we need him here. Jean-Sébastien's isn't Jean-Sébastien's any more.'

'But what does your dad have to say about that? It is still *his* restaurant, isn't it?'

Alexander shrugged. 'He agrees it's time for a change. Without Jean-Sébastien at the helm, we need a hook to draw customers. Ethan is that hook.'

She sighed. 'Look, I can't work for him, Alexander. I won't. And the others won't like him either.'

Alexander put one hand in the pocket of his suit trousers and held the other up. 'It is what it is, Maggie. Anyone who doesn't want to live with it can move on, yourself included.'

Then he turned on the heel of his polished Italian leather shoes and he was gone, leaving Maggie staring after him, her legs weak beneath her.

This was the beginning of the end, for her, and for Jean-Sébastien, his family legacy and everything he had built.

Before her vision clouded over with tears, she noticed Nayomi staring at her through the open doorway from the pot-wash station, her face offering nothing but pity. Maggie couldn't work for someone as arrogant as Ethan James. She didn't want to. She didn't want the restaurant to become some kind of experimental zoo for food that was the antithesis of traditional French fine dining.

She was going to be out on her ass, then what would she do? Jean-Sébastien was the one who had given her a chance in the first place, what if no one else saw in her what he did?

Isabella would be devastated. How would she tell Isabella?

She took a deep breath and attempted to calm the whirl of panic-stricken thoughts going through her mind. She had a kitchen to run and she would be damned if she let Alexander get in the way of her putting out food tonight worthy of Jean-Sébastien's name.

And if she pictured Ethan James's stupid, smirking face every time she sliced her knife through a duck breast, so be it.

Chapter Nine

Nayomi

Nayomi had no idea who Ethan James was but she couldn't believe that anyone wouldn't want Maggie as the head chef of their restaurant. From what she had seen, Maggie's food was second to none.

She was no stranger to the unfairness of life – why did her husband get sick and die two years ago? Why did it cost everything they owned to try, and fail, to get him better? Why couldn't her boys have everything she wanted for them now? But Nayomi had figured those injustices came from being poor. From her being a housewife for years while her husband brought in the sole wage. It had been what was expected of her but in trying to be a good, traditional Sri Lankan woman in an American world, she had to accept that she had failed her family.

It hadn't really occurred to her that people like Maggie – white, American, well-off, smart, talented and pretty – had to fight for their place in the world too.

She watched from the porters' station as Maggie pulled herself together outside and went back to her post in the kitchen. It seemed so unfair that you could be good at your job – great, as far as Nayomi could tell – yet be replaced at the whim of someone else. Didn't Alexander see how much of herself Maggie poured into her work?

Didn't he care about Maggie's future and what bills she had to pay?

Speaking of bills, just as the dishwasher beeped to let her know the cycle was complete, Alexander appeared at the porter station holding two payslips.

'Christ, it stinks back here,' he said, scrunching his face and holding the back of his hand to his nose.

'Ah, that'll be the fish stock pot from prep. It's next for a scrub,' Bill said cheerily, seemingly oblivious to Alexander's derogatory dramatics.

It did smell, but Nayomi tried not to focus on it. In her opinion, the worst part of their job was cleaning the drip trays from the poulet and duck. That fat stench seemed to permeate her clothes more than even fried onions and spices, and at least the latter smelled nice.

'It smells like these have been hard-earned,' Alexander said, holding out a payslip to Bill first, then one to Nayomi.

The weightlessness of that piece of paper belied the enormity of the information inside. She wanted to tear it open and confirm that her first week's pay was safely in her bank account, but knowing that would be a little uncouth, she rolled up the paper and stuck it into the pocket of her porter pants, feeling a little warmer and brighter inside.

She was already missing seeing her boys in the evenings and making fresh food for them, rather than instructing Farah what to reheat for their dinner. But it would be worth it to say *yes* to the next school trip and to buy Roshan the sneakers he so desperately wanted. It would be worth it just to know she could keep up the utilities in their apartment and put a nutritious meal on the table for her growing children.

As she set about unloading the dishwasher, she heard Maggie call 'Service!' from the pass. Saturday night was in motion.

But a stack of ten plates later, she heard the same call repeated.

'Service!' This time louder, snappier, unlike Maggie, she thought.

'What took you so long? This is wasted. Don't let me see you at my pass again tonight,' Maggie yelled. Then she called out, 'Again. I need both dishes again.'

'Oui, Chef.'

'Yes, Chef.'

What looked like two perfect dishes of big, juicy, shell-on prawns were slid onto the counter next to Nayomi and Bill.

They looked mouth-wateringly good.

'What happens to those?' she asked Bill.

He shrugged, pulled off his gloves, then took a large prawn from one of the plates, shelled it and popped it into his mouth.

'We can eat them or throw them. They won't be served.'

Nayomi stared at the untouched plate of prawns, perfectly presented. She wasn't a scavenger. But she hadn't had a chance to eat dinner before coming to the restaurant today and her stomach suddenly felt very empty.

She watched as Bill tucked into a second helping of the shellfish and thought, *if you can't beat 'em, join 'em.* And so, she took off her gloves, gave her hands a quick wash, then peeled and ate three delicious pieces of prawn. The meat was soft and tender but just cooked, not tough, the way prawns too often ended up in a curry. There was something in the buttery sauce dressing the dish that set her taste buds wild. She recognised fennel and star anise but there was more, so much more. She closed her eyes and let the sauce rouse her every sense. As seconds passed, new flavours emerged in her mouth.

'I can't believe they would put that in the trash,' she said to Bill.

'The amount of food that gets wasted here could feed a country, Nomey.' Nomey was Bill's particular way of semi-pronouncing her name.

'Don't they donate it or anything?'

'They can't donate a cooked langoustine now, can they?'

'It just seems like such a waste.'

Bill shrugged and got back to washing the fish stock pot. Nayomi continued stacking clean plates, her stomach now awakened and angrily begging for more food.

When it came around to eleven p.m., the rate of dirty dishes coming through for the dishwasher had slimmed to a trickle. 'Do you mind if I take off, Nomey?' Bill asked. 'The staff car has started up. You can go early next time, if you like. Doesn't take two to finish up from here.'

'Sure, no problem. Enjoy your two days off.'

'Not possible. The wife's got me a list of chores.'

'In that case, good luck,' she said, holding up a hand in farewell as he had already made to leave.

She interlaced her fingers and brought her hands above her head in a nice stretch, feeling the muscles in her sides purr. With no dishes currently to be cleaned and waiting only for dessert plates and coffee cups, Nayomi stepped out from her station to take a few minutes of fresh air outside. She approached the back door at the same time as Lucas, a junior chef, who was carrying a tray of sundried tomato bread, freshly baked for tonight's service.

'Is that for the trash?' Nayomi asked.

'Sure is.'

'I can take it.'

So she found herself standing outside with a tray of bread that would make an excellent breakfast for her boys tomorrow. Perhaps she could rustle up some eggs and invite Farah over as a way of saying thank you for looking after Roshan and Nuwan.

Glancing around, she saw there were no other members of staff in sight. *Could she? Could she get a carrier and just take this full tray of bread home with her?*

Hearing a rustle behind her, she jumped and turned to see Maggie stepping outside, taking off her chef's hat and wiping her brow with kitchen towel.

'Oh, hi,' Maggie said, sounding tired.

'Hi, Maggie. I was, erm, just going to throw away this bread.'

Maggie nodded.

Nayomi lifted the lid on the industrial bin but paused before trashing the food. She just couldn't do it. 'Maggie, do you think… I mean, would it be okay, if I took this home?'

'The bread?'

She bit her lip shyly as she stared down at the tray in her hands.

'Of course, please,' Maggie said. 'I'd be glad to see the food go to a good home. It'll be good for a couple of days.'

Was she a scavenger? Was this equivalent to begging on the streets?

Before she could answer her own thoughts, Maggie said, 'I'd take it myself but I've been doing some comfort baking of late and I have too much bread to get through at home as it is.'

Nayomi wasted no time in grabbing blue roll from the kitchen and wrapping up the bread. The boys would love it. Fancy food from her fancy new job. She wondered if Farah had ever tried sundried tomato bread. She would bet not the kind that tasted like the food from Jean-Sébastien's.

As she emptied the last of the crumbs from the tray into the bin, Nayomi thought Maggie looked sad. 'I'm a comfort baker too,' she said. 'Though my favourite go-to is Sri Lankan love cake.'

'What is Sri Lankan love cake?'

Nayomi breathed in the air, as if she were smelling her mother's recipe. 'Mmm, it's the most delightful sponge cake. I mostly make it like my mother taught me, full of orange peel, cherries and cashew nuts, cardamom, cinnamon and nutmeg. So many other things and whatever spices you like, really. I love playing around with spices in the kitchen, depending on my mood or whatever my boys want. My oldest loves nutty and earthy flavours but my youngest has the sweetest tooth.'

'Well, your recipe sounds delicious.'

'Oh it is, and perfect with a cup of tea. Sri Lanka is the home of the best tea you will ever drink. Every birthday or celebration, my mother used to bake a love cake and our family would come to our home in Kandy for tea and cake.'

'How long have you lived in America?'

'About twelve years. I moved here when I was eighteen, right after I got married.'

'Wow. I can't imagine moving halfway across the world like that. I'm ashamed to say I've never left the country.'

'You haven't?' Nayomi said, unable to hide her surprise.

Maggie shook her head. 'We didn't have the money when I was growing up and then I guess I've just been…' She shrugged. 'Gosh, I've no idea. I'm almost thirty years old and I think I've spent my entire adult life just *working*. That must sound so sad, huh?'

'Not at all. We all have different paths to follow. Your time will come.'

Maggie stared at Nayomi then, as if she was searching her face for the answer to an unasked question. 'You think so?'

Nayomi nodded. 'I think we can do anything we put our minds to… money permitting.'

Did she believe that? If she could do anything, what would she want to do? Something to make the boys proud? Something for herself? Imagine.

'What is it like? Sri Lanka, I mean,' Maggie asked.

'It depends where in the country you are but nowhere is too far. It's a relatively small island. The beaches are plentiful, soft sand, big waves and a peaceful breeze. There are parts where elephants roam free amongst locals. Those areas tend to have warmer, still air. In the tea country, there are lush green rolling hills, perfect for walking and much cooler in the summer months than other parts of the island.'

Maggie closed her eyes. 'Hmm, maybe I'll go someday. Sri Lanka, Asia, somewhere.' Then she opened her eyes and seemed to tune back into chef mode. 'We have drinks in the kitchen after service every Saturday, whatever you like from the bar. You're part of the team now and welcome to join us.'

'Oh, that's very kind but I still have some dishes to finish up and then I really should get home for the boys. The sitter will likely be crashed out on my sofa already.'

73

Maggie smiled. 'Tell you what, then, you can take yours to go. What do you drink?'

'Ah, wine, I guess.'

'Great. Any preferences?'

Nayomi shrugged. *The five-bucks-a-bottle stuff?* 'White?'

Maggie's smile grew wider, friendlier. 'Don't let Charles hear you say that, he'll be horrified.'

'Too late, Charles heard it.' The head sommelier appeared at Maggie's side. 'What kind of flavours do you like?' He directed the question to Nayomi.

'Ah, cinnamon, vanilla.'

Charles closed his eyes and pressed his index finger to his pouting lips. 'I know just the ticket, and I've got about a third of a bottle left that you can take away. Give me a minute.' Then he was off and Nayomi told Maggie, 'Thank you.'

Back inside, Nayomi could hear the chefs in the main kitchen, unwinding from a busy service with their well-deserved drinks. The kitchen had felt a little downbeat since she had started but tonight she heard the occasional playful jibe and short bursts of laughter.

'We're just waiting on one table to see if they want to order any dessert.' The voice startled Nayomi and she spun on the spot to see Ashley, the dessert chef, his arms folded as he leaned against the back door, enjoying some fresh air.

'Thanks for letting me know,' Nayomi said.

She expected the conversation to be over. She was, after all, the invisible employee. Then Ashley asked, 'Where do you live?'

'Me?'

He chuckled, the act bringing creases to the light brown skin around his eyes and at the corners of his plump lips. 'Yeah, you.'

'Queens.'

He nodded. 'I thought I overheard that. We can share the staff cab. I'm that way on too. I'll call it when I'm done to save you waiting any longer than necessary.'

'Oh, ah, great. That'd be great, thank you.'

The maître d' came into the kitchen then and confirmed that the last table couldn't fit in dessert. Ashley said he would call for a lift in ten minutes, once he had cleaned down his station and changed out of his uniform, so Nayomi set about shutting down the machines and cleaning the porter station too.

At the end of the night, back in her jeans, T-shirt and a denim jacket, she dumped her uniform in the communal laundry bag and carried her rucksack full of fancy bread and wine to the staff cab, where Ashley was already sitting in the back seat.

'Good to go?' the driver asked and waited for two affirmative votes before setting off.

'Do you live in Queens?' Nayomi asked Ashley, feeling the need to make conversation, given he had been decent about sharing the ride home and waiting for her to change.

Ashley put away his phone, which Nayomi had been trying not to view as he typed WhatsApp messages to someone, perhaps a wife or a girlfriend to say he was on his way home.

'Technically, I live in Brooklyn now but I'm right on the divide. Born and raised in Queens.'

'How did you come to work at the restaurant? Have you always been a chef?' Nayomi would have guessed he was in his mid-thirties, so it was plausible that he'd had a line of work before being a chef, she figured.

Ashley smiled, showing large white teeth, though not too big for his other features. 'I feel like I'm on a job interview.'

'Oh, sorry, I didn't mean to… You don't have to answer, I was just making conversation.'

He was still smiling as he said, 'I used to be a kitchen porter, too. I had an interest in food. Used to hound the chefs a bit, you know, looking for tips and all that. Then, one day, Jean-Sébastien says to me, "You're distracting my staff".' He paused to laugh. 'He tells me, "I can't have you hanging around while you're collecting pots and waiting for dishes to wash, my chefs need to concentrate". So there I am, thinking, *damn* I'm gonna get fired, right?'

Nayomi nodded. She must remember not to distract the chefs.

'Anyways, JS, he says to me, "So what if you're not in the pot-wash station, any more?" And I'm like, oh *man* here we go. But then he tells me he has a sort of charitable programme that will help me go to chef's school and I can work my way up in the restaurant. And I did. So, I owe everything to JS, Lord rest his soul.'

'Wow, that's amazing.' She barely knew him yet she was pleased for Ashley. Imagine washing dishes one day and the next someone offering to help make your dreams come true. 'It sounds like Jean-Sébastien was a great man.'

'He was. And Maggie is just like him. I mean, JS trained her but she's got a good heart like him, you know. It sucks that they're kicking her out. She's better than that.'

Nayomi couldn't agree more but she also knew too little about the world of fine dining to suppose she could make a sensible comment.

They fell into silence until Nayomi told the driver, 'Make a right up here. It says no entry but this time of night you'll be fine.'

Though he eyed her cautiously through the rear-view mirror, the driver did as instructed and pulled up outside Nayomi's apartment block, where a group of youths were smoking and generally looking up to no good outside.

'You, ah, live with someone? A husband or a boyfriend?' Ashley asked.

'Just my boys, Roshan and Nuwan, but don't worry, I see these guys hanging around all the time. They're okay.'

Nayomi started gathering her things as the driver switched the doors to open.

'How old are your boys?' Ashley asked.

'Ten and seven,' she replied, slinging her rucksack across shoulder. 'Well, goodnight. Thank you for the ride.'

As she rounded the car, the group of youths made various grunts and chin-lifts of greeting, which always reassured her, no matter how many times she passed them.

'Hey, Nayomi!' Ashley had rolled down the car window and was holding out a foil package. 'Take these. For the boys. You'll be doing my ass a good turn.'

'Ey, she's got herself a mule,' one of the youths called behind her.

Not wanting to attract more attention, she took the package without protest. 'Thank you. See you on Tuesday.'

Then Ashley casually held up a hand and she didn't hear the cab roll away until she closed the door to her block behind her.

Inside, she checked her mail box, then climbed the stairs to the third floor, laden with fine food, French wine, and a pay slip that meant she could treat her boys.

Feeling a warm glow of contentment, she turned her keys in the lock quietly and gently pushed open the apartment door. On the sofa, she saw Farah sleeping, the small TV playing on low volume in front of her. That was electricity she couldn't afford to waste. Crossing the room, she turned off the TV and lay a throw across Farah, her angel friend.

Slipping off her sneakers, she tiptoed to the boys' bedroom. Satisfied they were just fine when she heard them snoring in unison – they took after their father, in that respect – she closed the door and went back to the kitchen, where she unpacked her bread and set the bottle of wine on the counter. She opened the foil packet Ashley had given her to find two slices of tarte tatin, much larger than those they served in the restaurant.

She grinned from ear to ear. Tomorrow, her boys would eat like kings.

Next, she tore open her payslip and breathed a sigh of relief that her earnings – the most she had ever earned in one week – were correct.

Finally, she opened her mail and found that between two bills alone, her entire week's earnings, from the restaurant and the alterations shop combined, were already accounted for.

'At least I can pay them,' she whispered to herself. And as a reward, she poured herself a glass of wine she could never afford to buy, pulled out two chairs at the kitchen table and plonked her bottom in one with her feet up on the other, toasting herself for a job well done.

Chapter Ten

Emily

Emily was on her way to the office loos with a bottle-green silk blouse on a hanger in one hand and her make-up bag and a wig in the other. Her boss almost knocked her off her Louboutins as he marched past, reading mock-up pages of the next print edition of the paper, not looking up to see where he was going. Emily could imagine him as one of those kids in school who sat in the library at lunch rather than playing football in the yard with the other boys.

'Emily, you haven't sent me a draft article for the next edition yet,' he said, not apologising for Emily's near tumble.

'I haven't eaten anywhere that I want to rave about yet. Janey and I are going to a new lobster bar tonight. If that doesn't give me ammunition, I'll pull something out of the stocks.'

'Well, here's hoping it's fantastic or fantastically crap,' he said, already walking away with his head back in his paper.

As a general rule, Emily only wrote up a dining experience when it was worthy of the extra clientele it would garner from being featured in the *NYT*, or if it was undeserving of the actual or anticipated high praise it had had, or would receive, from other critics. Her preference was certainly for the former and, of the five or six restaurants she visited in a week, she would usually find one to sing about. But sometimes, negative reviews, while they always brought with them more grief than they were worth, were justified. For example, she had once written a negative review about a celebrity chef who brought his British gastro pub concept to Manhattan and, frankly, it blew. New Yorkers wanted subtly delicious food that they could make up for with just one extra hour of gym time or HIIT, not dripping-in-butter stodge like you might find in the pubs in England, which you couldn't burn off in a month of daily spin classes.

But she was mindful that what went to print in her name had the power to make or break a restaurant, especially one that was new on the scene or that had undergone major change. She wouldn't kick a fledgling without good reason, just as she wouldn't pretend an ugly duckling was beautiful in its own way.

Janey was already in the ladies' room and had changed from her comfy skater-boy dress and flat boots into wide-legged couture pants, fiercely pointy Dior shoes and a ruffle-neck white blouse. She had tamed her sometimes frizzy hair into a chic chignon and drawn cat's eyes with her liner.

'*Tu as l'air très chic, mon amie*,' Emily told her, hanging her blouse and wig on the back of a cubicle door and setting her make-up bag in a dry patch around the sinks.

'I heard chic and I'll take it,' Janey said. 'New blouse?'

'Mmmhmm. I felt like a pick-me-up.'

'A pick-me-up, why whatever could be the matter with you?'

'Ha. Ha.'

'Is this you finally admitting that perhaps your father's death has, understandably, got to you?'

Emily frowned as she peeled her body-con tee over her head and hung it over the cubicle door. 'Actually, I had a hangover on Saturday. The bad kind.'

'Like you did or said something bad?'

Emily hesitated. *Had falling out with Oliver been in part her fault? Had the hideousness of breakfast at her mom's house with Maggie been in part her fault?*

'Like I mixed multiple whisky sours with champagne and wine on an empty stomach.'

Janey sucked breath through her teeth. 'Ouch. That'll do it.'

'Nothing this beauty couldn't fix,' Emily said, tucking the silk blouse into her soft leather pencil skirt and admiring the outfit in the mirror.

She tied back her hair, covered it with a hair cap and slipped on the wig that was a dead ringer for Isla Fisher's auburn locks. A quick blush, a liner touch up and a swivel of lipstick and she was ready to wipe it all off again with fresh, succulent lobster meat.

Crustacean was the new venture from renowned seafood chef and Saturday morning TV personality Ellis Sawyer. The interior was 'Manhattan seafood bar', a central kitchen surrounded by glass cases of fish on ice and wooden stools so guests could pitch up at the bar, enjoying the sights, the sounds and the smells of the kitchen. Emily loved the general feel. What she didn't love were the overkill fish decorations cast around the walls. She made a quick note once she and Janey had been seated at the bar – there were tables and booths but their preference was to be upfront with the chefs.

The same waiter who had seated them appeared at their side, in black trousers, a crisp white shirt and a black apron emblazoned with the Crustacean logo – an unremarkable gold threaded lobster crawling out from behind the *a*. The staff were dressed traditionally but looked clean and groomed, an important look to get right in a place that sold raw fish. That the staff could go unnoticed was a plus. Emily made another note.

'Our signature martini, courtesy of Mr. Sawyer,' the waiter explained, setting down two martinis and a small plate of various amuse-bouches, which he informed them were a spiced seared tuna, beluga caviar and ceviche on crostini.

That Mr. Sawyer had sent free drinks meant two things. Firstly, despite her efforts at disguise, the head chef knew Emily was here and exactly what she could do for him, if her experience was up to scratch. This was great in terms of quality for her and Janey but not so good in terms of her ability to get the true diner's experience. Second, she and Janey could order the most expensive items on the menu and know that they would be entirely complimentary. And, from experience, Emily knew her friend would do just that.

'So, what did you and Oliver fight about this time?' Janey asked, rinsing ceviche from her mouth with a large sip of martini. 'That's too good to be legal.'

'A cliché line from a journalist, if ever I heard one,' Emily said, though she had to admit, if the amuse-bouches were anything to go by, she may have found herself something to write about tonight.

'The fight?' Janey urged.

'It was less a fight, more a drunken disgruntlement.'

'On your part, or his?'

Emily gave Janey the side-eye as she sipped her drink. 'I'm just… It was just…' She sighed. 'I guess, I got drunk. Like I said, I was drinking on an empty stomach and it didn't sit too well. That's it, in a nutshell.'

Janey nodded as she twizzled her olives on a stick in her glass. 'Was everyone else drunk?'

'No. That was half the problem. Cassandra and William told us they're having a baby and we were supposed to be celebrating. Olly felt like I ruined it.'

'Did you?'

She scoffed. 'I certainly put a dampener on mine and Olly's evening. In my defence, I hadn't wanted to go. We'd rescheduled from the weekend my dad died and I couldn't be bothered. I also didn't know they would be sharing good news with us.'

'That's not like you. Next you'll be telling me you would have rather stayed in and cooked tonight.'

'I'm not sure it would have been a bad idea on Saturday, except for the fact I can't cook.'

'There's a big difference between can't cook and won't cook, Ems. Training from being in diapers until you were twenty-six years old with your Michelin-celebrated father qualifies you to cook, I'd say.'

Emily didn't like where the conversation had drifted. So when the waiter returned to clear their glasses, she told him, 'Let's go for another round of those, thanks.'

And when the second martini arrived, Emily didn't hold back. She finished the drink in three long mouthfuls, pretending she didn't see the scrutinising look she received from Janey.

'Hell, I'm a mom who's been let out. If you want to drink on a school night, I'm in. But just let me say this, then we can get drunk and eat as much lobster as you want.'

Emily inhaled deeply. 'Let's hear it.'

'It's okay not to be okay, Ems. Everyone's situation is different and no matter what went on between you and your dad, no matter how well you try to hide it from other people, you're entitled to grieve in your own way. Okay?'

Emily nodded, her throat suddenly tight. 'Okay.'

'And if you want to talk, you'll reach out to me. Promise me, then I'll leave you alone to lobster.'

'I promise,' Emily said, then bared her teeth in a mock angelic grin. The truth was, she didn't know whether she wanted people to care that her dad had passed or not. She didn't know whether *she* wanted to care. But at least Janey offered to care if Emily wanted her to, which was more than her fiancé was offering. 'Now, what wine shall we have with dinner?'

'Something extortionate.'

And as the friends laughed, Emily figured that Janey, a new silk blouse and a plentiful supply of booze were just the recipe to make her feel okay.

Without those things, Emily was starting to think that she had no idea what she wanted any more. Her figured out life – food critic, Wall Street fiancé, gorgeous Brooklyn Heights apartment, a wardrobe to rival Carrie Bradshaw's and free fine dining on tap – didn't seem to plug all the holes inside her any more.

Or maybe, as she hoped would turn out to be the case, she just had a temporary hole that would close up of its own accord. The sooner the better. Because if her paper-perfect life didn't tick all the boxes, what on earth *did* she want?

Chapter Eleven

Maggie

Maggie's arm ached as she furiously hand-whisked a third batch of cake batter in a mixing bowl. She could have borrowed the electric KitchenAid from the pastry station but she wanted to do things the old-fashioned way this morning. More than anything, she wanted to drag out the process of making an abundance of surprise-centred, butter-iced cupcakes.

It was approaching ten in the morning and she had been in the restaurant kitchen for nearly three hours. She had been awake for something like seven. She didn't want to count how few hours that meant she had actually slept – if tossing and turning and dreaming like she had eaten a kilo of cheese before bed even counted as sleep.

She had let herself into the kitchen with her hair still wet from the quick shower she had at home and slipped a JS apron over her jeans and sweater. After finding everything she needed from the stores, she set off weighing her fears and anxiety and mixing them with sugar and spices in a bowl until they looked less vivid than they had in her nightmares.

But she was still whisking with rage at what was left behind. *Ethan James.* Of all the people Alexander could have chosen to take over the kitchen, why did it have to be Ethan?

She had first met Ethan at chef school eight years ago. Her very first thoughts were something along the lines of *this guy is distractingly good-looking*, all leather jacket, motorbike, sunglasses and ruggedly messy hair. But as soon as the class were asked to stand in a circle in the kitchen and introduce themselves she had realised he was one hundred per cent up his own ass.

He had reeled off every celebrity chef connection he had in the world, then finished his monologue by declaring he was only in chef school at all because his experimental style of cooking scared people. *Who even says that?*

'They want to tame me,' he said. As if he was some sort of exotic cat.

The stink of it was, Ethan *could* cook. If they were given a freestyle assignment, Ethan stormed ahead of the class. He won *every* competition.

Then one day, he was paired against Maggie and they were tasked with producing a French classic with a subtle twist of their choosing.

This is my chance, Maggie had thought. She knew she was good at the classics. She had read every book she could get her hands on, often falling asleep at night with the book on her chest. She had cooked all the classic dishes Jean-Sébastien had on the menu in his restaurant countless times.

She was up for the challenge and excited to wipe the – admittedly very attractive – smirk off Ethan's face.

Then she overheard him talking to the popular guys in the class – the loudest, most arrogant guys.

'Nervous? *Pfft*. What is her name? *Maggie?* You know where she worked before this, right? A cafe. She's just a glorified baker, not a real chef. She's dreaming if she thinks she can out-chef me.'

Dreaming. That word had thrown her right back to New Jersey. She heard her mom calling her a *dreamer*, a *fantasist*, an *accident*.

And just like that, Ethan had stolen her resolve.

She came second in class to Ethan but she knew she could have done better, should have done better, *would* have done better if she hadn't overheard him badmouthing her. If he hadn't planted that seed of doubt in her mind.

She was *always* second, and always fighting harder than every man in the kitchen just to retain that title.

Finally, she had a shot at being first and once again Alexander had stepped in and made her second to Ethan egotistical James.

Her parents were right. They had said she would be mad to move to the city; that she would never make it as a somebody just because she could make a few cakes. And now, they'd be sitting on a cloud somewhere looking down on her and saying, *we told you so*.

She whisked her cake batter so hard that it started to spit out of the bowl.

'I thought I could smell cake. I assumed it would be Ashley getting a head start on the window decorations for the hotel bakery. But I am delighted to find a princess rather than a frog.'

Charles swept breezily into the kitchen with a full cafetière of coffee, two mugs and a milk jug, oblivious to her foul mood.

'Ashley isn't a frog,' Maggie told him, setting down her cake batter that was now over-beaten.

'Ah, next to my Maggie, anyone is a frog.' Charles poured two coffees without needing to ask whether Maggie would benefit from a caffeine hit. 'Though most princesses aren't onto their...' He considered the racks of cooling sponges, then peered into the oven where another batch were rising. 'Third, perhaps fourth, round of cakes by this time of day.'

Maggie accepted a mug full of coffee and held it between her hands, enjoying the warmth in the otherwise cool kitchen. Charles's presence alone had distracted her and taken the edge off her anger, leaving her feeling drained and very much in need of coffee. 'Third large batch,' she confirmed. 'Why are you here already, Charles?'

'Stock count. I have the pleasure of going wine-tasting this afternoon. Can I interest you?'

'I have the pleasure of going raw meat-viewing this afternoon but thank you for the invitation.'

'Well, since we both have busy days ahead, why don't you tell Grandpa Charles what has you baking cakes this morning?'

Maggie shrugged. 'I thought I'd do something nice for the guys.'

'Yes, a very manly choice, the... ah, cupcake, is it?'

Despite her low mood, Maggie laughed. 'I'll do blueberry icing.'

Charles nodded. 'And now for the real answer.'

'Couldn't sleep.'

Charles sipped his coffee. 'Might this have something to do with a certain Ethan James?'

'You've heard, then?'

'Sadly, yes.'

'Then you know I've let everyone down.' Feeling herself well up, exactly what she was trying to avoid by burying herself in cupcakes, Maggie set aside her coffee and began spooning batter into a baking tray. Angry was much better than weepy.

'You've let no one down, Maggie.'

She dropped her wooden spoon and bowl to the counter unintentionally hard. 'No? Charles, of course I have. I've been training for this job for years. I've put everything into this kitchen and Alexander is hiring someone like Ethan James. Who, don't get me wrong, I know is better than me, his accolades say as much. But he's new-age. An experimenter. He isn't French classic. And that's what this restaurant is supposed to be. That's what Jean-Sébastien founded every menu and every dish on.'

She thought of how hard Jean-Sébastien had worked to make his restaurant the prestigious establishment it was. 'I'm just not good enough and I have to face facts. I can't stop Ethan James from taking over everything Jean-Sébastien built.'

It was no use trying any more, her tears broke free. She didn't bother hiding them from Charles as she turned to look him in the eye.

'He gave me a chance, Charles. Before Jean-Sébastien took me under his wing, I was wasting my life, earning a rock-bottom wage making cupcakes and selling them in a tiny store to people who could drop six dollars on a cake they may or may not eat.'

What Maggie didn't say out loud was that Jean-Sébastien had given her Emily, too. A friend whose love and support she hadn't known she needed until it came into her life. It had been Emily, after all, who bought one of her cupcakes and saw her potential, challenging her to make bigger and better cakes. It had been Emily who pushed her to become a chef under her father's tutelage.

Charles handed her a pocket square to dab her tears and blow her nose. Shaking his head, he brought a hand gently to her shoulder. 'Maggie May.' He tutted. 'Never have I seen you so defeatist. You're right, you will be letting someone down – you'll be letting yourself down, and only yourself, if you don't wipe away these tears and prove your critics wrong.'

Sniffing, she asked, 'What do you mean?'

'You have ten weeks to run this kitchen the way *you* want to run it. The way I see it, you have ten weeks to convince Alexander that he made a mistake in hiring Ethan James a.k.a. the wizard chef. And if he doesn't change his mind, at least you will have shown the world what you can do and the next move you make will be to head chef of your own kitchen. You have to prove your worth, Maggie. So get your tears out and put them behind you because the Maggie I know wouldn't go down without a fight. Do you know how I know that?'

She shrugged.

'Because neither would her mentor.'

She took a deep breath and stood up straighter. 'Fighting.' She nodded. 'I can give that jackass Ethan James a fight. His dry ice and shock value have no place here.'

'That's more like it. Now, when can Grandpa Charles have one of these cupcakes?'

Maggie chuckled. 'I'm going to pop these trays in the oven then fill and ice the batch that's cooling over there. I'll bring you one to the cellar. Let me see… lemon curd centre and a strawberry top?'

'You know me too well.' Charles swaggered out of the kitchen, coffee in hand, singing Rod Stewart's 'Maggie May'.

—

After an afternoon of viewing, feeling and smelling raw meat, Maggie returned to the restaurant ready for Thursday night's service. She slipped through the back of the kitchen, depositing a bag of fresh herbs and cherry tomatoes from the market that had smelled so good she couldn't resist buying them. She headed straight through to the staff changing area, where she swapped her casual clothes for chef pants, jacket and shoes. Scraping her hair back into a tight bun, she looked in the mirror to make sure her hat was on straight.

'Okay, Maggie, time to prove your worth,' she told her reflection.

Feeling like a different woman to the one who had walked into the kitchen to bake cakes that morning, Maggie made her way to *her* kitchen, the smells of prep for the evening menu leading her there like Hansel and Gretel's breadcrumb trail.

Only her good mood wasn't interrupted by a wicked witch. Oh no, what stopped Maggie in her tracks was something much eviler.

'What are you doing in my kitchen?'

Her words left her mouth with uncommon malice and must have been loud enough to draw the attention of every nearby chef in the kitchen. As one, they turned from their stations to look at her – or, perhaps, they had been working with pricked ears, anticipating this very moment.

Just how long had Ethan James been in her kitchen?

Ethan was leaning across the shoulder of Josh, who had recently been promoted to temporary sous chef as part of the forced reshuffle in the kitchen. In front of Josh were four pans, each containing a different sauce, and clearly Ethan was sticking his nose in where it didn't belong, at least not for ten weeks.

As Maggie pushed back her shoulders and folded her arms across her chest, Ethan stood up straighter and mirrored her position, drawing her attention to what was still, seven years on from chef school, a sculpted torso. *Who did he think he was, standing up to her, the head chef, in her own kitchen?*

'I came to check out what will be my new kitchen and to meet the members of my new team.'

Maggie bristled at the slight – but very much there – emphasis on 'my' when he spoke. 'Well, you've seen now. So unless you're hanging around to gloat, I'd appreciate if you let us concentrate on tonight's service.'

A small frown marred his otherwise perfect features and he uncrossed his arms. 'Why would I want to glo—'

'And another thing,' Maggie interrupted, trying and failing to keep a lid on her irritation. 'If you *are* in *my* kitchen, you can leave your leather jacket at the door. It's not sanitary. You've had that thing for years.'

He snorted. 'Always a stickler.'

At the risk of saying something to undermine her position further, Maggie decided to say nothing at all, though she did give him a deathly scowl.

'Your kitchen, your rule, Chef. For now. And helping with tonight's service was what I was doing. I was just telling your sous chef here, that his red wine reduction could use more—'

Maggie held up a hand to silence him, then took a clean teaspoon from a pot on the counter. Josh held up the pan towards her and Maggie spooned, blew on and tasted the reduction.

'A little more salt, chef,' she said.

'I agree,' Ethan told her. 'If you'd let me finish, I was going to suggest a pinch of salt and, to make it interesting, next time try frying off pancetta first and adding it to the base. You can sieve it out later but it will add depth and bring out those key flavours, especially the thyme. Once the jus is half reduced you could whisk through some butter and dark chocolate, at least seventy per cent—'

'We're aiming for classic, not *your* kind of interesting,' Maggie bit. 'That's what Jean-Sebastian's is — a classic French fine dining restaurant. You can save your potions and wand-waving for when you're in post. Okay?'

Ethan held up his hands but laughed indignantly. 'Just as much fun as you always were Maggie, huh?'

'Maybe your kind of fun isn't for everyone, Ethan. Some of us can't afford to play. Now, did you want to borrow a uniform or are you leaving?'

Shaking his head with a smirk, he took the sunglasses that had been hooked into the V-neck of his white T-shirt and covered his eyes, despite still being indoors. 'It's been good to catch up, Maggie. I'll see you soon.'

He waved a hand flippantly as he left the kitchen, leaving Maggie burning holes in his back with her eyes. 'Ten weeks will be too soon, Ethan.'

'Oh, and, ah, thanks for the cupcake. A real classic dish.'

Urghhhh. He boiled her blood. Ethan James was nothing but a womanising, cocky, frustratingly good-looking and irritatingly celebrated chef. 'I can't stand that guy.'

'For what it's worth,' Josh said, tossing salt into his red wine reduction, 'I love your cupcakes.'

Rolling her eyes, Maggie started to make rounds of the kitchen, observing and tasting the hard work of her chefs. But she couldn't get Ethan James out of her head – what would Ethan think about this balance of flavours? What would he suggest to add more acidity to that dish or something else to lift it? Betrayal, that's all she got from her silly mind. Betrayal.

She didn't know then that her mind would betray her again in her sleep. That she would see the way those dark jeans had hugged Ethan's butt just so, and how his feet had looked big, very big in those boots. That his toned chest and bad-boy leather jacket she pretended to hate would play a prominent role in her hormone-infested imagination. That she would dream of kissing those annoyingly full smirking lips, as she had dreamed many times years ago in chef school.

Chapter Twelve

Nayomi

Once the pan of water on the cooker came to boil, Nayomi turned down the heat and carefully cracked in four eggs to poach. For the second week in a row, she had taken leftover bread from the restaurant and now set about arranging the sourdough onto plates.

'Can I do something?' Farah asked from where she was sitting at Nayomi's kitchen table, still in her love heart print pyjamas and slippers, which she had worn to venture the fifteen yards from her apartment door to Nayomi's this morning for breakfast.

'You could make coffee, if you like? There's a new pot of instant in the cupboard but I'm out of milk.'

'Do you want me to grab some from my place?' Farah asked, already out of her seat and filling the kettle.

'I can take black coffee so it's up to you,' Nayomi said, taking her Saturday morning pièce de résistance from the refrigerator, which now had a working lightbulb, thanks to her pay from the restaurant hitting her bank account last week.

'Ooo, what have you got there?' Farah asked, hovering at Nayomi's shoulder as she unwrapped the paper bag and breathed in the scent of four slices of proper ham from the local deli.

'A Saturday breakfast treat,' Nayomi said, holding up the ham for Farah to sniff.

'I think I like your job at the restaurant,' Farah said with a smile and playfully flirty eyebrows dancing up and down.

'At least *you* do. Roshan is giving me the cold shoulder this week.'

'I got that impression. He'll come around; he just misses you in the evenings.'

'If only he appreciated that the job is mostly for him and Nuwan, you know?'

'He's a kid, Nayomi. He'll get it a decade from now. When he likes you again.'

Then she laughed and Nayomi had to laugh at the sad state of affairs too. When it came to Roshan, Nayomi was firmly within the old adage – damned if she did and damned if she didn't.

She often wondered if her eldest son's attitude would be different if his father was around. *Was she strict enough? Did she guide him enough? Did he get everything he needed from her or did he need a man in his life?*

She buttered the sourdough on the plates, laid a slice of thick ham on top of each and scooped her almost round poached eggs out of the pan and placed them on top of the ham. Then she checked the taste of the Hollandaise sauce she had made from scratch, happy that her experiment of cooking coriander seeds into the butter base had worked wonderfully, and spooned a dollop onto each egg.

Farah called the boys from their respective positions – Roshan in his bedroom, sulking, and Nuwan drawing in the lounge, under strict orders to stay away from his big brother until at least after breakfast following their fisticuffs over something and nothing at eight thirty that morning.

Farah put four glasses of water and two mugs of black coffee on the table as the boys took their seats. When Nayomi set down their extravagant breakfasts in front of them, she savoured their wide-eyed surprise. She was sure it meant more to her than to the boys that she could afford to set them up for the weekend with a fancy breakfast, but this moment of excitement in their eyes before they demolished their food was an image of joy she would deposit straight into her memory bank.

'I'm going to get too used to these weekend mornings,' Farah said, piercing her egg and delighting in the yolk running across her ham and soaking into her bread.

Nayomi also delighted in the precision of her egg timing. She smiled as she watched her boys and her best friend devour their meals, reminded of how wonderful a family meal used to be in her village growing up. In Sri Lanka, food brought people together. It was a celebration and rarely had she experienced this in all her time living in America. But these weekend mornings, with surprises constructed around what she had managed to save from the trash at the restaurant, had started to remind her of the wonder of food. The pleasure of seeing happy faces and full tummies.

She wondered if this was how Maggie and Ashley felt during every service at the restaurant. *Did they cherish that sense of achievement in bringing people together to celebrate exquisite food?*

She had never known a true sense of job satisfaction. When she moved to America, she was expected to be a housewife and that had been the role she adopted until Shan died. Now, work to her was what put bread on the table – more literally these days than ever before. How amazing it must be to feel accomplished at serving happiness. And as she tucked into her ham, eggs and delicious sourdough, she had a moment of clarity. *That is why they suffer the stress of the kitchen*, she thought.

While she was happy for Farah to have a second mug of coffee once their plates had been cleared, Nayomi decided not to have one herself and save the granules. She could get hot drinks for free at the restaurant.

Nuwan rested back in his seat, pushing out his stomach and patting it with both hands. 'Oh boy,' he said, like a man of many more years. 'That was good, Mom.'

Nayomi smiled. A smile which grew when her more stubborn child conceded, 'It was good. Thanks.'

'Maybe my new job doesn't seem so bad on a weekend, huh, Roshan?' she asked, which turned his face into a frown.

'What do you boys want to do today?' In truth, the options were limited to free activities because even with a second wage now, they were far from flush and she was still catching up on settling old bills. 'Maybe we could go to the park?'

'Yeah!' Nuwan shouted.

'We always go to the park,' Roshan muttered. 'Anyway, I'm going to Brent's house today. His mom said he could have some of us over for pizza and Nintendo.'

'Well, I thought we could spend some time together today, before my shift later. Just the three of us.'

'That's so unfair. It's not my fault you never see us. I already told Brent I would go at school yesterday. I'd be the only person not going.'

'Roshan, this hard-done-by attitude needs to change.' Nayomi's argument was cut short by the ringing of her phone. 'This discussion is not over,' she told her son, moving to the lounge to answer the call, which was flashing up as *Work JS* on her screen.

'Hello?'

'Nayomi? It's Maggie. From the restaurant.'

'Oh, hi, Maggie.'

'I know this is short notice but Bill has called in sick and I was wondering if you'd be able to start your shift early today?'

Nayomi peered around the lounge wall into the kitchen where Roshan was sitting with his arms folded as Farah appeared to be trying to reason with him.

'I'm not sure, Maggie, I—' *Really don't want to let my boys down.*

'We'll pay you double for the extra hours and send the staff car to pick you up.'

Oh. Bill started four hours earlier than she did on a Saturday. That meant eight hours of pay and with Nuwan's birthday on the horizon…

'Can you give me five minutes to see if I can make some childcare arrangements?'

'Sure. Call me back.'

After a call with Brent's mom to 'okay' Nuwan tagging along with Roshan for the afternoon, Nayomi called Maggie back and agreed to work the extra hours. All she had to do then was break the news to Roshan, who hated having his little brother accompany him to *anything* because it was *so* uncool.

—

Once he was over the life-trauma of his younger brother attending Brent's computer party, which had now turned into a sleepover since Brent's mom had offered to keep Roshan and Nuwan overnight, Roshan had walked into Brent's house with a grin. His manners were hit and miss at home, but to Brent's mom he was polite, thanking her and handing over the cheap flowers Nayomi had bought on the way over as a 'thank you'. Three bucks wasn't much of a gesture, yet the flowers had been received with grace and for Nayomi's part, she was grateful to have the gift of childcare.

By contrast, Nuwan had looked forlorn on the threshold of Brent's house. Though he was a tough cookie and, for his age, remarkably more intuitive than his older brother, Nayomi felt the sadness he was holding back when he hugged her tightly goodbye. That cracked her heart more than if he had kicked and screamed or openly sulked, the way Roshan tended to do.

So when the staff car beeped outside her apartment block, Nayomi was torn in two. On the one hand, she was doing the best thing by her boys in earning money; on the other, she wished she could spend all her time making their lives fuller and richer with her time.

She was so consumed by her own thoughts that she didn't notice Ashley sitting in the back of the car until she was inside and closing the door.

'Hey there,' Ashley said.

To her surprise, Nayomi found herself checking him out. *Why?* She had no idea. It was just a general perusal, she supposed. But, for the record, she approved of his manly jeans – not like those tight, skinny low-rise things that seemed so popular nowadays, but a solid stonewash, with little shape at all. She liked his hooded knit sweater, that showcased what appeared to be naturally strong arms. The kind of arms that could be very handy around the home. He smelled clean and fresh, as if he had recently showered – an image Nayomi forced from her mind the second it appeared.

'Hi,' she said, feeling a little guilty for having scrutinised his appearance. It was something she didn't like others to do to her, conscious that she couldn't always afford the latest fashion trends or the most flattering clothes.

Yet, when Ashley caught her off guard by declaring, 'You look nice,' she didn't feel annoyed. In fact, she was pleased that due to her pit stop at Brent's house, Nayomi had showered and blow-dried her hair before putting on the fancier of two pairs of jeans she owned and tucking in a striped shirt.

Despite her relief, though, she felt her skin heat at the compliment. She wasn't used to compliments, nor did she feel entirely comfortable receiving one. She couldn't remember a man complimenting her since her husband had died.

'I had to take the boys to their friend's house. They've gone to a sleepover.'

She wasn't sure why she was justifying her appearance but Ashley probably thought she was overdressed to be heading to work as a porter. It was one of the smartest outfits Nayomi owned. And now, with the driver glancing at her through the rear-view mirror and knowing that Ashley had given her appearance a once-over, she felt uncomfortable and silly. She was even wearing the body spray that Farah had bought her for Christmas, which she used sparingly.

Taking the elastic from her wrist, she quickly braided her hair into her usual work style and tied off the end.

'I didn't think you worked Saturday afternoons,' Ashley said.

'I don't, usually. Bill is sick.'

'Ah, gotcha. It's good that you could jump in at short notice, then.'

She hummed. 'What do they normally do? You know, if Bill is sick or on holiday or something?'

'They'd get the most junior apprentice or commis chef to stand in or they'd ask the hotel to borrow one of their porters. They'll be pleased you could work.'

'Well, me too. Every little helps.' She hadn't needed to say that and wished she hadn't, so quickly added, 'It's my son's birthday next Sunday and I'd like to get him something nice.' *As opposed to reviving something hand-me-down from Roshan*, she thought.

'Your youngest or oldest?'

'Youngest. He'll be eight.'

'That's Nuwan, right?'

She couldn't help but smile as she nodded. He had listened. In her experience, men had very selective hearing, even her husband had opted in or out of conversations as it suited him.

Then Ashley apologised as he pulled his phone from the front pocket of his sweater.

'Hey. You okay? I'm on my way to work… You know I work Saturday afternoon through to evening… I'll be home around the same time as I'm always home on a Saturday… I did say goodbye… I shouted goodbye on my way out… It's in the cupboard above the cooker.'

Nayomi pretended not to eavesdrop but it was tricky in a confined space. She also pretended not to see Ashley shaking his head as he ended the call, gazing fixedly out the window. 'Sorry about that.'

Nayomi turned her focus back to Ashley. 'No trouble.' But she was really thinking, *your wife or girlfriend sounds high maintenance.*

Still, Ashley had someone at home to call him about nonsense and nag him about not saying goodbye properly – which probably meant with a hug and a kiss. On that basis, Nayomi couldn't feel too sorry for him. And she really had no idea what Ashley was like at home. Perhaps he was lazy and messy and drove his wife or girlfriend half to distraction. Nayomi had once known that well.

Other than going out to work, her husband had assumed the role of a true Sri Lankan man and expected Nayomi to be the doting wife, her life revolving around pleasing him and caring for their children. It was the role she came to America to fulfil and it had led to many wonderful memories. She and Shan had cared for each other and they had both loved the boys more than life itself. When Shan worked as a lecturer, they weren't flush exactly but they had money to enjoy days out at Coney Island and Staten Island. They had ventured to Boston and Washington for Shan's work and made mini family holidays of the trips.

But that role had not stood her in good stead for being alone and having to provide for the boys herself.

Since her husband had died, Nayomi had been forced to start a new life, learning what it was like to be a working mom, fending for her family with few skills and no qualifications. It was far from a breeze but she was trying. Maybe one day, she'd even do something for herself.

Chapter Thirteen

Emily

Emily had woken early for a Sunday, even earlier than Oliver, and slipped out of bed without disturbing him, which hadn't been tricky, since he was a heavy snorer and they weren't the cuddling type, preferring to each have their own share of the bed. Even when they made love, they didn't end with a post-coital snuggle. Rather, they would roll over, back to back but not touching, and say goodnight, if they remembered.

After pulling on a pair of yoga pants and a zip-up, she had decided to go for a stroll. She stopped off at her favourite bakery, picking up two newspapers, two lattes and pastries for Oliver's breakfast. Now, she was sitting at the window of their lounge, the sun defying the imminent autumn weather and beaming through the floor-to-ceiling window panes. Emily was relishing the heat before Oliver inevitably turned on the air conditioning.

She heard Oliver pad through the apartment and move directly to the kitchen but she was too engrossed in the latest Trump scandal to look up, sipping her latte on autopilot.

'This man is single-handedly saving the print press industry,' she said.

'What's that?' Oliver asked, mumbling through a mouthful of pastry from the kitchen bench, carrying a second croissant on a plate.

'Trump.'

'Right.'

'I got you a latte and a paper.' Emily gestured to the space on the opposite side of the table where she had left a plate, a sachet of butter, a small pot of his favourite strawberry jam and a newspaper.

'Thanks.' He took a seat wearing only his lounge shorts and a thin T-shirt, yet still said, 'It's roasting in here. Aren't you having breakfast?'

Emily had her head back in her paper but raised her take-out cup and gave it a gentle wiggle from side to side. 'Just coffee for me today.'

'A skinny day, huh?'

She figured the answer was obvious so didn't bother offering a response. Oliver didn't seem to need one as he unfolded his paper, took another bite of pastry and settled back into his seat.

And there they stayed, each sipping coffee, each silently reading the news, until…

'Oh my word!' Emily leaned forward and pulled the newspaper even closer to her face, as if the act might change the words written on the page. 'I can't believe it.' She continued to read, chortling as she did. 'This is too good.'

'All right, I give in, what is it?' Oliver asked, lowering his own paper to look at her.

Emily could barely contain her excitement as she read aloud: '*Following the death of legendary Jean-Sébastien, the executive chef of his eponymous restaurant at the Grande Parisienne Hotel, the three-Michelin star French fine-dining restaurant has agreed terms with celebrity and two-Michelin star chef, Ethan James. Critics will no doubt be eagerly anticipating the shake-up, which is set to take place in November, desperate to see what the notorious experimental style of James will mean for the restaurant. And the question everyone will be asking is, will the move land Ethan James his third star?'*

Emily chortled. 'Maggie will have been sitting in the wings, waiting to take over the kitchen.' She clapped. 'In swoops Ethan James. This is gold.'

'I thought you couldn't care less about the restaurant?'

'I don't care. That's the point.'

Oliver's brow scrunched, showing increasingly prominent signs of ageing despite his desperate bids to erase them. 'You seem to care.'

'Well, I don't. It's just funny.'

'Isn't it a shame? I mean, if I understand it correctly, Ethan James is very new-age and a bit wacky, right? Don't get me wrong, when we ate at his current place, I loved it, but it doesn't fit with French fine dining.'

Emily wafted a hand through the air and sipped what were now cold final dregs of latte in a move that simply gave her something to do as she suddenly felt uncomfortable. 'That place has needed a shake-up for a long time. My da— Jean-Sébastien couldn't let anyone have a say. He wouldn't be told his ways were archaic. He couldn't even accept a tweak on French classics. That's what's ironic. He wanted to build this huge legacy and he would have wanted Maggie – his sous chef – to follow in his shoes. Lord knows she's just the sheep to his shepherd. But that won't happen with Ethan taking over.'

'You're the critic,' Oliver said, shrugging as he raised his newspaper back to eye level. 'Just seems like a shame.'

Emily's giddiness turned to anger. *What did he know?* Then, just as abruptly, it turned to sadness. Because her father *had* wanted to grow a legacy. He had wanted to pass that down to his next of kin, as his father had, and his father's father. He had wanted to pass on Jean-Sébastien's to Emily.

But that had been a long time ago, back when Emily wanted to be a chef and take over the restaurant. Before he drove her mad every single day with his constant nitpicking, shouting at her, refusing to even listen to her ideas. Before every day in the kitchen became a chore, an argument, a cloud of anger waiting to burst. Before super-Maggie took Emily's rightful place.

Folding her newspaper, she slammed it down on the table.

'What happens to people like her, anyway?'

'Who?' Emily snapped.

'The sous chef. Maggie. Is it just like being fired in any other industry? Does she just go get another job? Or are there, you know, chef talent scouts or something?'

But Emily had tuned him out – his words, his actions, her ability to see and hear him. She stormed off to the shower room.

A shame. The only *shame* was Oliver being another man in her life who failed to support her. She twisted the shower knobs violently to start the water and began to undress.

Although, on this occasion, perhaps she had to accept that Oliver hadn't actually done anything wrong. No, Jean-Sébastien had done something wrong. He had been bull-headed and selfish. He had doted on Maggie as if *she* were his daughter. All because Maggie simply did as he told her to do. *Make my French classics, Maggie. Yes, sir, please, sir, three bags full, sir.*

As steam began to fill the bathroom from the hot shower, Emily slumped down onto the toilet seat. *Urgh.* Maggie was just a clone. Nothing but a *yes* girl. She'd had more verve and innovation when she was working in that cupcake store. Even when she and Emily had spent Sundays rustling up a storm in the kitchen for Jean-Sébastien and Isabella – how fake she had been, acting like the best friend Emily had ever known, all the while just schmoozing her dad. Now, Maggie was nothing but unoriginal, at best.

And Emily would make damn sure that the food industry knew it.

With her resolve, she felt some of her anger begin to dissipate. But as she stepped under the shower spray, she wished she could cling onto her anger, because what was left was sadness.

She should have taken over Jean-Sébastien's. If she had, she would have certainly tweaked the menu, played around with the classics in ways her father would never have entertained. Despite her father – and Maggie – thinking otherwise, she wouldn't have obliterated any sense of the classics or the legacy of the restaurant and, yes, her father. Rather, she would have breathed new life into tradition – added a little flair and originality. She and Maggie could have worked alongside each other, like they had in the beginning, having fun together, always tag-teaming the guys when they tried to make wisecracks during their shifts, serving perfect dishes.

But Ethan James was coming in instead and he was certain to make Jean-Sébastien's unrecognisable.

'I'm sorry.' With her wet hair still wrapped in a towel, Emily draped her arms across Oliver's shoulders and pressed her lips to his hair where he still sat at the lounge coffee table with his newspaper.

He stroked her arm. 'What's going on, Ems?'

Moving to his side, she retook the seat she had been sitting in before her shower.

'Am I supposed to ask you if you're okay? Are you grieving? You've got to let me in on what I'm supposed to do here. We've been together for nearly two years and any time your dad has come up, you've dismissed your relationship with your parents as nothing. In fact, you've near chewed my head off for asking anything about them. So I don't. And when he died, I figured that was what I was supposed to do then, too. You said you didn't care. Now, I'm thinking you do care. I don't even know in what direction to take my next step.'

The funny thing about having someone state the obvious, Emily thought, was that it was so obvious, yet she had completely missed it. Did she want him to ask about her dad and how she felt about his death? If he did, how would she answer when she didn't know herself? But was she nevertheless pissed that he had never asked? Yeah.

She heaved a sigh. If she was confused, Oliver must be.

'How about this,' he suggested. 'Let's start small. Why don't you tell me who Maggie is and why you seem to want to stick pins in her eyes?'

Emily felt her lips turn up at one side. 'To tell you who Maggie is would take at least one more coffee. To tell you why we don't get along would take… ooh, a lifetime, maybe?'

Oliver folded his newspaper, set it down on the hard-wood floor and stood up.

Of course, Emily thought, *he didn't really want to know.* That was their relationship. In the early days, it had all been about sex and food. Then holidays. Then a new apartment and what had felt like a rushed, perhaps even forced, engagement. They never delved into anything beyond the superficial, which seemed to suit them fine, except now, when it didn't suit Emily at all.

But Oliver surprised her. Leaning down, he lifted her chin until she looked at him, then he gently kissed her, like he loved her. 'Let's start with coffee, then.'

Emily watched his perfectly tight bottom move under his lounge pants as he walked to the kitchen and smiled. *He gave a damn.*

And so, when he returned with two large mugs of coffee, Emily pulled her legs up onto her chair and started from the beginning.

'Maggie and I met about eight years ago. She was working in my favourite bakery then, making the most delicious cakes. They were cupcakes but had surprise fillings, like lemon curd, jam, peanut butter. I was working at the restaurant at the time—'

'Hold up. Take a step back. You were working in which restaurant? Your dad's?'

She nodded, sipping her coffee. 'I was a chef.'

Her words garnered exactly the reaction she had anticipated. 'A chef? But you can't cook.'

Leaning her head to one side, she said, 'Hmm, more like *won't* cook. I grew up around a celebrated chef, Olly. My life was about food and restaurants. It was only natural, I suppose, that I'd follow in my dad's footsteps. He assumed I would, in any event.'

Closing his eyes, Oliver shook his head, as a confused cartoon character might do after their eyes ballooned out of their head. 'I thought you studied creative writing? Now you tell me you were a chef in a Michelin-starred restaurant?'

'I guess I've left out a few details about my life, here and there,' she confessed. In her defence, they had rarely had deep conversations about the past. There had always been something to do, somewhere to go, people to see. They had been busy having fun, rather than dredging up history. Like her, Oliver had dropped hints and snippets of childhood memories he would rather forget and, she supposed, if two people wanted to forget, one was unlikely to encourage the other to talk. That had been the basis of their mutual understanding. Before today.

'I did study creative writing.' She let out a sombre laugh. 'Perhaps that was the first thing that really ticked him off. See, my dad thought that I should focus solely on establishing myself as a master of the French classics, as he had done, and my grandfather before him. And, at first, studying creative writing wasn't the antithesis of me being a chef. I continued to work in the restaurant while I studied and my father assumed that my writing skills would come in handy when one day I had my own cookbook to publish. But I had a dream of one day writing a book. I wanted to go to France, the home of the classics, and drive around, sampling dishes, drawing inspiration, and putting a twist on the style that was my own. The book would have been about travel, France and food. And actually written by me, not a ghost writer like most chefs have.'

Emily took a sip of coffee as she remembered what had followed. 'My mistake was letting my dad in on this dream. He never saw it as an extension of his work, of the work we did together. He thought it was defiant in some way. Like, me saying I didn't want to continue his legacy, or something.'

Emotion caught her off guard, causing her to look to the East River, staring at the glare of the sun against the water until her wet eyes were dry.

'Fast forward a few years. My dad was increasingly nitpicky with me in the kitchen when I went back full time. I was bursting with ideas to make the menu pop, and he hated them all. Sometimes I think he just hated them to spite me. He saw every idea as some new insubordination. He used to shout in the kitchen, non-stop.'

Oliver, who hadn't moved since she had begun speaking, now pulled the foot of one leg across the thigh of his other and leaned back in his seat. 'Based solely on my knowledge of Gordon Ramsay shows, isn't that what all head chefs are like?'

Emily smiled. 'They can be. Not quite as ridiculous as Gordon, though. But in my dad's case, it felt like it was always targeted at me. *I* had ruined a dish. *I* had made an entire table late. Sometimes it was my fault, others it definitely wasn't, but I always seemed to take the brunt of it. At first, I just took it on the chin, as part of the politics of a professional kitchen – the hierarchy.'

'What happened to change that?' Oliver pushed her forgotten coffee towards her, perhaps sensing she needed a break, and she took a sip.

'I had met Maggie. We became friends. Best friends. It was clear to me that Maggie could do more than make cupcakes and she and I became inseparable. In some ways, both of us had been working so hard trying to prove ourselves to our parents that we hadn't had a chance to make the kind of friendships we had together.'

Emily drifted with her own thoughts, remembering days spent showing Maggie the city. Standing outside on the Staten Island ferry with rain teeming down on them as they laughed, just so that Maggie could get a better view of the Statue of Liberty. Falling in a heap on top of each other as they skated around Rockefeller ice rink in December before warming up with hot chocolates heaped with whipped cream and marshmallows. Those days were gone but Emily couldn't forget how much fun they had been.

'So, anyway, when Jean-Sébastien's was looking for a new junior pastry chef, I suggested Maggie. She had been around my parents, in our house, and they both really liked her. So, my dad gave her a shot.'

Emily sighed, standing with her coffee between her hands and moving to the window. Sitting next to Oliver, under his scrutinising gaze, was just too much.

'At first it was great. We were best friends, we worked the same unsociable hours and spent time together when we weren't in the kitchen. Maggie went to chef school alongside work and started churning her way through the ranks fairly quickly.'

Just like that, the old rage that Emily felt six years ago rekindled. She was back in the kitchen, watching her dad and Maggie with their heads together as they dissected a dish. Oh-so-perfect Maggie understanding her dad's vision, the restaurant vision, the importance of the classics. She never broke ranks, never questioned him.

'My dad continued sniping at me, embarrassing me in front of the staff, shouting down my suggestions in team meetings. But what was new, was that he started to compare me with Maggie. He would listen to anything she had to say, because it was never even slightly off piste. And Maggie…' She shook her head. 'She never spoke up for me with him, not once.'

She broke off, surprised to hear the rasp of her accelerated breath. It was incredible how much it still *hurt*.

'I'm not defending him, Emily, but do you think it's just that you and your dad weren't matched, creatively, to work together? It sounds like you had a healthy relationship up until when you started working full time in his restaurant.'

Emily could feel her anger rising as she squeezed her coffee mug with her fingertips and explained, 'Things changed. I would turn up to my parents' house and Maggie would already be there, helping *my* dad cook Sunday lunch. Dropping off bread and cakes for *my* mom. She loved it. She relished the attention because she had never got it from her own parents. Well, that wasn't *my* fault.'

She ignored the small voice in the back of her mind, reminding her that Maggie had done that before she'd started working at Jean-Sébastien's. That Emily had never had a problem with sharing her family with Maggie until her own relationship with them started to fall apart. She ignored the devil on her shoulder reminding her how she used to feel sorry for Maggie and the way she had been dragged up, without love and attention.

'And then, one night, he started screaming at me in the kitchen because my scallops were overdone – which they weren't. But he didn't tell me to make them again.' She exhaled so heavily that her nostrils flared. 'He told Maggie to re-do the dish. *My* dish. On *my* station. And I lost it. Fairly so, too. He might as well have fired me on the spot. I took off my hat and threw it at him. I took off my jacket and threw that at him too. And he just kept yelling at me. Everyone in the kitchen was looking. The restaurant manager came back to tell us the guests could hear us.'

Her jaw clenched with fury. 'I can never remember if he fired me first or I quit first. Either way, I walked out of his restaurant that night and out of his life. He was welcome to his precious Maggie – seemingly the daughter he had always wanted and never had.'

Oliver said nothing, or if he did, she couldn't hear him past the screaming in her mind, in her ears, as the events of that night played over and over in her head. She hadn't spoken to her dad for years and now he was dead. And it was all Maggie's fault. Maggie the *yes* girl.

God, she hated her.

'Was it?' Oliver said, in a tone that suggested he was repeating himself. His words brought Emily back to the room, which suddenly felt much cooler.

'Huh?'

'Was it Maggie's fault?'

She scowled, realising she had blamed Maggie aloud and irate at Oliver's insinuation. 'It sure as hell wasn't *my* fault!'

Oliver held up his palms. 'No, I know that. That wasn't what I— I didn't mean— Look, that wasn't the right thing to say. I'm thinking you'd rather I didn't say anything at all.'

She continued to stare at him, unable to redirect her rage because there was no one else in the room. 'If you can't say anything without being a dick, then I'd suggest you say nothing at all.'

He inhaled, then slapped his hands on his thighs and stood. 'That's my cue to head out for a run.'

Yes, go for a run, Olly. Run away. Open me up and leave me.

'I think that's the best thing you've said all morning,' she bit, knowing she didn't mean it, unable to stop herself.

Slamming her mug down dangerously hard on the glass table top, she stormed out of the room and got her laptop. Her dad was dead and it was too late. Too late to scream at him, to ask him why, to ask him how he could just let her go. But it wasn't too late to make Maggie pay. It wasn't too late to make sure Maggie never got snapped up by another restaurant, where she could ride on the back of Jean-Sébastien's legacy – the legacy intended for Emily.

Chapter Fourteen

Maggie

Things were starting to fall apart. The kitchen had lost its buzz and so had the food. She couldn't put her finger on what exactly was missing but every dish she presented to the pass seemed to be lacking… something. The flowers used to garnish the dishes didn't seem bright enough, the butter sauce not yellow enough, the fish not white enough.

For the first time since she had been head chef at Jean-Sébastien's, a customer had sent food back this week. Whether Maggie agreed that the duck was overcooked was inconsequential. The fact was, food had been sent back under her watch and, worse still, the plate had been carried back to Maggie by Alexander, who almost looked smug about it.

On Tuesday and Wednesday, Maggie had been handed letters of resignation from two of her more experienced chefs. Both claimed to be 'ready for a change' and felt that the 'time was right for a new challenge'. Yet, she wondered if they would have been as eager to move on to pastures new if Jean-Sébastien was still in charge.

The thing was, until she knew the what, why and how, she had no idea how to fix whatever was broken.

Just when she thought her mood couldn't get any lower, she heard a too familiar voice.

'Evening all,' Ethan said brightly as he breezed into the kitchen in a full *JS* chef's uniform that had clearly been tailored for him, as the trousers hugged his butt quite deliciously and the jacket made his chest look strong and scrumptious.

Maggie had been trying to focus on making a food list to place a farm order as the other chefs prepped for the Friday night service. Tucking her pencil behind her ear and folding her arms, she stood up from the pass.

'Is there a reason you keep appearing in my kitchen like an infestation?'

Ethan laughed, then flashed her what was, objectively, a fairly dazzling smile, creasing the skin at the sides of his mouth and reaching his cheeks. It made it quite difficult for her to maintain the level of frost she was trying to project.

'Maggie.' He dipped his head in greeting.

She raised an eyebrow. 'Well?'

'My restaurant is trialling a new chef tonight and I thought it would be only polite to give him a shot at running the kitchen without me around.'

'Huh. Don't get any ideas, Ethan. You can move in two minutes after I'm gone and not a second before.'

He winked at her. 'Feisty tonight, Maggie. It's a good look on you. Whatever happened to sweet Maggie from school, the teacher's pet?'

'She kept running into an arrogant jerk who was stealing her kitchen from under her feet. What do you want? Service is about to begin.'

Ethan's smile faded but his spirits didn't appear dampened. He looked around the kitchen, holding out his arms from his sides. 'I thought I'd swing by and see how you run things, help out. I want my team to know me and I want to know them before I'm in post. We're all on trial here. You too, if you'd like to work under me.'

Maggie outwardly recoiled. Inwardly, she cursed the tiny flutter in her stomach that his words had provoked – the same flutter she used to get at chef's school, back when she'd had an irrational crush on Ethan. She had been like a schoolgirl, secretly attracted to the popular guy, willing him to show her attention, even if only so she could throw him a snarky retort. How could she loathe a man and still find him sexy? Was it his attention she craved? Or was it just that she missed having someone to spar with? As much as everyone dismissed her as Jean-Sébastien's 'yes man', they'd had a brilliant working relationship and had often battled over each other's suggestions.

'Me? Under *you*? In your dreams, Ethan.' She silently cursed herself for sounding like a wounded teenager.

Ethan smirked, one side of his mouth lifting in a taunting gesture. 'Oh you have been, Maggie. Many a time.'

Thankfully, her anger at the looks and laughs Ethan received from her staff kept Maggie's focus off the resurgence of flutters in her chest and stomach.

'You're a pig,' she jibed, turning her back on him and refocussing on her shopping list. 'And if you interrupt service you'll—'

'Arghhh! Goddamn it!'

Maggie lifted her head sharply to the source of the noise and found her sous chef holding a towel over his hand, with more blood than she would care to see dripping down his wrist and soaking through the sleeve of his white jacket.

She moved quickly but Ethan beat her to the scene, raising Josh's arm in the air and carefully inspecting the knife wound. 'A Band-Aid isn't going to cut it for this one. No pun intended,' Ethan said, turning to Maggie who was now also inspecting the cut.

'He's right, Josh, I think we need to send you to get this stitched. Keep his arm raised, Ethan, I'll get the first aid box.'

Charles was on hand carrying a chair from the dining room just as Josh started to turn an unhealthy shade of grey. Maggie helped him onto the seat and as Ethan held his arm up, Maggie strapped the hand in a bandage. Meanwhile, Charles called for the staff car to take him to hospital.

'See, we make a good team. Me, first responder and supervisor. You, grunt worker,' Ethan said, that smirk firmly back on his face. Maggie could think of some choice words for him right now but bit her lip to keep them in.

Instead, she moved on to her new conundrum – she was a chef down and needed to reshuffle her kitchen, right as the first order was brought in from the restaurant.

Perfect. Just perfect.

'Look, I don't know the menu like you do but I'm here and happy to help, so why don't you take over from Josh and I'll man the pass?'

Maggie glared at Ethan. Five minutes. It had been five minutes and already he was trying to worm his way into her shoes.

She scoured the room. All other options meant rotating her staff from where they had been prepping all afternoon. Allowing Ethan to take the pass was the easiest solution and, realistically, the most likely to produce the best results. Plus, wouldn't she look petty and not at all like a team player if she said no, given that Ethan had openly announced his idea?

With the reluctance of an uncooked potato being asked to mash, she said, 'Fine. But it's a one-off and you'll follow my lead, my instructions. Understand?'

'Yes, ma'am,' he said, with a mock salute that made her rising temper fizz.

'It's yes, *Chef*.'

'Yes, *Chef*.' He winked and swapped places with Maggie at the pass, calling out the first check.

As every response of 'Yes, Chef' was uttered around the kitchen, Maggie grew angrier and more jealous. Soon, this would be how the kitchen looked. Except there was no way, not ever, that she would be standing at the sauces station while Ethan gave orders. She had come second to him once before and would *not* be in that position again.

She really needed to look to the marketplace for another job – preferably head of her own kitchen.

Though she had to block out the reality of the evening's hierarchy, halfway through the service Maggie was forced to admit that things were running relatively smoothly. She had had to guide Ethan through the presentation of some of the dishes the first time he set them but he was, unsurprisingly, a fast learner. More surprisingly for sure, was that he took her direction with grace and didn't try any of the tricks he was notorious for. He respected Maggie's role as head chef, despite appearing to take the lead in the kitchen from the pass.

What they served as a team were top-drawer French classics, presented as such.

They were taking two minutes of downtime as checks went quiet and headed outside to cool off. Ethan took off his hat and ruffled his golden-blond hair as he leaned back against the wall. Just as Maggie found herself watching him, their eyes met.

Recovering quickly from being caught in the act of ogling, she said, 'Thank you for tonight. Though it pains me to admit it, service has been smoother for not having to reshuffle the kitchen.'

'Still half to go yet.'

They both laughed.

'You're a good chef, Maggie. I forgot how particular you are.'

'Hmm, I'm going to take both of those statements as positives.'

'They were well intentioned.' He placed a hand on his heart. 'I swear.'

She pushed her hands into her pockets. 'And I should probably say, thank you for not trying to do anything quirky tonight. I'm sure it hurt being so... how did you used speak of the classics? If my memory serves me correctly, it was something like...'

'Bland and pretentious. I said you're a good chef, Maggie, but that doesn't change my opinion of what is being served up here. Not a problem if you're only targeting the market of wealthy, fifty-years-plus patrons, sure.'

Maggie opened her mouth in shock. Even if she had bad thoughts about another chef, she would never be so brazen as to disclose them.

'I played by the rules tonight because you're the head chef here, Maggie. But you can do better than this. What held you back years ago was being a stickler for the recipe and you're still doing it now but you don't have to. Trust yourself.'

Maggie's eyes narrowed as her jaw stiffened. 'You have no idea why I am the way I am. You don't know me.'

Ethan shrugged. 'So fill me in. You judge me on someone you think you know from eight years ago. At least I'm here, telling you how I see things right now, and as far as I can see, you're wasting your talent.'

She scoffed, shaking her head. 'Look around you, Ethan, I am the only female chef in the kitchen. Don't you get it? I *have* to play by the rules. I have to do everything better than my male peers, just to keep my job.'

'I don't think that's true at all. I think that's an excuse because you don't dare follow your instincts.'

'Oh yeah?' Her fists clenched at her sides. 'Tell your buddy, Alexander, that.'

And perfectly on cue, she heard Alexander's voice call out. 'Chef?'

Ethan followed her into the kitchen where they found Alexander standing on the restaurant side of the pass.

'What's up?' she asked, residual anger tinging her tone.

'Emily Blanchon is here and based on her order, I'd say she's here in her official capacity,' Alexander told her, handing over a check for food.

'Emily? Jean-Sébastien's daughter Emily? *New York Times* Emily?'

'The very one,' Alexander said. 'Not sure why she's decided to come in this interim period but she's here.'

There was a bitter tone to Alexander's words and it was obvious why. Alexander would have loved Emily to critique the restaurant but he would have invited her months from now, when Ethan was in post, the name of the place had undoubtedly changed, and he was looking for recognition from the *New York Times* of how great the new-look restaurant at the Grande Parisienne Hotel was doing.

Instead, she had come just weeks after her father's death, while there was an interim head chef, whom she happened to despise.

Maggie knew exactly why her old friend was in the restaurant tonight and no matter how hard she tried, no matter how perfect the dishes she served to Emily were, Maggie would not be receiving a glowing review.

Chapter Fifteen

Nayomi

Working two jobs was tiring.

Toni, Nayomi's boss at the alterations job, was being extremely supportive of her situation. He didn't even grumble when her tired eyes meant she sewed off line and had to unpick and re-sew almost an entire dress hem earlier in the week. Toni could have taught the general manager at the restaurant a few manners. Alexander was, in her limited experience of bosses, a terrible one. Always criticising, never praising, and always seeming to take personal calls as he swanned around the restaurant and kitchen like a peacock looking for a mate. Maggie, on the other hand, whom she had most dealings with and was, in Nayomi's eyes, her real boss, was wonderful. Helpful and kind.

Working at the restaurant also had other perks, like the free staff cab in the evenings, the general chatter and joking in the kitchen – though she rarely took part, she did find herself laughing at the jibes the chefs threw at each other. Then, of course, there was the fact that her boys had never eaten so well. Almost every night she would come home with waste food in her rucksack that Maggie always told her was free to a good home. Though at first she had felt uncomfortable taking the leftovers, she had come to realise that the chefs were always snacking in the kitchen on the 'just in case' food, the less than perfect dishes that they decided not to serve to guests, and sometimes the raw ingredients of their dishes. The only difference, she supposed, was that she tended to take her share home for the boys.

The best perk of the kitchen porter job – and the reason she was walking around the restaurant like a zombie at eleven a.m. on a Saturday morning – was the overtime. As the lure of New York in autumn brought an influx of tourists looking to get a head start on their Christmas shopping and witness the orange and red colours of the trees in Central Park, the number of visitors to the Grande Parisienne Hotel had increased. Not only did she get asked to work extra hours in Jean-Sébastien's but she had also been asked to cover a porter shift in the general kitchen. And today, she had been asked to fill in for a runner to keep the buffet cart topped up for the hotel's breakfast service.

She was, naturally, conflicted each time she accepted an extra shift, but she reasoned that she would spend the whole of Sunday with the boys and she would do school pick-up and drop-off on Mondays, even if she accepted a Monday night shift at the hotel. Because all the extra money was being spent on her family; their necessities and, this week, a modest birthday gift for Nuwan.

Because she was guest-facing, working on the breakfast buffet this morning, Nayomi had been given a spare chef uniform, which fit her relatively well. Her shift in Jean-Sébastien's didn't start for a few hours but she had left her rucksack in the porter station when she arrived this morning. She forgot entirely what she was wearing when she stepped into the kitchen, which was already full of busy chefs prepping for service.

'G'day, Chef,' one of the chefs said in a thick Australian accent as he swooped past Nayomi with tray of steaming water.

At first, she looked behind her to see who he was speaking to. Seeing only the door to the kitchen, she realised he was speaking to her because... *Oh*.

Feeling her cheeks flush, she explained, 'I was helping out on the breakfast buffet.'

Then Maggie raised her head from where she was stirring a pan of some kind of sauce, looking tense and tired. Still, she sent a gentle smile in Nayomi's direction and said, 'It suits you.'

Nayomi raised a self-conscious hand to the hat on her head and moved quickly to the far end of the kitchen to get her rucksack, an illogical smile forcing its way onto her lips. *Her. A chef in a fancy restaurant. As if.*

But for a fleeting moment, she allowed herself to envisage walking into a kitchen like this as a real chef and found she had a pang of excitement at the thought of being a *someone*.

As she rounded the pastry station, Ashley was leaning over one of his creations, seemingly immersed in his art. He glanced in Nayomi's direction, doing a double take.

'Check you out,' he said, setting aside a piping bag and wiping his hands on the towel hanging on the side of his uniform.

Nayomi slipped the white hat from her head and held it in front of her as she flattened her hair back into her braid. 'I need to change. I've been helping the main kitchen,' she said, for some reason feeling even more foolish in front of Ashley than she had the others.

Ashley flashed her a boyish grin. 'I was going to put this in the fridge until later but since you're here, you might as well be the first to see the finished product. Come here.'

He waved her closer and took a step to one side, displaying the most delightful celebration cake. A tall cylindrical shape, it was covered in perfectly smooth baby-blue royal icing, with white chocolate icing that was made to look like it was dripping from the top. Around the base were stars, circles and piped gems. But it was the decoration on top of the cake that made Nayomi bring her hand to her mouth.

Various shades of piped swirls and gems made a peak and on top of the peak was sugar art that read:

Nuwan

8

'You… You made my baby a birthday cake?' She struggled to get the words past the lump that had formed in her throat as she stepped closer to inspect the cake.

'I wasn't sure what he's into, so I just went with blue. The inside is vanilla sponge with jam and cream. Should be good for a few days, at least.'

Nayomi looked from the cake to Ashley. 'I can't believe you remembered.'

She shook her head in disbelief. Neither of her sons had ever had a cake as magnificent as this. She could have never afforded something like this.

'Ashley, I don't know what to say.'

He shrugged. 'Thanks is fine.' That beaming smile was still lighting up his face.

'Won't you get in trouble?'

'I came in early.'

'But the ingredients. Can I pay for the ingredients?' She wasn't sure how, exactly, but she knew it couldn't have been cheap to make a cake like this. Not to mention the time Ashley must have spent.

'You absolutely cannot.' Maggie was now standing nearby, wiping her hands on a towel. 'He cleared it with me first.'

'I... I can't thank you enough. Both of you.' She stared at the cake again. A marvel. Happiness escaped her as a giggle. Nuwan would be blown away by this. 'It must have taken hours.'

'Worth it for that laugh,' Ashley said. 'Now, I'm gonna get this bad boy in the fridge before the kitchen gets too hot. I'll take it out before we get the staff car later.'

Just like that, Nayomi's tiredness was gone, her awkwardness over the uniform was gone, and all she could think of were the million reasons she loved working at Jean-Sébastien's – the kindness of Ashley and Maggie top of the list.

–

She couldn't wait to get home, no, scratch that, she couldn't wait for tomorrow to come. Her Saturday shift had been as busy as ever, which was always the busiest shift of the week. People seemed looser with their cash on Saturdays compared to other days. More people went for the tasting menu and paired wine. More people squeezed in dessert when they must have been full to bursting already. And, from what she understood from Charles, the most expensive wines on the menu were ordered in abundance on Saturdays.

Nayomi would admit that, since Charles had been choosing wine for her staff drink, she had come to appreciate that a nice wine was very tasty. She couldn't really smell apples and pears, citrus and oak but she could tell when one wine lingered on her palate and another didn't. She got a pleasant sort of feeling sipping some and less so with others. But what she did know, no matter whether it took three sips to enjoy a wine or not, was that she would *never* pay four hundred dollars for a bottle of wine.

Naturally, since she was so desperate to get home tonight, there were two tables of people who lingered. The waiting staff reported that they had struck up conversation hours ago and as the wine had flowed, so had their buoyancy. Now, they were the only guests left in the restaurant and they had pushed together their tables to make one long, loud, slow-to-order-dessert group.

As one of the mixologists from the bar did the rounds in the kitchen with his pad and pen taking staff drinks orders, Maggie appeared between the porter station and the dessert station.

'Has Bill left?' she asked.

'I told him I would finish up,' Nayomi said. 'There's only dessert plates from the last table and any dishes Ashley makes.'

'Well you and Ashley might as well come around for drinks with the rest of us while you wait.'

Nayomi nodded but felt apprehensive. Usually, she ended up taking her staff drink home because she was never finished until after the chefs. A torrent of thoughts ran through her mind. *What will we talk about? Where will I stand? Should I change first?* And she found herself asking a question she used to ask herself a lot when she first moved to America when she was eighteen years old – *Do I belong?*

Back then, she had left the safety of her village in Sri Lanka to come with her new husband to America where he was studying. Despite being fair-skinned by comparison to many of her friends in Sri Lanka, people stared at her brown skin in New York. It hadn't been long before she replaced her sari with jeans and sweaters in an attempt to blend into the crowd. And although everyone in the kitchen was in uniform tonight, Nayomi's was burgundy and everyone else's was white.

Standing in the porters' station, she straightened her jacket and her trousers, not that they looked any different for it – they certainly didn't look any whiter. Then she thought of her boys and the melting pot that was their school. *If they can do it…*

She stepped out from behind her partition and made her way into the main kitchen. The other chefs were gathered around in a sort of circle. Nayomi remembered how she had felt the first time she attended drinks at Shan's work Christmas party and she didn't like it.

'Make room, guys.' Ashley's big voice preceded him into the area and the chefs in the circle shuffled apart.

'Hey, Nayomi,' Josh said. 'Have you ordered a drink? Hey, Brett, take Nayomi's order, would you?'

'And mine's beer,' Ashley called to the bar staff, coming to stand in the ring next to Nayomi and Josh.

'Uh-uh, I've got Nayomi covered,' Charles said, coming into the kitchen carrying a tray of full wine glasses. He handed Maggie a white wine he called Sancerre. Then he crossed the middle of the gathering towards Nayomi.

'Tonight, a light-bodied red. Do you like red, Nayomi?'

She wiped her clammy hands on her jacket and reached out to take one of two glasses of red wine from the tray.

'I'm not sure,' she said, honestly. 'I've only really had red once.'

'And what was it like?' Charles asked, setting the tray down on the steel worktop and taking the other glass of red wine in his hand, swilling the liquid around the sides of the glass.

She shrugged. 'Mmm, I'm not sure. Kind of...' She could feel herself getting flushed but Charles kept his attention trained on her. '...spicy? Like, erm, black pepper? Kind of... maybe... smoky too, like wood-smoked meat or something, maybe. And it went *straight* to my head.'

As it happened, that one prior experience with red wine had been at the same work event of her husband's where she had felt terribly out of place. They had told her to dress up, so she had. She had worn the sari she had worn to her sister's wedding. Shan had told her she looked beautiful, yet the eyes at the party that night had told her she looked like a freak show. She had been glad the red wine had travelled directly to her head that night.

Charles laughed, that belly laugh he did. 'Oui, oui. Red wine takes time to get used to but it's worth the effort, I promise. Now, swill a little, like this. We're aerating the wine.'

Nayomi followed the instructions.

'Then sniff. And sip. Draw air over the wine by sucking, like this.'

She smirked when he sounded like he was slurping – the kind of noise she'd tell the boys to stop making. But she did as instructed, then slowly swallowed the wine, letting it linger on her tongue before moving like velvet down her throat.

'What do you smell and taste?'

Nayomi closed her eyes. 'Erm, cherries? Black cherries? And maybe… cranberries?' She opened one eye and when she found Charles grinning, she figured she had said something right.

'She's learning. I will make an expert out of you yet, Nayomi.'

It was only wine, but Nayomi's smile threatened to be so big that she had to press her fingers to her lips to contain it.

'This is a pinot noir, most likely much lighter than the spicy wine you have drunk in the past.'

'Much nicer, too,' Nayomi said before taking another sip of the delicious drink.

Charles waved his free hand like the queen of England might and said, 'Voilà. Only the best for you, mon amie.'

'Say, Nayomi, were you cooking in the hotel this morning?' Josh asked. 'Just, I saw you in your whites.'

She swallowed another mouthful of wine, shaking her head. 'I was helping keep the buffet stocked up, that's all.'

'Do you cook?' Josh asked.

'Sure, but just for my family. My boys like American food. Like every kid, they want hot dogs and burgers but for special occasions I make Sri Lankan, my old family recipes from home.'

'Were you born in Sri Lanka?' Lucas asked, who was standing next to Josh.

'Yes. I lived on the island until I was eighteen, when I moved to America.'

'Do you speak Sinhala?' Jack asked from her right, a few bodies further round the circle.

'It was my first language but I learned English in school from a young age. I didn't learn Americanisms until I moved here.'

'You do sound a bit posh, some of the things you say, you know, like the Brits,' Ashley said.

Nayomi laughed as another question about her life was asked. She was being interrogated like the new kid in school but surprisingly, rather than making her feel *different*, she felt included. Like the people around her actually cared who she was and where she had come from. It felt... nice. She was almost sad when the last table decided to order dessert and she and Ashley had to get back to work, which seemed to bring a natural end to the post-work drinks as the chefs started to filter off home.

It was after midnight by the time Nayomi and Ashley sat in the back of the staff car, Ashley cradling Nuwan's birthday cake in a patisserie box like it was his first-born child.

'I don't want it to spoil,' he said, when Nayomi, who was feeling more relaxed than usual after her glass of pinot noir, had made a joke of it.

As usual, Ashley's phone started pinging – his wife or girlfriend, she figured. Only then did he hand over the box to Nayomi, who peeked inside one more time to see the spectacular cake.

When they pulled up outside Nayomi's block, they saw the group of youths who tended to hang around there, drinking out of brown paper bags and being more raucous than they normally were. Being careful not to knock the cake box, Nayomi unclipped her seatbelt and gathered her rucksack. Before she could consider the dilemma of opening the car door with no free hands, Ashley had opened the door for her and was offering a hand from the sidewalk.

Thanking the driver, she let Ashley take the cake box. She expected to take it straight back but Ashley started walking to the door of the apartment block, them both receiving wolf-whistles as Ashley held open the door for Nayomi to step inside.

In the hallway, standing amongst discarded flyers from the mail boxes lining the walls, Nayomi took the box from Ashley.

'Will you be okay getting into your apartment?'

She nodded. 'I'll be fine. Thank you for the cake. And for carrying it in.'

'I don't like those guys milling around here.'

'They never bother me,' Nayomi assured him. It was a product of the neighbourhood and there was nothing she could do about it.

Ashley nodded and looked to his feet as he put his hands in the pockets of his jeans. The air seemed to change around them. It was heavier, somehow, and Nayomi found herself thinking of what she should say.

'Well, thank you, again. Nuwan is going to love this,' she said, gesturing to the box in her hands.

'It was my pleasure.' Then his shoulder rose with his next breath and he said, 'All right, then. I'll be...' He waved a hand in the direction of the exit. 'Tell the kid I said happy birthday.'

Ashley made for the door as Nayomi made for the stairwell. Then, perhaps it was the wine making her brave, but something made her turn on her heels and say, 'Ashley? Since you made the cake and it's so... special... would you, erm, like to come here? Tomorrow? I'm making a Sri Lankan buffet for Nuwan's birthday meal and we always have spare. Plus, we need to leave room for this cake. And, believe me, the boys would much rather fill up on sweet treats.'

135

Ashley stared at her in silence. *Was it the wrong thing to have suggested?*

'I mean, your wife or girlfriend, from WhatsApp, she's welcome to come too, obviously. The more the merrier.'

Ashley pursed his lips, as if he was thinking and Nayomi's stomach sank. She had over-stepped.

'That'd be good. If you're sure. If the boys will be cool with it.'

Relief relaxed Nayomi's rigid body. 'Are you kidding? You're the source of dessert. They'll welcome you with open knives and forks.'

'All right then. So, maybe I should take your number? You know, just in case something changes?'

She called out her number and Ashley put it into his phone. As she mounted the staircase with aching arms and a smile, she thought about Nuwan's face tomorrow when he saw his gift and the birthday cake. She felt lighter and happier than she could remember feeling in a very long time.

—

Nayomi had managed only four hours of sleep and she didn't mind at all. She had been awake since shortly after five a.m. when she had started cooking. Now, returning from a wonderful morning at the park, in the sunshine with ten of Nuwan's friends from school, the apartment smelled of everything wonderful about Sri Lanka. Cloves, coriander, cinnamon, dill, garlic. The herbs and spices that had been marinating nicely in her curries all morning had filled the air and welcomed her home like her mother's arms wrapping around her. Closing her eyes, she hummed with contentedness.

She had acquired two of Nuwan's friends from school who had brought with them a computer game that apparently had all the kids buzzing at the moment. Nuwan had wanted to show off his new games console, which Nayomi had bought second-hand from a local store but which she had been assured was as good as new. She didn't bother asking Nuwan if he would like to help her finish preparing their banquet of birthday food but was pleasantly taken aback when Roshan offered to help.

Farah knocked on the door after Roshan and Nayomi had set rice to boil and turned on all of the curry dishes to reheat. Roshan's extra pair of hands came in very handy as, together, the three of them moved Farah's kitchen table into Nayomi's lounge. It wasn't ideal, splitting the group, but she figured the kids would enjoy their own space in the lounge while the adults ate in the kitchen. Regardless, she had no choice since neither the lounge nor the kitchen were big enough to take two tables.

Farah had brought with her a bottle of white wine that was identical to the one Nayomi had picked up on offer in the local store and she made quick work of pouring herself and Nayomi a glass.

'Remind me who's coming,' Farah said, plonking down into a chair with her glass of wine on Nayomi's assurance that the food was under control.

Roshan, her chief stirrer, was making sure the simmering curry dishes didn't stick.

'Nuwan's two friends from school are here. Obviously, us three. And my friend from work.'

'Oh yeah, the cake cook, right?'

'Shhh,' Nayomi said, her finger pressed to her lips.

'It's okay, I looked in the box when you were making roti,' Roshan said, causing Nayomi to poke him playfully. 'It's pretty cool. The nerd will like it.'

Nayomi chuckled. 'It *is* pretty cool, huh?'

Right on time, there was a knock on the front door. 'Oh, that will be Ashley.' Nayomi checked her braid was tame and that her shirt was neatly tucked into her jeans beneath her apron, then she went to answer the door.

Only, Ashley wasn't alone. Recovering from the surprise quickly, Nayomi welcomed both Ashley and the woman by his side into her home.

'Nayomi, this is my mom. Mom, this is Nayomi.'

'I'm Deloris,' the woman said. She was older and more feminine but otherwise a dead ringer for Ashley. Deloris had thick grey hair that had been sprayed into tame waves that reached her jawline. She was pleasantly plump, elegantly so, and had on a floral dress that was so lovely it made Nayomi think Deloris had spent the morning in church.

Attached to Deloris's arms were two silver crutches and on her left leg, she wore a cast.

'These are for you, dear,' Deloris said, gesturing to a bottle of wine that Ashley held in one hand, and a ceramic dish covered with foil in the other. 'My son chose the wine.'

'It's pinot noir,' Ashley said, a slight smile playing on his lips, which Nayomi reflected back at him.

'Thank you. That's so thoughtful.'

'Nonsense,' Deloris said, hobbling further inside on her crutches and moving towards the kitchen where Farah had stood up from the kitchen table to welcome the guests. 'I don't get out much these days, especially since I broke my leg. I made the dish myself.'

Nayomi was turning her head almost comically from side to side, looking at Deloris, on the move, and Ashley, who was now holding out the ceramic baking dish for her to take.

She closed the front door then lifted the foil lid on the dish. As thoughtful as it was, she was highly amused by the macaroni cheese that she suspected was intended as an accompaniment to her Sri Lankan banquet.

Ashley seemed to mirror her thoughts as she found him smirking down at her. 'It probably doesn't go with what you've prepared but my mom makes a mean mac 'n' cheese, trust me.'

'It's perfect, thank you.' She took the dish, which was still warm to touch. 'You've probably saved Nuwan's school friends, actually. They'll be much happier eating this than curry, I'm sure.'

'Oh, it smells wonderful in here,' Deloris sang out. 'And who might you be, sir?'

Nayomi heard Roshan and Farah making introductions in the kitchen.

'Is it okay that I brought her?' Ashley asked.

'Sure it is. Like I said, the more the merrier. It's a party now. I suppose I am a little surprised, though. I expected you to bring—'

'Deloris *is* my WhatsApp, just so you know. She's been living with me since she broke her leg. My place has easier access and she likes having someone to run around after her.'

Oh. So there was no...

'She's the *only* WhatsApp, by the way. She's a bit of a night owl and hasn't registered that I'm a grown man, you know?'

Nayomi wanted nothing more from Ashley than friendship and she had invited him here today out of gratitude only. *Really.* Yet she walked to the kitchen with an extra bounce in her step.

Roshan, on the other hand, had lost any bounce in his step as he stood rooted to the spot, boring holes into Ashley with his eyes, his chest as puffed out as a kid could puff out his chest. 'Isn't Ashley a girl's name?'

Oh boy. Nice start.

'It's unisex, Roshan. This is Ashley, my friend from work. He made—'

'The cake. I know. That's why I thought he was a girl.'

Nayomi glowered at her son. *Did she shout at him now or later?*

Thankfully, she didn't need to. Whether he recognised the error of his ways or an impending grounding, Roshan said, 'It's pretty cool though, the cake. My brother will like it.'

Ashley nodded. 'I think there's probably enough to go around.'

'Roshan, could you tell Nuwan and the boys that the food is ready, please?'

With his eyes still on Ashley, Roshan headed past Nayomi and Ashley, walking between them in a clear show of his feelings towards having a man in the house.

'Sorry about that,' Nayomi said as soon as Roshan was out of earshot. 'I guess we haven't had a man in the house since his dad died.'

'It was two years ago, Nayomi,' Farah added, suddenly making the kitchen feel even more awkward.

What exactly was she implying? That Roshan should move on? That Nayomi should move on? That Nayomi and Ashley—

'Right. You guys make yourselves comfortable,' Nayomi said, unwilling to finish that thought. 'Deloris, would you like something to rest your leg up on? I'll start serving.'

After a rough start, the birthday meal went remarkably well. The kids devoured the mac 'n' cheese in the lounge and *some* of Nayomi's cooking. In the kitchen, the Sri Lankan meal went down a treat, with Deloris audibly appreciating the first forkful of every dish she tried. The main thing was, laughter filled Nayomi's home from the belly-deep giggles of kids in the lounge, to the hearty chuckles of adults in her kitchen.

Nayomi treasured every second because she knew only too well how happiness could be with you one day and gone the next in as little time as it took to get the results of one scan or one blood test.

Deloris, it turned out, was hilarious. She had lived in Queens all her life and as a volunteer at the local church, she knew the ins and outs of the lives of anyone who had lived in Queens since the fifties. It was also quite obvious that she had never liked any of her son's girlfriends but, she made clear, she could tell Nayomi was a good one, even if she and Ashley were just friends (a sentence she had finished with a roll of her eyes).

When Nuwan's friends were picked up by their parents, it brought a natural end to the party. And, in any event, Deloris was getting tired now, she let it be known.

'Can we help you clear up?' Ashley asked, standing from the sofa.

'No, please, you've done enough, with wine, food and great company,' Nayomi told him.

'I'll help her,' Farah offered. 'While there's cake and wine left, that is.'

Nayomi walked Ashley and Deloris the four steps to the front door and held it open for them. 'Thanks so much for coming.' Then she called out to the boys to come and say goodbye.

Though Roshan's goodbye was curt, Nuwan rushed to the kitchen where Farah was already clearing away dishes and returned with a foil-wrapped package.

'You can have some of my birthday cake, for later,' he said, handing over the package.

Nayomi couldn't help but find him adorable. 'See, your hours of hard work weren't wasted. You get to take a piece home with you,' she said, unable to hide her amusement as Nuwan tucked against her hip, a sure sign he was worn out from a day of fun.

Ashley held up the package and thanked Nuwan for the gift.

'I had a good time today, thank you. I had no idea you could cook like that. Maybe you should mention it at the restaurant. Those whites suited you yesterday.'

Nayomi's cheeks burned. 'I can only do what I do. I could never cook the way you all can.'

'Well, I'd come to your restaurant, dear,' Deloris said, surprising Nayomi by shuffling forward and kissing her cheeks, her hands lingering there like a grandmother to a granddaughter. 'We women shouldn't underestimate ourselves. Bringing up two handsome young men on your own is harder than anything else you'll ever be asked to do.

'Right, son of mine, let's get me home.'

Ashley rolled his eyes and Nayomi wondered if Deloris and Ashley were on the same page about the longevity of their current living arrangements.

''Night then,' Nayomi said.

"Night then,' Ashley repeated. 'Oh, and, don't be offended but I noticed that your toilet flush sticks. It's corroded. My friend's a plumber so I've messaged him to get a new part. I can drop by later this week and sort that out for you.'

'Oh. Ah, thanks.' She was mildly embarrassed about the number of things that were breaking in her apartment but mostly, genuinely grateful. She had been struggling with the flush for months now and had no idea how to fix it or how much it would cost. 'Just let me know how much I owe you.'

'It's nothing. Tiny part. I'm owed a few favours anyway.'

When her guests had gone and Nayomi and Farah had restored the kitchen and lounge to their pre-party state, Nayomi tucked the boys into bed and fell back onto her own mattress for a much-needed sleep.

The last thoughts that crossed her mind were how nice it had been to have a man in her home and simultaneously, how guilty she felt for having that thought.

Nayomi had been brought up to wear a sari, avoid meat, never drink alcohol and, most importantly, to be a doting wife to one man, to the end.

What would her parents make of her life now?

Chapter Sixteen

Emily

'Are you sure you want to go to print with this?'

Emily stared down at her boss, one hand on her hip in her red 'Fluffer' wrap dress, standing tall in her heels as Archer leaned back in his office chair on the opposite side of his desk.

'Why wouldn't I?'

'Emily, this is the most damning review you've written for this section. Now, I'm all for throwing a critical review out there sometimes – some of our best traffic comes from negative articles. But I need you to promise me that there's nothing vindictive going on here.'

As he spoke, he repeatedly bounced his fingertips on the printed review of Jean-Sébastien's restaurant in front of him, a move that had Emily's reflexes twitching, one bounce at a time.

'Are you questioning my professionalism?'

He paused, clearly trying to read her expression and find any hidden meaning beneath it. 'I just need to be sure I can go in to bat for you if the shit hits the fan.'

'Well, you can. The fact is, the restaurant invited me to dinner, obviously expecting a review. I have to be honest.' The lie came easily and Emily didn't blink as she held Archer's gaze.

'See, that in itself strikes me as odd. When your dad has recently passed and the word on the street is that Ethan James has agreed terms to take over in a couple of months, why would they ask you to do a review *now*, of all times?'

'I don't know, Archer. Perhaps the interim head chef was hoping for a good review to boost her resume? Look, I'm not a mind reader, okay? I'm a food critic and I pride myself on giving *NYT* readers an honest critique. So, are you running it or do I need to write something else?'

He bounced his fingers one last time on top of the review, then balanced a pen between his upper lip and the base of his nose, which was as childlike as it was annoying. 'We'll go to press.'

'Great.' Rolling her eyes, she made quick work of leaving Archer's office, the hem of her dress sweeping after her.

'Bet I know what that was about,' Janey said, as Emily resumed her position at the adjacent desk to her friend.

When Emily chose not to hear the comment and turned her attention pointedly to her blank screen, Janey added, 'Are you sure you want to do this, Ems? That's a damaging review of the restaurant and the head chef.'

Emily began typing an email that didn't need to be sent. '*Interim* head chef. And that's the industry, Janey.'

'I know that but—'

'Have you ever questioned any of my other critical reviews?'

'No, but—'

'Then let's not start this now.' It was eleven a.m. and Emily had endured quite enough of the office. Shutting down her laptop, she said, 'I appreciate your concern, but this is just work. Not everything I do at the moment is in some way a product of my dad being an asshole. I'm going to work from home for the rest of the day. Are you still up for the new tapas place on Union Square tomorrow night?'

Janey nodded. 'Sure.'

'Great. See you there.'

Sliding her laptop into her handbag, Emily left the office, making a pit stop for coffee at Bryant Park.

Sitting on a bottle-green vintage chair at a table for one, Emily pulled her coat tighter around her, tying the belt at the waist. *Was she going too far? Did she want to ruin Maggie's career?*

She reached into her handbag, found her phone and dialled Archer. If her review was published, she would regret it, she just knew it.

Ring. Ring. Ring.

'This is the voicemail of Arch—'

Damn it.

Hanging up, Emily thought about running back to the office and stopping the wheels she had put in motion.

No. Maggie got to where she was by being a yes girl. She deserved that review.

With her new resolve, Emily sipped her coffee, scrolled through Twitter, Facebook then Instagram, then set off home to Brooklyn.

When she got home, work didn't come easily.

Time ticked past the print deadline for her review, meaning any decision was now out of her hands. Still, she didn't feel like a weight had been lifted, like she had a lighter mind to be able to get on with work.

'I'm just not interested,' the negative version of herself told her chirpier self, who seemed to have taken a back seat these days.

And she wasn't interested. What *was* writing restaurant reviews? Maybe one day she helped someone get some extra footfall but those places still had to put in the effort to keep customers coming. Maybe another day she lessened the footfall in a restaurant and those restaurants had to up their game to get customers coming back. Did she really *do* anything?

There was no art to what she did. No creativity. She commented on the efforts of others – wrote them up or tore them down – but she did nothing herself.

She used to want to do something. To create art, in the kitchen. Where had *that* Emily gone?

'Your dad killed you,' her negative self muttered.

Oh God, was she losing it?

She leaned forward, her elbow on the table, her chin planted in the base of her hand, and sighed.

If not for the sound of her WhatsApp pinging, she could have sat there for hours, lost in the abyss of nothingness.

> **Janey**
> Just checking in to make sure you're all
> right? Xx

She stared at the message. *Was she all right?* The fact that staring at such a simple message made her well up told its own story.

No, she wasn't all right. But why? What would make her better again?

It was rare that she wanted her peace to be interrupted by Oliver, but today she checked the time on her phone, wishing he would come home and distract her from… herself. Her hideous, bored, pointless self.

She had thought that her conversation last week with Oliver might have helped her get her head straight. Instead, relaying her past to a clearly ambivalent Oliver had done absolutely *nothing*. She had thought that writing a scathing review about Maggie and Jean-Sébastien's would be a release and, though it had lessened her anger, it had also numbed her, and she wasn't sure that was better.

Procrastinating from doing nothing, if there was such a thing, Emily clicked into the photos icon on her Mac. She scrolled through pictures of coffee, parks, food and shoes, all of which had appeared in her Instagram stories at some time. She had to scroll back around four months to find a picture of her and Oliver – a selfie in a rooftop bar, both of them pout-smiling and holding a vodkatini. She remembered the day. They had met for lunch at a restaurant Emily had been asked to review. Despite the breeze, which meant they had needed to wear light jackets, the weather had felt like the start of summer and worthy of a picture. Staring at it now, she wished she could see Oliver's eyes and her own. She wanted to know if they looked happy behind their designer shades.

'Happy people smile with their eyes,' her mom had told her once.

Emily suddenly needed to know the last time she had smiled with her eyes.

Scrolling back further, she found pictures of her and Oliver in the Hamptons, where they had gone for the weekend and stayed in his parents' beach home. Looking at a picture of herself sitting in a chair on the veranda, her hands wrapped around a mug of coffee, she saw what her mother meant. She had been smiling with her eyes last autumn. It had been that weekend she and Oliver had decided to move in together.

Three weeks before that, she found a picture of her and Oliver in Hawaii, both laughing as someone had told them to say tequila, right before he snapped the shot. And, yes, they had both been smiling with their eyes.

But when was the last time? She didn't know.

Something akin to morbid fascination made her scroll further still. Years back, she clicked on a picture of her and her dad, both wearing their chef whites and hats proudly, both smiling with their eyes. It had been a promotional photograph for a documentary about French cooking in New York, for which her dad had been the focus. They had cooked classic dishes together in her parents' home for three days of filming. Looking back, she needed pictures to remind her of the dishes they had cooked together but she didn't need a still to remember how much they had laughed and enjoyed cooking together.

She had loved her dad then and she knew that he had loved her. *When had that mutual affection stopped? Could she honestly say she didn't love him now? Could you love a person, respect them, and just not like them?*

Those days filming had been exactly what Emily had wanted to do back then. She had wanted to film in her own kitchen, experiment with twists on the classics, make her own recipes and write her own book.

In fact…

Clicking into her files, buried amongst examples of work from her creative writing course, she found the notes from her never-to-be cooking book. A list of inspirational places in France she wanted to visit. Restaurants she wanted to eat in. Recipe ideas.

The dream had died. *When?* When her father and Maggie killed it.

Her WhatsApp pinged around four p.m.

She started typing a reply, deleted it and wrote:

Sorry, I'm working. Have fun x

She wouldn't see him again today, she knew. He would roll home after midnight and she would already be curled up in the spare bed so that he didn't disturb her with his drunken snoring.

All she had wanted for hours was for Oliver to come home and relieve her from her self-wallowing. Usually, she would have jumped on the invitation, put on a pair of heels and headed out for the night. Right now, she couldn't be bothered with people. She couldn't be bothered with Oliver. And… she fancied a glass of wine, on her sofa, watching something trash on Netflix.

–

But Oliver did come home before midnight and Emily's one glass of wine had turned into a bottle and a half. And Netflix had not been interesting enough to steal her thoughts from the last time she had smiled with her eyes.

So, when he stumbled through the front door, Emily watched him, unsure if he was spinning or if it was the room that was spinning, and more curtly than she intended, she asked, 'What are you doing here?'

'It's my home.'

'It's *our* home. I hate when you say *my* home, like you earn all the big bucks and I squat here.'

He staggered over to the sofa. 'I came home to make sure you're okay. Now, I wish I hadn't bothered.'

Yes. She wanted this. She wanted to fight. 'I wish you hadn't bothered either.'

'What the fuck is that supposed to mean?'

'Why wouldn't I be okay, Olly? Huh? Because maybe we haven't been happy for months?'

'Oh, Emily, fuck off. I can't be bothered with this psycho shit.'

He walked to the kitchen and with fury, Emily stormed, unsteadily, after him.

'Don't tell me to fuck off. Tell me when you were last happy.'

He finished downing the glass of water he held and slammed the glass down on the countertop. 'Tonight, Emily. I was happy tonight.'

'Without me?'

'That's not what I said.'

'But it's what you meant.'

He walked out of the room, his shoulder clipping hers as he passed.

'Walk away. Don't talk. Bury your fucking head in the sand. That's you, Olly.'

He spun on the spot, catching her off guard, his face suddenly right above hers. '*I* don't say what I'm thinking? That's rich. You're like a freakin' yoyo, Emily. One minute you're up, the next you're down. I don't know if you're grieving or you couldn't give a damn that your dad died. I don't know if I'm supposed to bring you flowers and love hearts or sleep in the spare bed. How can that make me happy when you're so clearly unhappy?'

'Of course I give a damn that my dad is dead!'

And right there, face to face with her fiancé, she realised she did care. She cared so much it ached in her heart and her head and every limb of her body.

Oliver took a step back and ran his hand through his hair. 'Then stop pretending like you don't, Ems. Stop telling me stories of your past – your dad, Maggie, the kitchen – and making out like you don't have a heart.'

'I have a heart.' But even she heard the weakness in her words as she cast her clouded gaze to her feet.

'Really? Because I read your article on Jean-Sébastien's. You left your laptop open and I read something cold, malicious, hateful. You want me to speak? Here goes… You told me last weekend about Maggie. How she stepped on your toes and stole your dad from under you. But do you know all I heard? Jealousy. You were jealous of your dad's success and envious of Maggie's ability to please him when you did everything you could *not* to. The fall-out wasn't Maggie's fault; you used her as a scapegoat because you wanted to please your dad but you didn't have it in you.'

'Fuck you,' she said through her teeth.

'Wanting something different isn't a bad thing, Ems. Maybe even not being as good as your dad at *his* game. That's okay, too. But you couldn't walk away and do your own thing, nor did you want to stay. You definitely didn't want Maggie to stay in your shoes.'

'You don't know what you're talking about.'

He scoffed. 'Right, so now I should shut the hell up, huh? That article proves me right and you know it. You want to know why we aren't happy, Ems? Take a look inside.'

His words burned like hot oil through her skin – slowly seeping deeper and hotter.

As Oliver turned his back on her, Emily knew he had left a scar. One that she would carry with her wherever she ended up. But that place wouldn't be with Oliver.

–

It was three a.m. when Emily knocked on her mom's front door and waved the yellow cab away.

The light went on in the hallway, and as Emily watched her mom's outline through the stained glass door as she made her way downstairs, wrapping a robe around herself, her unshed tears finally fell.

'Emily?'

'Could I—' A sob broke her sentence. 'Could I stay here for a while?'

Her mom's embrace spoke more than words, as she welcomed her daughter home.

Chapter Seventeen

Maggie

The concept of 'fine' is saved only by the wine at Jean-Sébastien's.
Emily Blanchon for the New York Times.

Jean-Sébastien's at the Grande Parisienne Hotel has long been considered one of the finest restaurants in New York. From the elegant interiors of the dining room to the flawless preparation and service of true French classics. In a previous review in The New York Times in 2011, the restaurant was referred to as 'the stuff of dreams'. And a dream it was for proprietor, William Boucher and chef de cuisine, Jean-Sébastien, who had worked closely for more than twenty years and saw the restaurant gain and retain three Michelin stars for more than a decade.

But with the sudden death of Jean-Sébastien a month ago, has the dream come to an end for the once cherished eatery?

I was greeted on arrival at the restaurant by Alexander Boucher, the son of the long-reigning proprietor, who is being groomed to step into his father's shoes. Alexander was attentive and charming, exchanging pleasantries without being overly familiar, and ultimately handing off service to waiting staff who were impeccably dressed and cheery enough, without giving the feeling of ever-presence.

Opting for the prix fixe menu ($175) over the seven-course tasting menu ($250 for carnivore or $225 for vegetarian), I started my culinary experience with traditional coquilles Saint Jacques. The large, meaty king scallops were succulent, cooked to perfection, allowing their subtle flavour to flourish through the light gruyère, breadcrumb and parsley topping. My friend who had attended the dinner with me, allowed me to taste her duck liver foie gras appetiser – the restaurant's renowned bestseller. The foie gras was delectable and slid down the throat like silk.

Pomposity coupled with superior raw ingredients made for two tasty dishes but which were, sadly, utterly lacking in imagination. Frankly, we could have gotten the same plates at any traditional French restaurant in the city worth its salt (and likely for much more affordable prices). Both first course dishes were garnished with colourful flowers, the absence of which would have made for nothing more than a precisely cooked but mundane classic dish, the recipes for which were unchanged since the post-war era. The only culinary surprise we received with our appetisers came from an expertly chosen wine that brought character to the dishes that was otherwise not present at all.

My main course of Dover sole left a distinctly similar impression to the appetisers. Though the sole was just cooked, exactly as it should be, and the accompanying sauce light yet buttery, the after taste was one of disappointment and missed opportunity.

Many diners, the loyalists of history and nostalgia, would have enjoyed the cast back to traditional fine dining and the pretention of recipes unchanged for decades. But in 2021 New York City, a food mecca, gone are the days when a spoonful of caviar granted your dish an automatic five stars. Gone are the days when doing the classics simply and well with the highest quality ingredients was enough. Diners now have a wealth of food options from low value Mexican with big, rich flavours leaving a full stomach, to affordable fine dining. To stand out (particularly at the prices of Jean-Sébastien's), you have to offer something better, something grander than a well-cooked dish.

While some dishes – one per course offerings – vary in the restaurant from week to week, the menu at Jean-Sébastien's has been largely unchanged for years. This seemed to work for the late executive chef but with his sous chef, Maggie Hill, temporarily filling very big shoes, she had to bring something inspiring to the table or be a match for Jean-Sébastien's decades of experience. Unfortunately, she offered neither. The dishes, though well-prepared, have lost that certain je ne sais quoi of her predecessor and she brought no flair of her own. No modern twist on the classics. No mystique. No pizazz.

Today's diners want to be walked through the culinary experience like an art gallery. At first sight, immaculate presentation. At first bite, fine ingredients and flawless cooking of them. Then, the pizazz: the intricacies of creativity assaulting one's senses on the eyes, the nose, the palate. It is this latter element that appears to be extinct at Jean-Sébastien's.

The bottom line is that Maggie Hill, though a perfectly adequate cook, does not appear to have what it takes to be a master of a three-Michelin star kitchen.

Alexander Boucher has his work cut out as he takes over the reins. With only the temporary head chef in post, his guidance will be needed more than ever if he wants to prevent the good name of Jean-Sébastien's going to ruin. Alexander has already announced the impending introduction of celebrated experimental chef, Ethan James. Perhaps it would be worth revisiting the establishment several months from now, when James has had an opportunity to give Jean-Sébastien's some much-needed modernisation. Until then and only on the basis that nothing more exciting is on offer, though they may enjoy good service and unexpectedly exciting wine, readers can expect nothing more than dining mediocrity at some of the highest prices in the city. And who needs mediocrity in a haven of food choices? Nobody.

Maggie read to the end of the article, again, and closed the lid of her laptop. Reaching out for Livvy, who had been perched on the arm of the sofa, she held the cat in her lap and stared into nothingness. Because nothing was exactly what she would be able to achieve in the culinary world after such a scathing review.

The day had started well. After her alarm woke her at four forty a.m., Maggie had pulled on a pair of skinny jeans, a sweater and a rain jacket and made it to the fish market for opening at five a.m. She got a great deal on the best turbot she had found so far this year, then went to her preferred farmers' market for opening, where she picked up bunches of herbs that had the kitchen of her own home currently smelling like the most delectable perfume she had come across.

Then, as she had stepped through the door to her apartment, her phone had rung. Between gasps and what sounded like spitting as he projected his words so profusely, Alexander had let her know that there was a review in the *New York Times* that had ruined him. And that the catastrophe was entirely Maggie's doing.

After reading Emily's words three times in full, for once, Maggie had to agree with Alexander.

Lack of imagination.
Mundane dishes.
Disappointment.
No inspiration or experience.
Mediocrity.
Perfectly adequate but no master.
Maggie had killed Jean-Sébastien's dream.
And Emily had killed Maggie's career.

She didn't realise she was crying until her tears began to drip onto Livvy's soft fur.

'Sorry, baby,' she said, stroking the cat. 'It's just…'

As her silent tears turned to sobs, Maggie walked to the bathroom for tissue with Livvy tucked under her arm, unable to give up the comfort of her fur baby.

'Jean-Sébastien was the only person who believed in me, Livvy,' she said, slumping down on top of the toilet seat and loudly blowing her nose. 'It's not like my parents didn't want me to do well, I guess, they just never pushed me or encouraged me. They'd have been happy if I worked the till at the local mini-mart, as long as I paid them lodgings.'

She blew her nose again and sighed. 'It was me who had had enough of being nothing and left New Jersey. Me, who got a job in one of the best bakeries in the city. Me, who shared a house with four other people just so that I could have enough money for rent. But it was Jean-Sébastien – or, ironically, Emily, then Jean-Sébastien – who showed faith in me being something more. And now I've let him down.'

Livvy purred as Maggie rubbed her cheek against the cat. 'Emily is right. Alexander is right. Even if he changes things, the restaurant will be better off with—'

Her door buzzer sounded and Maggie carried Livvy to answer the intercom.

'It's Ethan.'

It was the unmistakable voice of the very last person she wanted to see right now. Well, penultimate last, one up from Emily.

'What do you want and how do you know where I live?'

'Alexander and could you just buzz me in? I've got heavy bags and it's about to start raining again.'

She blew her nose again, fiercely, and wiped under her eyes to remove the stains from the mascara she'd applied in the early hours. Ethan rapped on the door again and she reluctantly unlocked and opened it.

She hoped her scowl was prominent enough to convey just how displeased she was to see him.

He stared at her for a few seconds, not smugly but, she thought, compassionately.

Then he said, 'You look like crap.'

'Gee, thanks, Ethan. Now you've shared that, you can feel free to crawl back under whatever rock you came from.'

In response, he held up two large brown paper bags. 'I brought breakfast.'

She continued to scowl, folding her arms across her chest, unmoving from the doorway. In an untimely fashion, her stomach growled.

'What kind of breakfast?'

That arrogant smirk of his was back. 'French toast. At least it will be, once I make it. Fresh oranges to juice.'

She didn't budge.

'Eggs. Smoked trout. Muffins.'

Hmm, that did sound like a good feast.

He set one bag down on the ground and from behind the wall, he magicked a tray holding two take-out coffees.

'One almond milk latte and one cow's milk latte. You get first dibs.'

That would do it. 'Fine.'

Stepping to one side, she accepted the coffee tray and told Ethan, 'The kitchen's that way.'

Livvy followed behind him, hot on his heels. *Traitor.* Reluctantly following the source of her breakfast, Maggie momentarily dropped her wariness of the impromptu visit and sipped, unable to stop herself admitting, 'This is the best coffee I've ever tasted. Truly.'

Ethan turned from where he was unpacking ingredients from his paper bags and filling the benchtops as if he was welcome in her home. 'Good, isn't it? My favourite after a long night of no sleep.'

She rolled her eyes, knowing exactly Ethan's reputation and what generally kept him up all night. 'Well, I didn't have a night of…' She waved her hand through the air, allowing the gesture to finish her sentence.

Ethan scoffed. 'Yeah, I figured as much. Which is why my assumption must be correct.'

'That I got up in the early hours to have a sordid affair with turbot at the fish market?'

Ethan tossed a bar of butter into the air and caught it again with the same hand, pointing it in her direction like a wand. 'You've spent the morning reading a rather damning assessment of your cooking abilities by someone who used to be your friend. And, correct me if I'm wrong, but you, Miss Goody, don't have all that many friends.'

Was this guy for real? 'All right, that's it. Time for you to leave, Ethan.' She set her coffee on the kitchen table and tried to usher him towards the door, growing more irate as he laughed. 'And next time Alexander gives out my personal details, I'm making a complaint to Human Resources.'

On the threshold of the kitchen and the hallway, Ethan turned to face her, pressing his arms into the doorframe, un-budging. 'Look, I'm sorry.' He held up his palms. 'I come in peace. We all get bad reviews from time to time. It's like a punch in the gut. I get it.'

She leaned her head to one side, as if to say, *you've had a review as bad as this one?*

'Okay, it's a particularly bad review. Hence the French toast.'

'You're here to gloat,' she bit. 'This is perfect for you, isn't it? The restaurant and its *temporary* head chef are slammed. Rock bottom. Then in sweeps Ethan James, coming to save the day. The rescue of all rescues. Super Chef.'

He twisted his lips as if in thought. 'Super Chef does have a certain ring to it.'

'Get out, Ethan.'

He laughed and caught her off guard by taking hold of her face in his large palms. There was a split second in which she welcomed his touch. Then it passed.

'I'm here as a friend.'

'Since when have you been my f—' Squeezing her cheeks, he pressed her lips into a wide O until she couldn't speak and was forced to laugh at her fish-like state.

'That's better.' He moved his hands away and moved back to his bench full of ingredients. 'You don't laugh enough. It suits you.'

Pleased that her betraying smile fell on his back, she retrieved her coffee from the table and told him, 'Don't you try to flirt with me, Ethan James.'

He flashed her a grin and a wink across his shoulder. 'Never.'

Again, she smiled. A remarkable feat after her morning.

Oh, no, Maggie. You do not fall for his boyish charm. He's the guy who has always thought of you as second best.

'Are you just going to watch or are you going to get your hands dirty?'

If she could forget that it was Ethan, Maggie would have been quite happy to watch a handsome man moving around her kitchen with ease, admirably predicting the home of every pot, pan and utensil he needed.

But it was Ethan. She stood from where she had taken a seat at the kitchen table. 'What can I do?'

He tossed her an orange, which she caught one-handed. 'Juice.'

'Actually, I picked up some amazing mint this morning at the farmers' market. I'll add some.' She tore a leaf from the bag of herbs she had left on the table to take to the restaurant later. Rubbing it between her fingers, she held it under Ethan's nose. He closed his eyes and inhaled.

'Add a pinch of cinnamon, too.'

He even thought he could juice better than her. *Urgh.*

As he set about slicing fresh bread and Maggie went about juicing the oranges, they worked in comfortable silence. She supposed any company was better than none as a distraction today.

'You know, the best place for veg and herbs is in New Jersey. I'll take you out there some time. But know that the best produce always has my name on it,' Ethan said, as he set two plates of French toast down on the table.

She tried and failed not to appreciate aloud what was, genuinely, the best French toast she had ever tasted. *Damn him.*

'This is very good.'

He nodded, chewing a giant-sized bite. 'It's even better if you leave the brioche soaking in custard overnight. But I didn't know quite how bad that review was going to be last night.'

'And just when I thought there was something I could like about you, you go and ruin it.'

He scoffed as he took another bite the BFG would have been proud of. Maggie on the other hand, had suddenly lost her appetite. 'God, it's so bad.' She could feel her eyes welling up again. She would *not* cry in front of Ethan. 'Some might call it career-ending.'

'Meh, the Shake Shack is always hiring.'

She understood his attempt at humour but it failed to amuse her in the slightest.

'Do you want to unravel it?' he asked, perhaps his remote streak of emotional intelligence acknowledging their differing moods.

She inhaled deeply, staring at her remaining French toast. 'No. I want to eat as much French toast and smoked trout as you'll serve me. Then I'm going to wash my face and go to work with my chest puffed out like nothing has happened.'

He sucked icing sugar from his finger. 'Bury your head in the sand instead of working on your problems.' He stood from the table, clearing his empty plate and getting back to cooking the main course. 'Whatever works for you, Maggie. But it seems to me like burying your head in the sand is precisely the reason you've received that review in the first place.'

'Oh really? You don't think on any level this is a personal attack from an old friend who is bitter that I have the job she always wanted?'

He was leaning back against the worktop, looking at her. 'Do you?'

'Yes.'

'You don't recognise any truth in that review?'

'I know that if Emily knew Alexander like I do, she would *not* be singing his praises. He's the kind of man Emily and I used to despise.' A man as self-absorbed as Ethan James, they would have said. Though admittedly, with none of Ethan's talent and an added dose of misogynistic pig.

'And your cooking?'

'Excuse me?'

He shrugged. 'If she wasn't being vindictive but honest, do you think she'd have made the same comments about your food?'

'Are you completely devoid of any social awareness?', she asked angrily. 'Mundane? Mediocre? Are you seriously asking me if I think my food is those things?'

'Are they?'

'No!'

'Well then, you have nothing to worry about. The dust will settle and you'll get another job where you can make the French classics *exactly* as Jean-Sébastien taught you.'

Every muscle in her body tensed as she stood, clenching her fists at her sides. 'You mean, not using any imagination of my own?'

'I didn't say that, you did.' He turned back to the pan on the cooker and lifted out perfectly round poached eggs, carefully placing them on a plate on top of muffins topped with smoked trout pâté.

He topped the dish with a tiny sprinkle of smoked paprika and black pepper and carried both plates to the table, inclining his head for Maggie to take a seat opposite him. He picked up the knife and fork Maggie had laid out and waited for her to sit.

When she didn't, he set down his cutlery and shuffled in his seat to look at her, where she still stood with clenched fists. She had half a mind to pour her glass of orange juice over his head – many others would have, she was sure.

'There's a reason I cook the way I do, Ethan. I can't put a foot wrong, don't you see that? I have to be better, more perfect that any man in the kitchen, just to be thought of in the same light. And I won't… I *can't* let myself down.'

'Look, you're a great chef. I can't deny it. When it comes to the classics, you're fantastic.'

Her fists slowly relaxed, as her shoulders dropped from where she had been holding them near her ears.

'All I'm saying is, and maybe some of the truth in that review is saying, don't just be a chef, Maggie, be an artist. Create. Bring *your* personality to the dishes you produce, not Jean-Sébastien's. You've been trained by the best. Now take that platform and build on it, manipulate it. Who are you, Maggie? Who are you as a chef, as an artist? Let your culinarians know. Let your diners know.'

Was there truth in his words? Was there truth in that godawful review?

'Now, would you please sit down and eat your lovingly prepared breakfast before it goes cold. Or worse, before that egg yolk solidifies. Countries have gone to war over lesser things.'

She wouldn't return his smile but she did sit. She picked up her glass of orange, contemplated pouring it over Ethan's product-styled hair, then chose not to waste the juice. The plate of food was, she confessed, a delight.

But she otherwise ate in silence because her mind wasn't in her kitchen at home, it was in the kitchen at the Grande Parisienne Hotel, where in a few short hours her dignity would be thwarted again, when she had to face the staff she was supposed to be in charge of.

And Emily's words came back to her, *Maggie Hill, though a perfectly adequate cook, does not appear to have what it takes to be a master of a three-Michelin star kitchen.*

-

There was an air of melancholy, or perhaps despondency, in the kitchen when she arrived at work. With each chef that came through the door, the mood seemed heavier. Were they grieving the end of Maggie's career? A friendship? Or the excellent reputation her predecessor had spent years building?

Maggie had never been in this position – not only receiving such a resolute level of criticism but being in charge of a kitchen she had let down. She had no idea if she was supposed to act like nothing had happened, go on with the show, as the saying went. Or if she was supposed to openly address the review and do something about it. On the one hand, what was the point? She had less than eight weeks left before she was out of work and, thanks to Emily, possibly indefinitely (excluding getting a job at a fast food place, like Ethan had suggested). On the other, if she gave in now, she wouldn't be fighting for Jean-Sébastien's honour, for the pride of her chefs, for her own pride.

As she called the team into a huddle around the pass to explain the turbot special – which wasn't necessary because it was a special they had cooked many times before with Jean-Sébastien at the helm – she felt all eyes on her, questioning and full of expectation.

She was braving herself to apologise to the team when Alexander snapped from behind her, 'Chef. A word.'

She could have written the script for what Alexander said to her in his office without turning up.

Basically, Maggie had added fuel to his fire, justified the impending arrival of Ethan when, apparently, Alexander's father had questioned the decision. He reiterated every negative line of Emily's review, going so far as to embellish the adjectives.

'Thank God I was here to put the only positive spin on that disaster,' he said, slapping his hands down onto his desk where he perched, half-seated, half-standing, making Maggie feel like the naughty kid in school.

And if he would treat her like a child, she might as well behave as a petulant one…

'She liked the wine, too,' she said, smiling innocently.

'Is this a joke to you, Maggie? Because the only farce here is what you're doing in that kitchen.'

'Is that so? Well, you were perfectly happy for me to wind down my three months in the manner of that "farce" before Emily's article. I didn't see you complaining about full covers and happy guests.'

He shook his head, clearly exasperated as he roughly rubbed at the stubble decorating his cheeks. 'The sooner Ethan gets here, the better. For now, if you don't want to be out on your ass, get back in the kitchen and make sure the next two months don't ruin this restaurant for the long term.'

Maggie scoffed and turned to leave.

'And, Maggie, if you can't do it for me and all the men in that kitchen who will be out of work if you ruin us, do it for *him*. Jean-Sébastien wouldn't want to see his protégée destroy everything he worked for now, would he?'

She left the office and, in the corridor, pressed her back to the wall, looking up to the ornate Artexed ceiling until her vision unclouded.

Hate was a very strong word.

But she truly *hated* Alexander.

She needed to do something, not because he told her to, but because she couldn't stand the thought of her unemployment proving the asshat right.

Chapter Eighteen

Nayomi

'Is that nice?'

Nuwan nodded vigorously, grinning, as much as was practical, around the straw dipped into the fresh orange juice Nayomi had bought him as a treat on their walk to Queens subway station.

They were sitting side by side on a relatively quiet train, given the early hour on a Sunday morning.

'Thank you for coming with me today, buddy. I know it's not the best Sunday.'

'Are you kidding? Mom, I'm *so* excited.'

She smiled at his enthusiasm and the way he could sound much older than his years sometimes.

'You are?'

'Yup. I've never been to your work before.'

'You've been to the tailor's.'

'Yeah but that's just Toni's house, really. This is a huge hotel and a real, proper restaurant. I've never been to a huge hotel and a real, proper restaurant.'

His words tinged her smile with sadness. She hoped that she gave her boys a good life but always worried about how far short she was falling.

Then Nuwan slurped the last of his juice and leaned his head against her arm. 'Mom, I'm so proud of you.'

'*Proud* of me? You're eight years old, how do you know what it means to be proud of someone?'

As the train dipped into a tunnel, she watched his reflection in the window of the car as he told her, 'You always say you're proud of me.'

And right then, she had never been more full of pride. She kissed his coconut-scented hair and let her lips linger on his head as she composed herself.

Given that no one had answered the kitchen phone when she had called ahead to explain that she would need to bring her son along to work, Nayomi was apprehensive when she slipped in through the front door of the restaurant and found every chef on the books sitting around one large table that had been formed by pushing the smaller dining tables together.

As the door was stolen by a wind and banged shut behind them, all eyes in the dining room fell on Nayomi and Nuwan.

'Wow!' Nuwan gasped, completely ignorant to the awkwardness Nayomi felt, gawping at the opulent space. 'This is cool.'

Then his eyes fell on Ashley, seated halfway down one long side of the table.

'Ashley!' Nuwan called out, running to the chef.

'Hey, buddy, how's it going?' Ashley pushed out his chair, giving himself a better angle to fist-bump Nuwan.

Meanwhile, Nayomi sought out Maggie's gaze at the head of the table. She was about to apologise for the additional person when Maggie said, 'Thanks for coming in on your day off, Nayomi. Help yourself to coffee or juice. We're just about to get started.'

Nayomi nodded, grateful. She would explain her predicament after the meeting. For now, she had intruded enough and clearly her son had no concept of the fact that Nayomi was just a side-part in the kitchen.

'Nuwan, come over here. Ashley's working.'

Having caused enough of a scene, she opted against coffee and juice and pulled out a seat at one of the few smaller dining tables around the sides of the room.

'There are enough seats at the table, Nayomi,' Maggie said, gesturing to the head of the table opposite her, where two seats remained empty.

Oh.

Nayomi nodded and led Nuwan to the seat next to her. 'We have to be quiet now, while the meeting goes on, okay?' she whispered.

In response, Nuwan demonstrated closing a zip across his lips and throwing away the key. The kid had a *lot* of personality.

'All right, guys, let's make a start,' Maggie said. 'There's no point hiding from the things going on around here, so let's get them on the table. As you know, in less than two months, Ethan James will be coming in as permanent executive and head chef. You'll have seen him around in the kitchen. He's likely to step up his presence as his shoes are filled at his current place and he looks to fill mine here.'

She paused to sip her coffee and Nayomi felt for her. Those must have been hard words to say.

'*But* for now, *we* are still a team and I'm the head chef here. As individuals and collectively, we have important work to do. There'd be no use pretending that Emily Blanchon's review wasn't very bad news.'

'Or bitter and twisted news,' Jack said, receiving almost roundtable endorsement for his comment.

'Be that as it may,' Maggie said, 'the vast majority of *NYT*'s readership won't know that Emily was

Jean-Sébastien's daughter, that she used to work here and that she may be just a little bit bitter and twisted.'

It was obvious to Nayomi that Maggie's attempt at a light-hearted expression was founded in discomfort.

'And, I have to hold my hands up and apologise to you all.' As a couple of the chefs made to protest, Maggie held up a hand. 'No, please, let me finish. I thought we could continue through this time until Ethan takes over, in exactly the way Jean-Sébastien had done things. But the reality is, I am *not* Jean-Sébastien. I take full responsibility for that review but we're here today because I need *your* help. We need to help each other.'

Maggie's gaze seemed to scan the table, then landed on Nayomi. She tried to offer encouragement in response.

'I don't want to see the name of this restaurant pummelled and I'm sure you don't either. Partially, out of respect for Jean-Sébastien. But also because, well...' She shrugged. 'I need a job after this.'

Maggie's laughter seemed to lift her own spirits and those of the others around the table.

'I also want you to know that Ethan has said that he intends to keep staff on under his management, though he does have a few chefs he wants to bring with him and he caveats any intentions with you guys being up to scratch. So, if not for the name of the restaurant, if not because I'm asking you, then please, let's work together to make sure that you guys can shine. I want you to be able to showcase what you can do for Ethan.'

'What's the deal, Chef? What do you want from us?' Josh asked.

'I want us to make some changes. I'm not talking Ethan James-style magic tricks and potions here. What I mean is, let's add that "mystique", that "pizazz", that "*je ne sais quoi*" to our dishes.'

Nayomi joined in the amusement around the table as Maggie used her fingers to quote Emily's words. Clearly, the review in the *NYT* hadn't escaped anyone's attention.

'What I want from today is every chef in the room, me included, to come up with three new ideas by the end of the day. Not necessarily the overhaul of dishes. The restaurant is renowned for French classics and that's what we'll serve. But we might add a different technique, a new component, a new taste. If you have ideas for specials, it's your chance to show off. But don't forget that any dish must be rooted in the…'

'Classics,' the bodies around the table said simultaneously, giving everyone cause to laugh.

The smile that played on Maggie's face then seemed more real and Nayomi watched her boss with admiration. She was owning the adversity she faced and was graceful in the face of it. And every person in the room listened to her.

Nayomi had noticed that Maggie was quieter than the other chefs in the kitchen. On a Saturday night at drinks, she wasn't always involved in the jokes. She wasn't always involved in the chatter in the kitchen during a shift. And where Nayomi had wondered about there being a gender issue in the kitchen – the basis of that really coming from Alexander's treatment of Maggie and the clear gender imbalance in the kitchen – now, she figured some of the reluctance to make Maggie the source of jokes was a mark of respect.

There was an electric pulse in the room, a vibe of excitement, as the chefs ended the meeting and headed to the kitchen. Nayomi had been asked to work purely to help with cleaning dishes but she still felt part of something thrilling. She even felt a little envious. Her hands itched to join in the food games in the kitchen.

When only Maggie was left in the dining room, Nayomi moved to her, her hands resting on Nuwan's shoulders as he walked in front of her.

'Maggie? I just want to say sorry for not giving you a heads-up about Nuwan coming along with me today. I tried to call the kitchen but no one answered. My friend who usually sits for the boys had plans today and my oldest boy was invited to a—'

Maggie reached out a hand to Nayomi's shoulder and offered a friendly look to Nuwan. 'It's absolutely fine, Nayomi. It's your day off and I'm grateful you could come in. The only thing is, he can't be in the kitchen for safety reasons. I hope that's not too much of a problem? He's welcome to set up out here and we can keep you guys in food and juice. Obviously, be out here as much as you need to be.'

'That's fine,' Nuwan said. 'I have my work books and colouring and my Lego in my backpack.'

With mock excited surprise, Maggie said, 'In that case, maybe I'll have to spend some time out here with you, too. I love Lego.'

'Will Ashley be allowed to play too?'

Maggie looked to Nayomi, raising an eyebrow in a way that made Nayomi giggle. 'We're just friends.'

'He made me a birthday cake,' Nuwan added.

'I saw that cake. It was great, huh?'

'Yup.'

'Okay, guys, I'll let you get sorted. Any problems just give me a shout. And thanks, again, Nayomi.'

When Maggie left, Nuwan told Nayomi, 'I like her.'

'She's one of the good ones.'

–

After three hours and a heap of dirty pots, the kitchen was still humming with energy. Spirits were jovial. Maggie was not only making dishes herself but also wandering the kitchen, helping other chefs, tasting their creations. She was the mother hen to many chicks. And those chicks were creating smell sensations that had Nayomi's empty stomach yelling at her for food. It was past lunch time and with the logistics of the morning – dressing two boys and getting them out of the house, dropping Roshan at a friend's home, and taking the subway into work – she and the boys had managed only two slices of leftover bread from the restaurant for breakfast.

Though he had been maintained with a plentiful supply of sugary juices from the bar, if she was hungry, she figured Nuwan must be starving.

She followed the sound of Maggie's voice into the pastry end of the kitchen and found her tasting something Ashley had created, and seemingly enjoying it.

'Maggie? Would it be okay if I take a break? I just need to pop out and get Nuwan some lunch.'

Holding her fingertips across her mouth as she finished eating, Maggie replied, 'Sure. No need to ask. Though you're welcome to rustle up something here, if you like.'

'Me? In the kitchen? I wouldn't dare use the equipment in here.'

'You should,' Ashley said, wiping his hands on a towel. 'What about those coconut things you make? Oh, man, I'd kill for one of those. And I've got spare coconuts.'

'Pani pol? The rolled pancakes?' Nayomi clarified.

'Ashley tells me you're a great cook,' Maggie said. 'And we have the crêpe pan. I don't think anyone is using it.'

Nayomi's cheeks heated. 'I only cook at home. And pani pol are incredibly easy to make. Ashley's being generous.'

'Well, it's up to you, but if you're making anything with coconut, I'd love to try it. Coconut is one of my favourite tastes.'

Ashley gave a subtle nod of encouragement from behind Maggie.

Nayomi cooking in this incredible kitchen? The temptation to feel part of what was happening in there today was too much to resist.

'If you're sure...'

When she told Nuwan she was making food in the kitchen, his eyes lit up. Despite spending most of the day building Lego in the dining room, where Charlie had now arrived to match wines to new flavours but was in fact building a pirate ship with him, Nuwan was unfathomably excited about his day at mom's work. When she told him that he could come into the kitchen to sit on a countertop while Nayomi made lunch, provided he didn't touch anything, she thought he might never come down from his high.

Her son felt like her superpower when Nayomi moved the crêpe pan and set up a cooking spot in the pastry end of the kitchen, where there was less action and fewer hot pans to create hazards for an eight-year-old boy. She was still nervous and felt out of place, nestled amidst the chefs' white uniforms in her maroon jacket and blue apron, but Nuwan gave her a dose of confidence. She felt impressive, like someone her son could look up to. Though she tried to be those things by being a good mother, this was different somehow.

Ashley helped her gather ingredients for her dish and even gave her a coconut carver, which she had been pleased to find the kitchen had. Carving and shredding the whites of a coconut by hand was not easy and fresh always tasted better than desiccated.

She bopped along to the music playing over the kitchen radio as she hand-mixed pancake batter in a bowl – adding a Sri Lankan secret, a pinch of turmeric for yellow colouring but not so much for taste. Her hips jiggled of their own volition as she ground out the whites of two coconuts. She hummed the parts of songs she knew as she mixed shredded coconut, lashings of dark honey (the best she had ever tasted), a splash of coconut milk and indulgent amounts of cinnamon and cardamom for the filling.

When the first pancake was ready, she turned it onto a plate and guided Nuwan to spoon the right amount of filling into a line down the centre. Then she quickly tucked and rolled, the way she had done a thousand times before, and cut the roll into bite-sized pieces for her son.

Then she made a second pani pol for Ashley, who ate standing up, leaning back against the worktop. 'This is so good. How many is too many in one sitting?'

Feeling a little flattered and a little giddy, Nayomi continued to cook the tasty treats – another for both guys.

'Oh my, is this what smells absolutely divine?' Maggie asked, just as Nayomi was turning out the fifth pancake onto a plate.

'This one is yours if you want it?' she said.

'I'd love it.'

So, Nayomi tucked and rolled and handed off her fifth pani pol to Maggie, nervously awaiting her feedback.

'Oh my goodness. Nayomi, this is amazing. Ashley, you were so right.'

Buoyed by the praise and the flutter of happiness in her chest, Nayomi poured more batter onto the crêpe pan.

As Maggie licked her fingers, she asked, 'How do you make these?'

'I'm glad you like them but don't be fooled, they're really easy to make,' Nayomi said, concentrating primarily on not letting her pancake get too crispy. 'They're a little thicker than usual crêpes but not as thick as American pancakes. And you mustn't let them get crispy. That's important because the texture makes them easier to roll and hold in shape.'

'What about the colour?' Maggie asked.

'The yellow? A tiny pinch of turmeric. Not so much that you can taste it. If you have the—' She paused, embarrassed but shrugged and continued. 'If you have the money, saffron is really great. For colour but also to taste.' She brushed over the comment quickly. It was quite obvious, she figured, that she was far from wealthy, but she didn't need to draw attention to it, especially not in front of Nuwan. 'At home, in Sri Lanka, we would have used jaggery – a large block of hard, dark sugar. It's not too easy to find here, so you can use muscovado or dark sugar, but I often use honey in America and the one you have here works really well.'

'What's in the filling?'

Nayomi relayed the recipe as she filled a pancake for herself. 'Does anyone want another?'

'You have that one, you must be hungry. We've all been snacking as we cook,' Maggie said. Then she stared at Nayomi as if she were looking straight through her and spoke almost as if to herself. 'Cinnamon and cardamom, huh?'

'Sri Lankans put cinnamon in everything,' Nayomi said.

'*Everything*,' Nuwan added, making all four of them laugh. 'My mom makes the best food, Chef.'

Maggie laughed heartily then, a sound that pleased Nayomi to hear.

'You can call me Maggie, Nuwan.'

He twisted his lips in contemplation. 'I like calling you chef. It's important, isn't it? Like talking to the president or something.'

Maggie chuckled again. 'I think you should come back here every day, Nuwan.'

'I would but I have to go to school most days.'

Then they were laughing again. And when something made Nayomi glance up to Ashley, she found his eyes on hers. That fluttering moved from her heart to the pit of her stomach.

—

Later in the day, when the kitchen was beginning to quiet down and Nuwan had crashed after multiple sugar peaks and troughs, now fast asleep across three chairs in the dining room, Ashley appeared at the porters' station.

'Do you want to share the staff car?'

Having assumed she would be getting the subway home, not realising that the staff car might be running on a Sunday, Nayomi was delighted by the offer.

An hour later, she flicked off the lights in the dazzlingly clean kitchen, and Ashley carried Nuwan out to the staff car, as Nayomi followed behind with a backpack and a Lego pirate ship that she had been told must come home in one piece.

After a brief detour to collect Roshan from his friend's house, Ashley asked, 'Are you guys hungry? I'm starving. There's a Mexican place right by you. If I got some take-out, would you be interested in sharing?'

Before Nayomi could decide either way, Roshan had agreed that they would all eat burritos and Nayomi caved, on the basis that the boys got washed and put on their PJs first.

Once the boys were tucked up in bed, Nayomi sat down on the sofa with Ashley, folding her legs beneath her, increasingly comfortable in his presence.

'Thank you for dinner. The boys loved it. I think you may have had Roshan won over there for an hour.'

Ashley laughed. 'That's about fifty minutes longer than I managed last time.'

'They're no pushovers, my boys,' Nayomi joked.

But Ashley was perfectly serious when he told her, 'You've done a great job with them. How long has it been just the three of you, if that's not too personal?'

She shook her head. 'It's okay. Two years.'

'Did you ever think about moving back to Sri Lanka?'

'I did. But my life would have been so different in Sri Lanka. I never worked. I had no independence. America opened my eyes. Not all of it good, sure. I mean, I'd be in a lot better position financially if we were in Sri Lanka.' She shrugged. 'I don't know, I guess my home is more America now than Sri Lanka, even though I still call the island home. I grew up here, in the truest sense. I became an adult here. And the boys are, I think, more American than Sri Lankan. They have better opportunities here.

Especially now that I'm at the restaurant and can afford some of the add-ons at their school.'

Ashley nodded. 'Maggie was genuinely impressed with your cooking today.'

'Pfft, pani pol are so easy. I'm sure she was just being polite.'

'No, seriously. I could tell. You know, she asked me if I could have a shot at making a spiced ice cream that would complement your pancakes.'

'She did?'

He nodded. 'I think she might be contemplating making a dish from your idea.'

'Like a special?'

'Yeah, exactly.'

Nayomi's chest fluttered. 'Wow.'

'You know what I told her?'

Nayomi shook her head.

'I suggested she give you a shot at making the pani pol and I could make the ice cream. What do you think?'

Nayomi sat up straighter. 'What? Like, cook? Me? In the restaurant?'

'Don't get your hopes up, because Maggie didn't respond one way or the other. But I said, if it was a special, why not try it for a night or two and see how it sells. You can make them in advance, right? That's what you did when I had them here, I think?'

'They're actually better made in advance and left to settle.'

'So, I figure you could make them and still do your porter duties. I would just add the ice cream and serve them.'

'Do you think she'll go for it?'

'We'll see. I hope so.'

Nayomi held a hand to her chest in a bid to calm her racing heart. 'Thank you so much for even thinking that. For even having faith in me.' And before she knew what she was doing, her lips met Ashley's cheek.

She pulled back quickly and covered her mouth with her fingertips. 'I'm sorry. I didn't mean to do that.'

Ashley's chest noticeably rose and fell with his next breaths and his eyes fell to Nayomi's mouth when she removed her hand.

Panic stiffened her body. 'Ashley. I don't— I shouldn't have— We couldn't—'

'Hey, it was a polite kiss on the cheek. Friendly. Nothing more.'

But the way he stood and shoved his hands into the pockets of his jeans, his shoulders high, Nayomi felt horrible. Had she ruined a friendship? She truly hoped not.

'I should go. The boys have school tomorrow. You have to be up early.'

He walked himself to the door and had closed it gently behind him before Nayomi had a chance to say goodnight.

Nayomi sat back down on the sofa and held a cushion against her stomach. She pressed her fingertips to her lips again and replayed the softness of Ashley's skin against them.

The only man she had ever kissed had been her husband. Shouldn't he be her last? Wasn't that how she had been raised?

Chapter Nineteen

Emily

Emily woke feeling heavy – heavy heart, heavy mind. Heavy, heavy, heavy.

Since taking the ultimate leap backward in life and moving back home with her mom almost a week ago, she hadn't eaten out once. That might not sound strange for a typical person who had walked out on her fiancé and their home, written a scathing review of her late father's restaurant and verbally bashed an ex-best friend, and whose meals were being cooked by her mom who was constantly on at her to eat more. But for Emily, it meant she also wasn't working. She had a backlog of visits to restaurants and notes she could turn into reviews, but she didn't feel like writing anything.

In fact, she didn't feel like *doing* anything. Except watching re-runs of *Stranger Things* on her iPad, in bed, under the same floral sheets that had adorned her bed a decade ago.

Rolling onto her side, she hugged her pillow and stared out of the window, in a half-lucid state between awake and dreaming. She had been sleeping with the curtains open the last few nights, to see if she would feel any lighter if she woke in a morning with the natural light of day.

She didn't.

A big old tree was being blown in the wind outside, its leaves rustling loud enough to be heard through the windows. She watched a leaf break from a branch and twirl in the sky before gliding left and right, until it fell below her range of vision. It triggered a memory of her and Maggie sitting on a bench in Central Park, around this time of year. Maggie was helping her plan a trip that, years ago, she had desperately wanted to take.

She would fly into Paris and after a week or so of taking in the sights and incredible food, she would hire a car and drive to Champagne, to taste *real* champagne and pair it with the finest cheeses her parents' homeland had to offer. Then she would work her way around the country. North, east, south, west, middle. And when she was ready, she would rent a small place to stay in the capital. There, where all great writers found inspiration, she would write about her experiences, create dishes she had been inspired to cook on her travels and write up recipes.

Rolling onto her back, she stared up at the ceiling. An empty white canvass. Blank. *Who was she? Who was Emily Blanchon?*

Not a chef – she didn't so much as make toast these days. Not a professional writer – who could call her one after her recent vendetta piece? Not somebody special to anyone – Oliver hadn't even called since she had walked out.

'Emily? Are you up? I've made coffee and fresh bread,' Isabella called from the bottom of the staircase.

Not a good daughter – letting her grieving mother run around after her while she wallowed in bed day after day.

Her eyes filled in what was becoming an annoying habit of late. She wanted to cry constantly. Her tears were like a wind-up toy, fully braced and ready to be unloaded at any time but kept at bay by their captor.

She brought herself up to sit on the edge of her bed and pulled on a pair of slipper socks. A brief moment of dizziness passed over her and she realised she was famished. She also noticed her laptop and phone taunting her from the bedside table.

Like it or not, she had to get a review to her editor today. Until she thought of something better to do, being a food critic was what paid her bills, even those for the home she was no longer living in.

Had she ever actually wanted to be a food critic?

That was one question too many for her mental capacity today.

Trudging downstairs in her checked PJs – found in a drawer of her old things that she had never cleared out of her parents' home – laptop and phone in hand, her stomach growled at the scent of fresh bread and strong, rich coffee.

Isabella was sitting at the kitchen table, so engrossed in a stack of papers that she didn't notice Emily until she set her laptop down opposite her mom.

'Did you bake?' Emily asked.

'Just baguettes.' Her mom replied without looking up from what appeared to be a rather official letter.

Emily made herself coffee, sliced four large chunks from the delectable smelling baguette and smothered them all in butter and raspberry preserve.

Tucking one leg beneath her on the chair, she sat down opposite Isabella and opened her laptop.

Finally, her mom looked up, peering above the rim of her gold-framed reading glasses.

'I'm working,' Emily said. 'I have to submit a review today.'

She expected some kind of words of positivity from her mom — *well done for being proactive* or *I'm glad to see you're feeling up to it, darling*. Instead, the expression her mom wore was one of disappointment.

'Why are you looking at me like that?' Emily spoke through a mouthful of half-chewed bread.

'I'm not looking at you like anything,' Isabella said, returning her attention to her papers.

They hadn't discussed Emily's review of Jean-Sébastien's but given her mom had subscribed to *NYT* the moment Emily told her about her job with the paper she knew Isabella would have read the article.

Part of Emily wanted her mom to call her out on it. She wanted to yell and scream, argue that Isabella would have supported her precious Maggie and the restaurant no matter how much truth was in the article. The other part of her was becoming increasingly ashamed. There *was* truth in the review. Maggie *did* blindly follow Jean-Sébastien's ways. But Emily knew from the moment she made the reservation at the restaurant to the time she hit *send* on her article, that she had written her words with malice.

As she worked through her bread and coffee, she opened her laptop reluctantly and began to read her notes from three visits to Wag4U World Steakhouse — a terrible name that made the place sound like a pet store but which did showcase the restaurant's focus on wagyu beef from the prominent meat regions of the world.

Perhaps because she wasn't engrossed in what she was doing or perhaps because it sounded so defeatist and unlike her mom, Emily found herself very aware of the sighs and tuts coming from the opposite side of the table.

'What's going on, Mom? What is all that stuff?'

Isabella dropped the pages she was reading onto the table top and lifted her hands in defeat before letting out a sound of exasperation and walking to the kitchen window, her back to Emily.

Emily moved her laptop aside and picked up the last of the bulk of papers her mom had been reading.

> Re: Estate of Jean-Sébastien Blanchon.
> Transfer of equity interests in US corpora-
> tions.

She began to read, as her mom spoke with what sounded like sadness as much as exasperation.

'I just don't understand it all. Letters about his restaurants. His charities. His book royalties. Every day I get more mail, *Sorry for your loss but*. I have to sign things to accept equity interests in companies and restaurants I don't have any idea about. What about his charity work? Paying for those who can't afford it to go to chef school. How can I not keep funding his passions? But I don't know what money we have or don't have.' She brought her hands to her head, rubbing her temples. 'It's all so confusing. I have wardrobes full of his clothes to clear out. Cars to sell. People to contact to donate things that he left in his will.'

A new wave of guilt washed over Emily. *How had she been so self-absorbed that she hadn't recognised her mom's need for help?*

She set the letters down on the table and went to Isabella, folding her into her arms. 'I'm sorry, Mom. I'm sorry.'

As her mom – always strong and positive – broke against her chest, Emily's own tears finally released.

'I'm going to help you with all of this.' She pressed her lips to her mom's familiar scented hair. 'I promise.'

–

For the first time in a week, Emily stepped out of the shower and changed out of her pyjamas. Having fired off one of the most rushed and mindless pieces of writing she had ever composed about *Wag4U World Steakhouse* to her editor, Emily had sent her mom out into the garden. The morning wind had subsided and left a pleasant enough day in its wake. Isabella was pruning bushes under the shade of a floppy hat with an old radio playing next to her. She seemed in much brighter spirits than she had earlier in the day and for that, Emily was grateful.

Downstairs on the kitchen table, armed with her third coffee of the day, Emily spread all the legal and business mail Isabella had received in the last few weeks and began arranging it into piles – books, restaurants, television appearances, charities. By late afternoon, she felt like there was at least a semblance of order to the chaos brought to her mom's life.

'He was involved in so much,' Isabella said, approaching Emily from the outside door behind her, satisfied that the garden, at least, was in a better state than it had been this morning.

'I focused so much on the hotel and the restaurant because he was always there but he had so many things going on,' Emily agreed. 'They've suspended the upcoming documentary on Netflix and they are looking at replacing his episode with one by another chef.'

Isabella nodded. 'It's sad, when he had already done the work. I think I'd like to see him on our screens again. But perhaps it is too morbid for people. I don't know.'

Emily draped an arm around her mom's waist as they stared at the now orderly piles of admin Emily had to work through.

'How about, you go and get cleaned up and I finish up with this stuff for today, then I'll make us something nice for dinner. And, if you like, we can watch something old of Dad's – one of his judging contests, maybe?'

Isabella looked up at her daughter. 'You're going to cook for me?'

It was bizarre the way Emily's heart started racing. *Was she sure about this?* But she nodded. 'Yes. I'll cook.'

Isabella's frown turned into a soft smile. One she wore very well. 'I would like that very much.'

That was settled then. Emily would pop to the local grocery store, then she would do what she hadn't done for years. She would cook a proper meal.

It had been almost as long since Emily had wandered around a grocery store. She had come to her parents' favourite store – though local, it was beautiful and well stocked. Vegetables were stacked on shelves in wicker baskets, declined enough that she could easily see the contents and help herself to the perfect size of potatoes and onions for her boulangère and the chunkiest stems of asparagus for her white asparagus soup. She filled the basket that hung on her forearm and found herself humming along to the music playing in the background.

At the meat counter, she assessed the cuts on display, eventually asking to take a closer look at a duck breast.

Armed with ingredients for her starter and main course, Emily was about to head to the cashier, when a colourful selection of macarons caught her eye. *Mom's favourites.*

She had walked almost the entire way home before she realised that since leaving the house she hadn't thought about Oliver or work or the mound of estate admin she had yet to wade through. She had thought about food. About how to cook it – remembering old tricks as if she had never left the kitchen. She imagined her mom's delight at sitting down this evening to a home-cooked dinner. And she had hummed and sung, feeling something very close to happy, or contented, at least.

The quietness of the house stopped her from calling out a greeting as she stepped inside. In the lounge, she found her mom sitting in the stripy grandad chair in the bay window, a book open but face down on her lap, her head leaning sideways as she slept. Emily suspected she hadn't been sleeping well of late and it was pleasing to see her a thousand times more peaceful than she had been this morning.

In the kitchen, Emily closed the surrounding doors and set to work making cream of white asparagus soup. Her old recipe came rushing back to her, just, as people say, like riding a bike. She cut the tips off the asparagus and set them aside to add later, then sautéed onions in butter, added chopped asparagus and popped a lid on the pan to let the vegetables steam.

Meanwhile, she went into her dad's herb garden and began snapping off sprigs of the herbs she needed. Parsley to garnish her soup. A small amount of rosemary for her red-berry duck sauce. Lemon thyme for her potatoes. She rolled the herb leaves between her fingers and inhaled, her eyes closing as fresh lemon infiltrated her senses. And she heard her dad's voice in her ear, saying *lemon thyme; the most versatile of all the herbs.*

Feeling contented, she got back to the kitchen and, for hours, was swept up in the easy pleasure of creating something delicious, with the primary objective of bringing some much-needed joy to her mom.

At eight thirty, she hung up her apron, poured two glasses of the remaining dry white wine she had used to make her soup, and called her mom through to the kitchen, where she presented her with a temperate bowl of soup, accompanied with bread and butter.

'Don't eat too much bread,' she told Isabella, gesturing for her to take a seat. 'Something tasty might have slipped into my basket for dessert.'

But Isabella didn't take a seat. She stood, staring at the table with surprise. 'Emily, this is just wonderful.'

An old feeling of pride filled Emily. A feeling she used to get when her dad praised her in the kitchen... before he didn't any more. She pushed that thought from her head. Tonight was about being happy. It was about her mom.

'Come on now, Mrs. Sentimental. That soup is the perfect temperature. Don't let it get too cold.'

Moving to her seat, Isabella said playfully, 'Just as bossy as your dad.'

Emily bit her tongue to stop herself from responding. *Be nice.*

But with the first spoonful of soup, Isabella said, 'This is delightful, Emily. Very light. Do you know, I always preferred your soups? Your dad didn't have the patience for a good soup.'

Emily paused, mid-scooping a spoonful of soup from her bowl. 'Mom, can we *not* do that? Can we just eat a nice meal without the comparisons?'

'I'm sorry, I didn't even realise I was doing it. It was just how you two always were. Always competing with each other. Trying to outdo one another. You used to love it.'

'I used to hate it.'

Isabella shook her head. 'No you didn't, Emily. You and your dad made each other better chefs.'

Emily took a large swig of wine from her glass. 'Until he didn't want to listen to my ideas any more.'

'It was his kitchen, Emily. He was doing what he knew worked well. Just as Maggie is trying to do now.'

'Oh great, here we go. Let's talk about dad *and* my review. Anything else you'd like to ruin a good night with, Mom?'

Isabella put her spoon down in her bowl and sat back. 'I'm sorry. You're right. You've prepared this marvellous meal and it's been a wonder to see you happy today, singing while you worked. Let's start again as if we just sat down, shall we?'

So, they did. By the time Emily switched their white wine for two glasses of the red wine she had paired with her duck and presented a close-to-perfect plate of food for main course, their stilted conversation had turned to one which flowed. Emily was brought up to speed on family and friends of her mom's that she hadn't kept up with in recent years. She learned that her mom had started to crochet and was painting again, as she had enjoyed when Emily was a young girl.

They skimmed over the topic of Oliver and left it that Emily wasn't sure what she wanted and Oliver hadn't tried to contact her either, so perhaps he wasn't sure, or perhaps he thought their break-up was for the best.

'Do you think you're well-suited?' her mom asked.

Emily answered honestly, 'I just don't know. I'm not sure he gets me. Like, really understands who I am.'

'Perhaps that's difficult for someone else to understand if you aren't too sure yourself?'

Where Emily would have tended to give an off-hand quip in response, something made her fall quiet tonight. It was a question she would think about again and again in the days and weeks to come.

But when she and her mom took decaffeinated coffees and a large plate of too many macarons to the sofa, Emily decided not to think about much beyond the crispy almond outsides and luxuriously creamy centres of the desserts.

Tonight, she was enjoying a kitchen triumph and her mom's company. Everything else could wait.

Chapter Twenty

Maggie

Her batter was thin and light. It hissed when it contacted the heat of the crêpe pan and the familiar smell of pudding rose to Maggie's nose.

She had decided to trial the new dessert in the restaurant tonight, for the first service of the week, and had been in the kitchen since first light perfecting the recipe – the filling of Nayomi's pani pol, with a lighter, more typically French crêpe.

As she waited for the crêpe to cook, she shuffled the four alternative bowls of filling she had been working on so that her preferred mix was closest to her.

'Sweetheart, making me breakfast? You shouldn't have.'

Maggie spotted Ethan – sunglasses in his hair, arms folded across his chest in that leather jacket he *knew* he looked good in, leaning back against the pass, one ankle crossed over the other. Casually sexy. If you liked that kind of thing, or man, or… *whatever.*

'I'm so far from being your sweetheart and don't worry, I didn't.'

Smirking, Ethan moved to her side, inspecting the bowls of sweet filling and scrutinising the crêpe batter, lifting the spoon from the bowl and eyeing the viscosity as the mixture poured from it.

'What are you doing here?' Maggie asked.

'I've got a meeting with Alexander.'

She didn't care much what about but Ethan was clearly proud to announce, 'I've been approached about a new documentary, following me through my next career venture.'

'Good for you. Well, enjoy your meeting. I'm sure you and Alexander can enjoy blowing smoke up each other's asses.'

He laughed, short and sharp, snorting in a way that was so goofy it had Maggie hiding her grin as she gently lifted the crêpe from the pan and onto a round plate. She was funny, when she wanted to be. Everyone seemed to think she was Mrs. Serious but Maggie made jokes, even if they were usually heard by only her and Jean-Sébastien, or her and her cat these days.

She spooned her preferred filling into the middle of the crêpe and began folding and rolling into a neat exotic twist on the traditional French crêpe.

'Is there a reason you're still here?' she asked, drizzling dark honey lightly across the crêpe.

She could sense Ethan smiling without looking at him. 'You seem happier today,' he said, completely at odds with the impression she was trying to give.

But it was true. She couldn't change Emily's review. It was damaging; it was out there for the world to read and judge Maggie. Right now, though, she was creating something in what was still her kitchen, and she was having fun.

Maggie scooped the cinnamon ice cream that she and Ashley had perfected the day before and slipped it on top of a small dial of coconut and sugar brittle, then gently lifted a light sugar nest from a plate where she had left it to cool and set it atop the ice cream. Finally, she added three edible purple flowers at evenly spaced intervals along the rolled crêpe – a nod to the purple water lily, Sri Lanka's national flower.

'It looks beautiful, Maggie. Then, your food always *looks* beautiful.'

She frowned at him. 'Can't you just give a compliment and leave it there?'

He chuckled, making Maggie shake her head. She wouldn't dignify him with a smile, even if she did find him *mildly* entertaining.

'The proof is in the pudding, Chef. Literally, in this case.'

Maggie took two forks from a utensil pot on the counter and confidently handed one to Ethan. 'Be my guest.'

They each forked opposite ends of the crêpe, taking a healthy amount of filling and a slick of ice cream. Despite telling herself that Ethan's opinion didn't matter, she watched him wrap his lips around the fork, chew and swallow. *Waiting.*

As she waited, she ate her own forkful and was sure this batch of filling was the closest she had gotten to Nayomi's sublime recipe.

'Well…?'

'I love it. Honestly, it's delicious. The crêpe is light, just crispy enough. The ice cream is subtle, which it needs to be to cut through that filling, which is… Mmm, mmm, mmm.'

Maggie blushed. His opinion *didn't* matter. It was just nice to hear, that was all.

'As far as I'm aware, this isn't a conventional French classic,' Ethan said. 'Who are you and what have you done with the Maggie I know?'

She pursed her lips and scowled playfully at his mock panic-stricken face. 'It's a Sri Lankan twist on a French crêpe.'

He stared at her, his expression softening then suddenly serious. His eyes fell to her mouth and, for no sensible reason, she wanted to feel his lips pressed to hers. She wanted to step into him and feel what it would be like to be folded into his arms, pressed against his firm chest. She remembered the ferocity of her crush on him at chef school. How her stomach would flip when he walked into a room. Then she remembered how utterly dismissive he was of her and her cupcake baking, how he ranked her as second best in the kitchen, declared her as such to all his guy friends, and preferred tall blondes with really long legs and no inhibitions when it came to everything else.

As she snapped out of her moment of imagined passion, Ethan pointed to the corner of his lip. 'You have coconut. Just there.'

'Oh, thanks.' She swiped quickly at her mouth, embarrassed by her wayward thoughts.

Ethan took another forkful of dessert. 'I need the recipe for this. My daughter would love it. She loves pancakes any which way she can have them.'

Maggie almost choked on air. 'Daughter? I didn't realise.'

Ethan seemed to force a smile but there was an undertone of sadness. 'Who would let a jackass like me have a kid, right?'

'No, I— I didn't mean anything by it. I'm just surprised. I don't know why. I didn't get the impression you were, you know, *with* anyone. Let alone a long-term—'

'I'm not *with* anyone. Not for our lack of trying. Not everything is conventional, Maggie, despite how your world looks.'

She wanted to snap at him that she knew all about fighting against convention, first with her parents and then with every arrogant male chef she encountered in this industry, but she bit back her words. *He's bitter at the situation, not you, Maggie. Let it slide.*

They fell into uncomfortable silence, Maggie trying to break the tension by asking, 'Do you want any more?'

'Are you done?'

She nodded. 'I've been at this for hours. If it's true that your stomach is only the size of a fist, I'm not sure where all the crêpes and filling I've eaten this morning have gone.'

She was pleased the lightness in Ethan's eyes returned. 'I don't like to see good food go to waste,' he said, taking hold of the plate and stepping back to lean against the countertop opposite Maggie as he tucked into the remaining dessert.

As she watched him, it occurred to her that just as Ethan didn't know her beyond his superficial impression of her, maybe there was more to him than his surface arrogance.

Probably not. But curiosity got the better of her, and Maggie blurted out, 'Do you mind me asking how old your daughter is?'

'She's five. Almost six.'

'Oh. So she was born not long after chef school?'

She couldn't imagine the version of Ethan she had known then ever becoming a father.

'Needless to say, she wasn't planned. But I cared for her mom. We tried to make a go of things. And I'm big enough to admit it was me who kept screwing things up. I loved them both. Annie, that's my daughter, she's brilliant. She's got this electric personality and she's so funny. Her mom and I are close; there's no animosity there. I just don't think I grew up quickly enough. Where she was a great mom right off the bat, I struggled to find my feet.'

He chewed a mouthful of food and shrugged. 'I guess I learned that it's not necessarily best to stay together because you have a kid, which is not how my own parents saw things when I was younger.'

His words made her pause. She recognised the sentiment entirely. If her mom hadn't been forced into legitimising her pregnancy with Maggie by marrying her dad, if her parents hadn't been forced to stay together by a lack of money, maybe they wouldn't have been so bitter and resentful. Maybe, they would have loved her.

He set his plate aside and sucked remnants of honey from his finger. 'It's a happier home without me in it. And, you know what? We make it work now. When I spend time with Annie, it's great. I hate that she has a second dad now, who gets to see her every day, but they're happy. We're happy. I wish I could see Annie more often than I do, maybe pick her up from school some days. But I can't so... it is what it is.'

Something Maggie never guessed she would think was that Ethan was human and might actually have a kind side. Something she never thought she would feel was sorry for him. And, even more unexpectedly, she found herself respecting him for his outlook.

'Couldn't you take Annie to school in the mornings sometimes?'

'She lives in New Jersey.'

'Oh.'

'Like I said, it is what it is.'

Maggie was lost for her next words. She recognised the unsociable nature of their hours, naturally. It was part of the reason she lived with Livvy and a herb garden and rarely saw anyone outside of work. But she hadn't been in a situation where she had been forced to choose work over a someone she loved before.

Ethan leaned forward and snatched her towel from where it was tucked into the side of her apron, wiping his hands. 'Actually, she lives near the farm I told you about. Whenever I go to see Annie, I go to the farm. They're both the perfect excuse for each other.'

He handed back her towel. 'So what's with the new dessert?'

The change in subject was surprisingly unwelcome. Maggie found herself wanting to know more about Ethan, intrigued by his moment of openness, and wanting to tell someone, *him*, things about her. But she suppressed that desire and told him, 'It's part of trying something new. It's actually Nayomi's inspiration, really. She's Sri Lankan and makes these things called pani pol. Very similar concept, I've just been refining it to make it lighter and more... French classic, I guess.'

'Obviously.'

She threw her towel back at Ethan, who caught it by his head.

'I can't get the filling as good as Nayomi's, though.'

'Who is Nayomi?'

'She's currently a kitchen porter.'

'Are you thinking about drafting her in?'

'I *am* drafting her in. To make the filling, at least. She just doesn't know it yet. I'll be able to give her some extra hours, and they'll be at a higher rate of pay than her porter wage, so I think she'll go for it.'

Ethan stared at her, eyes soft and the corners of his lips tilted up. 'You're a good soul, Maggie.'

She felt her face twist in confusion.

'It's something your predecessor would have done, you know?'

She hadn't seen it that way but she guessed he was right. Jean-Sébastien had given many people, including her, a hand onto the culinary ladder.

'Is it patronising if I say I'm kind of proud of you?' Ethan asked.

Her brows furrowed. 'Yes. It is.'

'Well, I am. You could have crawled into a corner and wept over Emily's review. Instead, you're trying new ideas. And look how happy you are today, creating something new.'

Maggie suddenly found interest in the tiled floor. 'I don't know if pride is something I feel.' She sighed. 'I feel like I'm going against his legacy and everything he built, Ethan. Jean-Sébastien was all about the classics. Pure. Elegant. Untouched. And here I am, running scared of a review and trying to save my own butt for future employment but taking everything he stood for and... ruining it.'

Ethan stepped closer to her. His presence compelled her to look from where their feet were almost touching to his face, tipped down towards hers, his stubbled square jaw and pink, full lips dangerously close for her senses. 'You're doing the exact opposite, Maggie. You're keeping him alive – his spirit, his love of food, of serving the public, of educating and supporting talent – you're keeping it all alive with your passion.'

She swallowed deeply, watching the skin of his throat stretch as he did the same.

'Do you know how pretty you are when you're happy?' He lifted a hand towards her face and her heart started thumping so hard in her chest, she wondered if he could hear it.

She braced herself for his touch.

Then his hand was snatched away as they heard, then saw, Alexander push through the door from the dining room.

Ethan stepped away from her sharply.

'There you are. Never on time,' Alexander said.

'I was on time,' Ethan replied. 'In fact, I was early. I've just been helping Maggie perfect a new dish.'

Maggie's mouth opened wide in shock.

'Let's go get coffee,' Alexander said, leaving the kitchen without so much as saying hello to Maggie.

'You lying jackass,' Maggie bit at Ethan, who glanced back across his shoulder and laughed at her.

Teasing, lying, arrogant, hasn't-changed-a-bit man-child.

203

Chapter Twenty-One

Nayomi

Nayomi dabbed her brow with a tissue and paused a moment to catch her breath before heading through the rear entrance to Jean-Sébastien's. She had agreed to come in early and was thrilled at the prospect that Maggie might ask her to help in the kitchen in a culinary role. But at two thirty p.m. she had been faced with a distraught bride-to-be, whose online order of four bridesmaid dresses had arrived late and all of them too long. Nayomi couldn't and didn't want to let Maggie down. But she couldn't and didn't want to let down a woman the day before one of the biggest days of her life.

The natural solution then, had been to make the best job she could of altering the bridesmaid dresses in very little time and then run to the subway station in Queens and from the subway station in Manhattan to the restaurant.

If there was a silver lining, at least she had been too lacking in oxygen to think about the awkward first meet with Ashley since she had too giddily kissed him on the cheek on Sunday evening.

'Nayomi, you're here!'

Maggie was standing next to Ashley's station, where she was drizzling thin strands of caramel from a fork and pulling them towards her in a continual process that seemed to be forming some kind of ball or basket of sugar.

Ashley was whisking ingredients in a large bowl and raised his chin in greeting. 'Hey. You okay?'

Nayomi wiped her brow again with tissue, her breathing almost back to normal. 'I ran from the subway station.'

'Oh, you could have been a little late, Nayomi, but I'm thrilled you're here.' Maggie stopped spinning sugar and turned to the countertop, where she set the art on top of a scoop of ice cream, which was placed next to something that looked very much like a fancy pani pol. She placed three purple flowers on top and held up the plate to Nayomi. 'What do you think?'

Nayomi set her rucksack on the ground and took the plate, closely inspecting the food that looked like it would cost a thousand dollars in a place like this. 'I think it looks lovely. But what is it?'

Maggie and Ashley smiled and Maggie told her. '*This* is the reason I asked you to come in early. We've perfected the crêpe, the ice cream and the presentation. But try as I might, I just can't make the filling as deliciously as you do. So, we were wondering if you would like to make the filling yourself. Exactly as you made it for me on Sunday?'

Nayomi felt her eyes narrow. 'You mean, here, in the kitchen?'

Maggie chuckled. 'Yes, exactly. You'll be paid more for your time spent working as a chef. I'd like to put the dessert on the menu as a special for a week from tonight and see how it sells. We figured, if you made the filling, Ashley would deal with the crêpe and the sugar art on an order-by-order basis.'

Ashley had planted the seed of possibility but Nayomi hadn't let herself fall into the trap of believing it could be a reality. Her, a chef. In a three-Michelin starred restaurant. Even if it would just be for a couple of hours each day.

'You wouldn't have to come in much earlier,' Ashley said.

'That's right. The same time as today would be great. Even a half hour later if you need it,' Maggie added.

She turned back to the counter and picked up a white chef's jacket that had been folded into a neat square. 'So, what do you say, a commis chef for two hours each day? Then your normal shift, starting a tad later, if needs be.' She held out the coat to Nayomi, who took hold of it in her spare hand, staring down at the dazzling white fabric.

Imagine what the boys would think of her in this.

A small giggle escaped her. 'I say, yes.'

Working alongside Ashley, wearing her gleaming chef's uniform, Nayomi ground the whites of coconuts and blended the ingredients of her filling. She marvelled at Ashley spinning sugar nests. She tasted his ice cream, which was entirely scrumptious and, she agreed, the ideal accompaniment to the light dessert that Maggie conjured up, still packed full of all the flavours Nayomi loved.

She tried not to think about what would happen at the end of the week, when her dish was no longer a special and tried, instead, to live in the moment, enjoy it.

Ashley talked as he worked. She had no idea how he could manage that so easily when his job seemed so much trickier than hers, which was really second nature. What she did know, was that any awkwardness she had feared between the two of them was non-existent.

When she had finished mixing the filling, Nayomi wiped down her area, ready to change into her porter uniform and get on with her normal job. 'Well, I wonder if we'll get lots of orders tonight, Ashley,' she said.

'I've got a feeling we will.'

She didn't mind if they did or didn't, she supposed. It would be nice if people liked the dessert but what mattered to her was that she had been given a chance at something new. Something bigger.

'Either way, thank you. I really appreciate what you've done for me.'

'You did the hard stuff,' he said.

She nodded and reluctantly made to leave. She would miss her white coat until tomorrow.

'Hey Nayomi. If we've got time tomorrow, I'll show you how to do the sugar. You know, if you want?'

'I'm not sure I'll be any good at it but I'd really like that. One day you'll have to show me how to make that ice cream, too. The boys would love it.'

Ashley lips tilted up. 'Sure thing.'

–

For two hours each day for a week of service, Nayomi felt like she was living a dream. Her white jacket was like a cloak with special powers. When she put it on, she was confident, not just that she could make pani pol filling, as she had been doing for years, but confident that she could fit in. The guys in the kitchen included her in jokes. They treated her like one of them. She wasn't invisible; she was a somebody. A somebody in a white cloak, with a swanky job.

Even when she dressed back in her porter uniform and went to the station with Bill, he would make a wisecrack or two about her new status. God love him, he wasn't a naturally funny man, but Nayomi laughed at his jokes regardless and she was grateful for his genuine support.

It was strange, to feel like she belonged.

At home, too, the boys had taken more of an interest in her days than ever before. There was still some animosity from Roshan, who would rather she could make their dinners and be home every night after school. But they were starting to slip into a routine. They were making more of their mornings together, taking ten minutes to enjoy the park on the way to school and once a week, usually on a Friday, Nayomi would buy the boys a treat breakfast. They would sit inside a bakery, drink juice and eat a decadent pastry, doughnut or waffle.

For the most part, the boys were excited about her temporary role as a chef.

'You get a white coat and everything?' Nuwan asked when she had first told them the news.

'Yep.'

'Like Ashley's?'

'Yep.'

Since Ashley made him a birthday cake, had stopped by to fix the toilet flush, bought burritos and wowed Nuwan during his one visit to the restaurant, Nuwan had become a little obsessed with all things Ashley.

Nayomi was careful not to bring any confusion into their home but she had to admit, seeing Nuwan enjoy a man's company was sweet. And despite their blunder last weekend, Nayomi liked Ashley's friendship too.

On Saturday morning, as they walked to Roshan's basketball game, he asked, 'So what, you're like a cook now?'

She didn't have the heart to admit that today would be her last service in the white coat because the dessert special would be off the menu next week. She didn't have the heart to admit it to her son, or herself.

For a week, she had learned new skills, felt the pressure of the kitchen, challenged herself. In a matter of hours, she would have to hand the white coat back.

So, she decided not to shatter either of their illusions. She told a little white lie and she smiled as she said, 'They prefer to be called chefs.'

But for the first time in her American life, Nayomi held a small belief that she and the boys could have more. Not just money but respect, pride. Her boys could look up to her for daring to do something new and trying to succeed.

Gosh, she was going to miss that white coat.

–

Saturday night's service had been as a busy as ever. Nayomi waved off Bill as he headed for the staff car and she unloaded what she hoped was the last full load of dishes from the machine.

Maggie appeared at the station, her collar unbuttoned and her apron removed, which told Nayomi that all main dishes of the night had been served.

'How have you found this week, Nayomi? I mean, juggling the kitchen and the porter station?'

Nayomi continued stacking plates as she told her boss, 'I've loved it. I feel like I've learned so much in just a few days. The boys think I have some kind of superpowers since I get to wear the chef uniform. And I think I feel the same. I've never really been pushed in this way. It's hard to explain.'

'I happen to think you have superpowers, too, Nayomi. Those desserts are mouthwatering.'

Nayomi beamed inside but said, 'I just make the filling.'

'Don't underestimate your value. You were the inspiration behind the entire dish.'

Nayomi's cheeks flushed. 'That's a nice thing to say, thank you. I'll, erm, leave the uniform in the staff laundry. I'm going to miss it.'

Maggie nodded thoughtfully. 'I don't have tonight's figures yet but I thought you'd like to know that your dessert was the most ordered dessert of the week.'

'It was?'

'Yep. Surprised?'

'I… yes. That's really… Nuwan is going to *die* when I tell him that.'

Maggie chuckled. 'So, Ashley tells me you're more than just a dab hand at sweet plates. And I guess I'm wondering what other dishes you have up your sleeve.'

'Oh, mostly curries. Traditional Sri Lankan food. That or hot dogs,' Nayomi said with a laugh.

'Well, how would you like to hang onto that white coat for another week and maybe show me some of what else you can do? If you like. I know you have the boys and I know it's been a rush for you to get here earlier in the evenings from your other job. But what I'm thinking is, if you came in at the same time each day next week, maybe you could show me what you do and I could show you a few tricks of the trade.'

Nayomi tried to be professional, stemming her wide grin to a normal range. 'I'd really like that.'

Maggie nodded. 'Settled, then. I look forward to working with you, Chef.'

As Maggie walked away, Nayomi pulled off her gloves and covered her mouth with her hand, replaying the conversation in her mind, unable to quite believe what had happened.

'Put it there, girl.' Ashley approached her from behind, holding out his closed fist, which she bumped with her own.

Okay, so it wasn't like she was a full-time chef or anything but Maggie wanted to see more of what she could do. No one, not ever, had wanted to learn anything from Nayomi. More than that, Maggie was going to teach her new skills.

And the whole time, she would be getting paid more than double per hour what she was making as a porter.

She shook her head. 'I can't believe it. Did you know our dessert sold more than any other dessert this week?'

Ashley bared his gleaming white teeth. 'I've been keeping a tally.'

She was so full of happiness, she threw her arms around Ashley's neck and he hugged her back, lifting her feet from the ground.

'Check on, Chef!' Someone called.

'Proud of you,' Ashley said as he left Nayomi to finishing unloading the dishwasher. Not even the red wine jus that had failed to wash off three plates could dampen her spirits.

In the staff car an hour or so later, Nayomi and Ashley discussed what she ought to cook for Maggie next week. Despite the late (or, rather, early) hour, tonight she didn't feel sleepy, she felt ecstatic. So much so, she was going to wake up the boys when she got home to tell them her good news.

When the car pulled up outside her block, Ashley walked her inside, as had become their custom.

As Nayomi checked her mailbox, Ashley asked, 'Do the boys like *Transformers*? Like, the movies?'

'I know what you mean. They love it, actually.'

'Don't poke fun at me but it's kind of a guilty pleasure of mine.'

Nayomi smirked.

'Hey, I said don't.'

'I'm sorry,' she said, pressing her lips together to stifle her amusement.

'It's just that… Well, I was thinking… You know, the latest movie is out right now and I don't have anyone to go with, so I was thinking maybe you and the boys would come with me tomorrow. I mean, if you're not busy. I know it's short notice. It's too short notice, right?'

Nayomi took a breath as she contemplated the offer.

It would be a real treat for the boys. One that she couldn't usually afford. And it would be nice for her to go out too. But…

'The thing is, Ashley, the boys would love it but I don't want to confuse them.'

'I get that. I'd make it clear we're just friends.'

She bit down on her lip, undecided.

'I mean, it's really Nuwan I want to take with me. He thinks I'm cool. Do you know how many people think I'm cool, Nayomi?'

She shook her head.

'None. Not one. Just Nuwan.'

She laughed. 'All right.'

'All right?'

'What time is the movie on?'

Ashley was already backing up, as if he could sense she was on the brink of changing her mind.

'I'll check. Afternoon but I'll message you the time.'

She held up a hand to wave goodnight but the door was already closing on Ashley.

So she was going to the movies tomorrow. Ashley, the boys and her. Four friends.

—

Roshan and Nuwan appeared in the lounge in matching outfits, which Roshan usually hated but it seemed he was willing to make an exception for their five-dollar market-bought *Transformers* T-shirts, which they both wore loose over a pair of jeans.

Roshan was sometimes so old for his years, it pleased her to see his boyish excitement. It thrilled her that she could afford to take them to the movies.

And she had convinced herself over the course of the morning that this was okay. Four friends going to the movies. It didn't mean she was trying to replace her husband or the boys' dad, or going against the morals her parents had instilled in her. It didn't have to mean anything except she had a new friend. A friend who had been good to her. A friend her boys – at least, Nuwan – really liked.

Nayomi slipped her cardigan over her shirt, which she, unlike the boys, had tucked into her jeans. She ran her hands over her long braid to smooth any rogue frizzy strands. Then she slipped the four bags of chocolate and four cans of Pepsi she had bought from the local store into her handbag.

'Okay, all set?'

Ashley was waiting on the sidewalk outside their apartment block, his hands tucked into the pockets of his jeans.

'Ashley!' Nuwan called, running to him but stopping short of crashing into him and holding out his clenched fist for Ashley to punch.

'Big man, how you doing?'

'They're both looking forward to the movie,' Nayomi said as she approached with a less vivacious Roshan by her side.

'You good, Roshan?' Ashley asked.

'Yeah, I'm good.' He shrugged, playing it cool.

They caught the subway to the cinema, a journey that was mostly taken up by Nuwan, Ashley, and even Roshan, enthusiastically relaying their favourite parts of the *Transformers* movies to date.

Inside the Cineplex, Ashley offered to buy all of the tickets but Nayomi refused, saying they should all buy their own. *Friends didn't need to buy other friends their movie tickets.* Ashley relented.

'At least let me buy candy,' he said.

Nayomi opened her handbag. 'No need. I've got you covered.'

'I like your thinking. The price of candy in here is insane.'

They sat in a row of four. Ashley, Nuwan, Roshan, Nayomi. She was relieved the guys had taken the seating arrangements out of her hands. No awkwardness, again.

And they watched the movie. Not exactly Nayomi's thing but her enjoyment came from seeing the boys utterly engrossed.

What was maybe normal to some people was so special to her and the boys that her heart was full.

Roshan flapped her away when she bent to kiss his brow but he did let her drape an arm around his shoulders and pull him into her for a two-minute cuddle.

She wondered if the boys wouldn't benefit from having a complete family again. *Would it be* so *wrong if she moved on? Did the 'rules' still apply if you lost your husband so young?*

Chapter Twenty-Two

Emily

She gripped her coffee mug tighter between her hands. At least if she couldn't see her hands trembling, she could pretend that they weren't. As she sat at a table for two at a cafe in Wall Street, her heart was racing.

If she had thought sending a WhatsApp message to Oliver and asking to meet was hard, sitting waiting for him to arrive was one of the hardest things she had done in her life.

The reality was, they needed to have this conversation.

Her breath hitched when she spotted him through the window, crossing the street. He had worn his blue suit and she wondered if he had done so because he knew she liked him in it. She had always loved the way the jacket drew attention to his broad shoulders and narrow waist, on display with his smooth white shirt tucked into his trousers. She knew how soft that shirt felt to touch, how she could trace the outline of his abdominals through the material.

Images of him smiling across a dinner table with candlelight shaping his face, and images of them frolicking half naked on a beach, came to her like sharp, painful flashbacks. As he looked right and left at the traffic lights, he swiped a hand through his hair and Emily wanted so badly to pull her own fingers through it.

They had been good together. Their relationship had been hot, passionate, intense and full of laughter. Until it wasn't.

Their eyes met and he smiled that handsome smile of his as he entered the cafe.

Oliver was going to make someone a fine husband one day.

Just not her.

Then he was in front of her, holding her in his strong arms, his scent filling the air around her, intoxicating her.

She held him close and breathed him in, feeling his chest expand with his breath as his hand slid into her hair.

'I've missed you,' he whispered, killing the resolve she had possessed just moments before.

Emily stepped out of his hold and retook her seat, gesturing to the coffee cup placed opposite her. 'I ordered you an Americano,' she said.

Oliver stared at the drink. 'I tell you I miss you and you tell me you ordered me a coffee?'

Emily twisted her face as she processed his words. 'Sorry.' She turned her mug between her fingers, waiting for Oliver to speak but he didn't. 'I have missed you,' she said, eventually. 'But what use is saying it?'

He stared at her and Emily thought she might never be able to look away. 'Why did you ask me to meet you if you can't even admit that you've missed me, Ems?'

It was a good question and one she couldn't articulate an answer to.

Oliver sighed. 'Janey called me. She's worried about you. She said you've been cancelling your scheduled dinners and turned in a review of a place you hadn't been to for months.'

'It's not as practical, from mom's place. And it hasn't really felt right. My mom needs my help right now. Dad's estate is bigger than either of us realised and there's a lot to either unravel or learn how to keep going. He had a lot of business ventures on the go.'

Oliver reached a hand towards hers but Emily pulled away, sliding her hands into her lap. Contact would make this harder.

Oliver held up his hands in surrender. 'I just don't know what to do here, Ems. Do I touch you? Do I tell you how I'm feeling? Do I ask how you're feeling and risk having my head chewed off?'

Emily looked up through her lashes and smirked. 'I'd start with your butt. More meat.'

His laughter was short-lived but it broke the palpable tension around the table.

'Olly, I think the truth is, I don't know what I want. I don't know what or who I am or want to be.'

He roughly rubbed a hand across his chin. 'I've got to tell you, Ems, I don't mean to get pissy with you but what does that even mean? What am I supposed to do with that?'

'I know. I don't know.'

'We've got a house together. A mortgage. Bills. We're good together, aren't we?'

'I know we have those things and I— I don't know if we *are* good together.'

He balled his hand into a fist, his anger betraying him. 'Where does that leave us? Me? I mean, you can hear yourself, right? You can hear how unfair this is to me?'

As he dragged a hand through his hair, Emily reached out to take it, their entwined fingers coming to rest on the tabletop. 'I do hear it, Olly. I've heard it turning around my head and making me dizzy for weeks now. And I love you so much.'

He pulled his hand away sharply.

'I do. I love you and that's why—'

'How can you say you love me and be living at your mom's instead of in our home with me? How can you say you love me, yet I'm sitting opposite you now thinking you're about to end us?'

His raised voice caused the eyes of other customers to glance in their direction.

Emily hated this. She hated that she was hurting him. 'Before you walked in here, I knew exactly what I needed to do, for both our sakes. Then as soon as I saw you and when you hugged me, I wanted to do the exact opposite. That's how sure I am that I have no clue who I am or what I want. And I think until I do, it's fairer on both of us that I walk away.'

'For now, or forever?'

She exhaled shakily. 'I don't know. And I'm not going to ask you to wait around to find out. At some point, I'm going to figure out where I got lost. When old, happy Emily disappeared and the current version of me took over. If we're meant to be together then, we will be.'

She slipped her engagement ring from her finger and slid it across the table to Oliver.

He picked it up, holding it in front of his face, scrutinising it like it might hold the missing answers Emily couldn't give.

After what felt like an age, he spoke. 'I wish you'd have thought about who you were and who you weren't before we bought a house together.' He stood with such force that his chair screeched along the floor, drawing more attention. Then he slapped his palm against the table, removing it to unveil Emily's engagement ring. 'Keep it. And let me know when you're coming to get your stuff.'

'Olly, please, don't be like this,' she pleaded. But her words fell on his back as he walked away.

Despite being aware of all the focus in the cafe being on her, Emily's tears fell and she buried her face in her hands as a sob escaped her.

Then two familiar arms wrapped around her and she tugged at her favourite blue suit as she cried against Oliver's chest.

'I'm sorry,' he whispered, kissing her head and stroking her hair down her back. 'Please don't cry.'

But she didn't have control of the stop tap and as he whispered soothing sounds to her, the tears kept falling.

She wished she knew what she wanted, now more than ever, but the only thing she knew was that, if she ever did change her mind, Oliver wouldn't be waiting.

-

That night, Emily made monkfish curry, which she and Isabella ate around the kitchen table. Her mom didn't ask questions; she simply hugged her and told her she was there whenever Emily was ready to tell her what had happened with Oliver. And she didn't protest when Emily declared she was ready for bed at eight o' clock.

Alone, in her childhood bedroom, Emily slipped a disc into the DVD-television combo that had stood on the same wall mount since she was a teen. She lay back on her bed as an old cooking documentary began to play, following her dad through a period of change at Jean-Sébastien's, back when Emily had worked alongside him.

'This is my daughter, Emily,' her dad announced proudly to the camera, placing a hand on her shoulder where she was filleting a fish on her station in the restaurant kitchen. 'What she can't do with turbot isn't worth knowing.'

Now, she smiled at his French accent, which he had never softened over years of living in America.

She watched as she and her dad were filmed sitting on stools beside each other, each with a coffee and a petit four on the bar behind them. She laughed, remembering how Charles had intentionally walked behind them polishing a wine glass, hoping to feature in the final cut, and how perturbed he had been when the director ordered him out of the shot.

'How do you find working alongside each other?' the interviewer asked.

'For me, it is a dream come true,' her dad replied. 'Fine food is to be celebrated and enjoyed with those we love. How better to enjoy fine food than creating it with your family?'

'Do you feel the same, Emily?' the interviewer asked.

On screen, Emily twisted her lips as if in thought and glanced to her dad from the corner of her eye. 'He can be a little bossy at times but I love him.'

Watching herself and her dad joke together on screen, she laughed now, in bed, and her eyes leaked tears again.

She had enjoyed working with her dad for so long. *When had it gone wrong?*

There was a soft tap on her bedroom door. Emily wiped her eyes quickly and called for her mom to come in.

Isabella looked at Emily, then up to the television screen and the sound of Jean-Sébastien's voice. 'This is a good one,' she said. 'Have you got to the soufflé cook-off yet?'

Emily shook her head, then lifted the throw she had tossed over her legs and Isabella came to sit on the bed next to her.

Beneath the blanket, they watched as Emily and Jean-Sébastien completed a timed challenge to make the best soufflé.

They whisked faster than ever, both light-heartedly teasing each other on opposite sides of the kitchen counter.

'In your haste, don't forget to season,' her dad told her.

'I learned from the best, Chef. You'd best concentrate on your own dish,' she retorted, as they simultaneously poured their fluffy soufflé mixes into ramekins.

Sitting on the bed, Isabella told her, 'He always wanted you to be the best.'

Emily watched herself on screen, as she stepped back from the oven, leaning back against the kitchen counter, her dad hanging an arm over her shoulder. 'You think you've beaten me?'

'The proof will be in the soufflé,' she told him, and he hugged her into his side.

Now, as she watched how close they had been, she told her mom what she knew to be the truth. 'I know he did, Mom. I know. I think maybe we just both wanted to be the best too much.'

They watched as Emily's soufflé was pronounced the winner by Charles, who winked at Jean-Sébastien as he declared him the loser.

'He loved you, Emily,' Isabella said. 'And you loved him.'

Her next breath was unsteady and she spoke the words she didn't realise had been troubling her since her dad's death. 'Do you think he knew?'

Warm tears trickled silently from her eyes and Isabella reached across to her daughter, using the corner of the blanket to dry her cheeks. 'He always knew, Emily. Always. He recognised his own stubbornness in you but he knew you loved him.'

—

It was as if a seal had been broken. When Emily wasn't speaking with lawyers about her dad's estate or tending to his herb and vegetable patches in the garden, she was cooking. Everything from Thai- and Indian-inspired dishes to American fare and French classics. She and her mom had eaten spiced tofu broths with steamed dumplings, palak paneer, loaded potato skins, steaks, pasta bakes, coq au vin.

Emily had found her old stride, her knack for combining flavours in new ways – matching equal and opposite tastes, like her dad had taught her. She remembered the fun she had had in exploring dishes and she was starting to remember herself. Slowly but surely, feeling lighter each day than she had in years, Emily was rediscovering herself.

She drew on memories – holidays in Texas eating smoked meats, two weeks in Southeast Asia eating street food, French meals her dad used to cook for her as a child. Like painting oils on canvas, she painted her treasured memories in food. She let the feelings she couldn't speak of be sieved, stirred, whisked, steamed and baked.

What she wasn't eating out, she and her mom were making up for in home cooking. Of course, finding her lost love of cooking might be cathartic, but it certainly wasn't sustaining her career. The last two reviews she had handed in had been based on old notes from her review diary and hadn't made the front page of the section, which had been unheard of for her reviews for almost two years.

She was ignoring calls from Archer and Janey, sporadically responding to their emails instead. And every day, she was cancelling reservations at restaurants. As far as the *New York Times* was concerned, she was off the grid. There was only so long they would put up with it before they allowed a shark-in-waiting to replace her in the prestigious role of head critic.

What she hadn't yet worked out was whether she cared. *Did she want to be a food critic for* NYT, *or anyone, for that matter? If she didn't, what* did *she want to do?*

As she waited for her game pie to cook, Emily sat down at her laptop on the kitchen table and submitted another sub-par review to her editor. Then she opened the old file on her computer, the one that had been taunting her since she last opened it, when she had still been living with Oliver. She sat back in her seat, her fingers hovering over the mouse pad, the cursor on the screen resting on the file.

Then she clicked and was reminded of her plans to travel around France and write a travel and cookbook.

But she didn't have long to torture herself with what could have been – or maybe still could be – because the front doorbell rang and two removal men began carrying boxes of her things from Brooklyn Heights into the hallway of her mom's house.

Chapter Twenty-Three

Maggie

It was five thirty p.m. on a Wednesday, one of the slowest nights of the week. Maggie had set up something between a training station and exploration station in the kitchen. Each night for more than a week, she and Nayomi had been exploring new ingredients and dishes.

Maggie was enjoying training Nayomi. She felt buoyed by it, excited by Nayomi's passion, which reminded Maggie of her own.

She was learning too, about new taste experiences, about Nayomi's life in Sri Lanka and the culture of people and a place she had never visited. More than anything, she felt like she was gaining a friendship.

As she learned more about Nayomi, she realised they shared a lot in common. Though from different places, they had both had modest upbringings. By the sound of things, relative to location, Maggie had grown up poorer than Nayomi. Maggie had never left North America, in the past because she couldn't afford to, then because she was so busy throwing herself into cooking. Now, even if she had the time and money, she didn't really know anyone she would travel with.

Where Maggie now earned a decent living, she had no family. Nayomi had a lovely family and lived on the breadline.

How did people come to have it all?

'Salmon,' Maggie said, placing a fillet of uncooked, deep red wild salmon on the counter.

She skinned the fillet, describing the process to Nayomi as she went. Then she sliced the fillet into six even portions and held one piece of raw fish out to Nayomi on a palette knife.

'Before we start working with something new, we need to really get under the skin of it because if we don't know this piece of fish, or whatever ingredient it might be, inside and out, we can't predict how it will behave.'

Nayomi nodded, tentatively taking the piece of raw fish.

'Don't worry, it's sashimi grade,' Maggie assured her.

A little more confidently, Nayomi tasted the fish.

'Taste it slowly. Absorb the texture, how it separates when bitten.'

Nayomi chewed slowly.

'Then we'll cook these other pieces. We'll try it seared, poached, grilled, baked and fried. We can see how it responds to different seasonings and accompaniments. Does it absorb them? Is it over-powered by them?'

Setting aside her knife, Maggie reached for two small pots, one of sugar, the other of salt and she held them up.

'A great dish is a simple dish. Equal and opposite tastes and colours. Tricks for the mouth, the nose and the eyes. Circles and squares. Cream and truffle. That's what Jean-Sébastien taught me. The earthiness of beef, the richness of red wine jus. The crisp skin of poulet and the softness of the meat beneath. The sugariness of pear with the spice of ginger. The acidity of vinegar with the sweetness of shallots.'

Nayomi hummed. 'That's a really nice piece of fish.'

'Let's see if we can make it even nicer.'

'Maggie, can I just say… Thank you. For everything you've done for me since I've been here. I mean, even giving me the porter job in the first place, when I'm sure I'd blown it with Alexander. And for all of your time with the cooking. I'm learning so much and, well, nobody has ever really invested time in me like this.'

Her words filled Maggie's chest. After everything Jean-Sébastien had done for her, when even her own parents had never taken time to educate her or shown an interest in her cooking, she was just so happy that she could give back. But in typical Maggie fashion, rather than accept the compliment with comfort, she blushed and told Nayomi, 'Remember I'm learning from you, too.'

It was true. Maggie was experimenting with spices in ways she never had. 'That beetroot curry you showed me last night… delicious.'

It was Nayomi's turn to blush. 'It's second nature by now.'

'Not for me. I've got an idea to incorporate it into a duck breast special, too. I'll cook it for you and you can let me know what you think.'

'Sure.' Nayomi nodded. 'Maggie, do you think…? Never mind.'

'No, go ahead.'

'Do you think I'd be good enough to get a job? As a chef, I mean. Actually, forget it. I'm crazy. A few lessons and I think I'm a professional. Just forget I said—'

'I think you'd make a great chef.'

Maggie meant it. More than that, she wished she could help Nayomi. Aside from just the food, Maggie admired Nayomi, her strength, the way she brought up her boys. If the situation was different and Maggie had

226

her own restaurant, or even a job lined up for when Ethan took over Jean-Sébastien's, for that matter, she would have employed Nayomi as an apprentice, maybe even a commis chef. She would have had the restaurant fund her to go to chef school.

Then she had a thought… Maybe she *did* know a way to help. Maybe.

'So, are we searing first?' Nayomi asked, retying her apron to tighten it around her small waist.

-

There were some exciting changes being made to the restaurant menu. Most of them so subtle, Maggie didn't bother to enlist Alexander's approval. The bigger changes, like the coconut crêpes, were special dishes over which Maggie had full control, unless Alexander asked. It seemed to her that Alexander was counting down until she was gone. Frankly, that suited her just fine. He could have the all-male kitchen he so desperately wanted in just a few short weeks and in the meantime, Maggie could go about her business in peace.

Quite what she was going to do at the end of those few short weeks was anyone's guess. She had been so focused on leaving Jean-Sébastien's on a good note that she hadn't even sought out job opportunities. She really must.

Just not right now. She had told her chefs there was no need to come in this Sunday. The tweaks they had made to the menu now would remain until she left. As for the specials, she was having so much fun creating them on her own, with ideas she had bounced off Nayomi in the week, that she was quite happy to have the kitchen to herself today as she got lost in her craft. Well, not entirely to herself. Somewhere in the background, Ethan was pottering, working on his new menus for the restaurant and making a list of new equipment he wanted to bring in. It seemed he was a big fan of the poaching bath.

Maggie had finished frying strips of beetroot with onions, garlic, curry leaves and turmeric, like Nayomi had demonstrated to her earlier in the week. As she let the beetroot settle amongst the spices, she had set about pan-frying a duck breast. The skin was perfectly crispy. While she waited for the meat to cook through just enough that it was still pink inside, she caramelised slices of fresh orange in cinnamon and sugar, then left them to simmer in Cointreau.

When the duck was cooked, she set it on a board to rest and blended her beetroot fry into a smooth purée. Finally, she assembled her dish, sweeping purée on the base of the plate, adding two baby carrots, halved, sitting the breast of the duck, sliced to expose the perfectly pink centre, on top of the carrots. She placed slices of caramelised orange carefully against the side of the duck and drizzled the sticky Cointreau sauce over the meat and around the plate. Lastly, she arranged one crisp spiral of orange zest and a sprig of mint leaves on top of the duck for decoration.

'Voilà,' she said, stepping back to admire her work.

'All right, you win, these smells are killing me,' Ethan said, appearing in the kitchen from the dining room. 'What's cooking, Chef?'

Maggie grinned, both at her new creation and that Ethan had been roused by the smells of the dish. 'Duck à l'orange with spiced beetroot purée.'

'I'm drooling. Pass me a knife and fork, then.'

'Who said you can have any of my cooking?' she said, pouting as she raised a brow.

Ethan moved from her side, coming to stand in front of her. Her breath trembled as his face moved closer to hers and she breathed him in, staring at those lips she had wanted to taste, it seemed, for too long. He came closer still. Her eyes closed under the intensity of his proximity.

She felt his arms moving around her sides.

Then he was gone. And when she opened her eyes, she realised he had been reaching for a knife and fork from the pot of utensils on the countertop behind her.

Urgh. Why did she let him get to her?

'Hey!' she said, scowling as he hovered over the plate of food, braced with the knife and fork.

He paused and asked, 'May I?'

'Fine,' she said petulantly but inside, she was hoping he liked it; she was yearning for his approval. For anyone's approval.

Ethan sliced through the duck and cut a segment of orange, then pushed a little of everything onto the back of his fork. Maggie watched him place the food in his mouth. She watched his eyes close, his jaw turn slowly, his Adam's apple move as he swallowed.

'Mmm. Oh, yeah. Maggie, that was... Mmm.'

Now Maggie swallowed deeply and willed certain parts of her body to cool off... quickly.

'Try this,' he said, beckoning her closer. Since she wasn't fully in control of her thoughts at that moment, she followed his instruction.

Ethan repeated the same slicing of the component parts of the dish. With a forkful of food, he turned to Maggie. 'Close your eyes.' She did, then she felt the warmth of the meat brushing her lips, the sweetness of caramel on her tongue, the creamy rich spice of the purée and the crispness of orange zest and mint.

She let the flavours explode in her mouth until she was humming her delight and craving more.

When she opened her eyes, Ethan was watching her intently, closely. Too close.

Kiss me, she willed him.

His gaze fell to her lips and she wanted to wrap her arms around him, pull him to her and make love to him right there on the kitchen counter.

Oh my goodness.

She snapped out of her trance. 'So you like it?'

Ethan similarly pulled away from her sharply. 'It's a delight, Maggie.'

Then she remembered. 'Oh. Stay there. Don't move. I've got something else for you to try.'

She returned from the large refrigerator outside to find Ethan had nearly finished the plate of duck. Laughing, she asked, 'It was that good, huh?'

He kissed his fingertips and made a smooching sound, Italian-style. 'Bellissimo.'

She tried to keep her smile to a level that didn't show her sheer delight at having impressed another chef and meanwhile, she blow-torched the top of two ramekins of green tea crème brûlée.

'I get dessert too?' He checked his watch. 'Eleven a.m. Meh, it's close enough to lunch, I guess.' He hopped up to sit on the counter – something Maggie would never have allowed if they weren't the only people in the kitchen.

As they were…

She handed Ethan a dessert and a spoon, then mirrored his position, coming to sit on the counter opposite him with her own crème brûlée.

'What do you think?'

Ethan nodded as he licked his spoon like a child licking an ice cream cone. 'Not as exciting as the duck but *so* good.'

I'll take it, Maggie thought, happily tucking into her dessert.

'Do you have another one?' Ethan asked. 'This is why I stay away from desserts. Once I get a taste, I'm like Comte de Reynaud.'

Maggie laughed at the reference to the village mayor in *Chocolat* who finally falls to the temptation of Vianne's chocolate. 'I loved that movie.'

Ethan took another spoonful of crème brûlée. 'You like the movie or Johnny Depp?'

Maggie laughed harder. 'Hey, I'm a single girl in the city, whose working hours mean she doesn't get a lot of dates.'

Ethan set his empty ramekin to one side and stared at her in a way Maggie couldn't read.

'Why are you looking at me like that?'

Ethan shrugged. 'I just wonder if it's really the working hours or if you don't date because you don't want to.'

Maggie scoffed. 'I suppose for someone whose *dates* take place between midnight and six a.m., you wouldn't understand it.'

He didn't respond to her quip, he just kept looking at her in the same inscrutable way, making her uncomfortable enough to get down from the counter and busy herself with tidying up. But she could feel his eyes on her.

'Ah, she throws me a dig to avoid being honest about herself. Why doesn't that surprise me?'

'Look,' she snapped. 'You don't know what it's like to be a girl who came from nothing. Your dad is a chef. You've always been in the industry. For me, I've had to really work hard to prove I'm… worthy. That my parents were wrong when they would call me a dreamer and a fantasist. That I'm more than just an inconvenience. I've had to put in one hundred and ten per cent.'

She felt herself getting upset, which was ridiculous. Then she felt Ethan by her side, his hand on her shoulder encouraging her to face him. Her jaw stiffened as she looked up to him, willing herself to calm down.

'You are worthy, Maggie. You're a great chef.'

With their attention fully on each other, he moved closer to her. So close, she could feel his breath on her lips.

What was she doing? This was Ethan James.

The one thing she needed less than a man in her life was a man who would break her heart when he sneaked out of the door the next morning.

She stepped away from him. 'Well, I'm just going to clear up here and…'

What? What was she going to do? Buy a coffee and wander the streets alone? Go to the movies, alone? Go for a run, alone? Sit at home with only Livvy and her herb garden for company?

'I'm heading out to the farm I mentioned in New Jersey shortly. The one I said I'd take you to, do you remember?'

Maggie nodded.

'Do you want to come? If you don't have other plans.'

–

Maggie had unpinned her long hair from where it had been loosely held in a clip and slipped out of her chef jacket and apron. Now, she sat in the passenger seat of Ethan's Volvo in her skinny jeans and a thin black blouse as they headed out to New Jersey.

It was a cool day but the sun was shining and they drove with the windows down. The fresh air and wind in her hair made her feel like she was taking a trip to somewhere exotic, as they crossed the Hudson River and headed north. The smog of the city cleared and left cleaner air, greener roads.

'I need to stop off to pick up Annie,' Ethan said, indicating to pull off the main road left.

'Your daughter?' She tried not to seem surprised but she was. Though she knew Annie lived in New Jersey and Ethan had mentioned that he saw her when he visited the farm, it just hadn't occurred to her that he would be picking up his daughter today. 'Sure, it's fine. But won't she mind that I'm intruding on your day?'

Ethan glanced to her fleetingly before returning his focus to the road. 'Are you joking? She'll love it. I drag her around this farm every other time I see her. You'll change the dynamics.'

That settled Maggie's nerves, as she was suddenly hyperaware of the impending scrutiny of a five-year-old girl. 'Okay, then, if you're sure.'

A few minutes later, they pulled into a suburban estate of detached houses, with immaculately pruned front lawns and bushes.

'This is nice,' Maggie remarked.

'Better than I could give her in the city.' Ethan pulled up outside a house and killed the engine. 'I'll be back in a mo.'

Maggie watched as a beautiful woman opened the front door of the home and before Ethan had even made it halfway from the car to the house, a gorgeous little girl, with her mother's blonde hair, falling in perfect ringlets down her pink corduroy dungarees, ran out to her dad.

'Daddy!'

Maggie couldn't help but feel warm and fuzzy as she watched Ethan scoop Annie up in his arms and twirl her around, kissing her cheek.

He didn't move closer to the house, holding up a hand to Annie's mother and saying, 'We'll be a few hours.'

The woman waved. 'Have fun. She's had lunch, Ethan, but she's kept some space in her dessert tummy, just in case.'

'Is that right?' Ethan asked, tickling Annie's tummy as he walked back to the car.

As they approached, Ethan bent to his hunkers, bringing Annie to the open window. 'This is my friend, Maggie,' Ethan said. 'She's a chef, like Dad.'

Annie pulled a dramatically shocked face – open eyes and open mouth.

'Hi Annie,' Maggie said. 'I hope you don't mind me tagging along today. Your dad is going to show me the farm.'

Annie shook her head. 'You can help me pick pumpkins for Halloween. Daddy carves funny faces in them for me. Some of them are so silly it's ridiculous.'

'That's not true.' Ethan exclaimed.

'It is too,' Annie said.

'Why do I get the feeling Annie is the one telling the truth here?' Maggie asked, receiving a vigorous nod from Annie in return.

'All right, you, let's get you in your seat.'

Ethan settled Annie into the child seat that Maggie hadn't even noticed in the back of the car and they headed out to the farm. During the ten-minute drive, Annie asked endless questions about Maggie – how old she was, where she lived, where she worked, if she had any pets, her favourite colour.

When they arrived at the farm, it seemed like everyone knew Ethan. They were greeted by a man called Gary, the owner of the farm, who was wearing stonewash jeans and a stereotypical checked farmers' shirt under his padded gilet. He shook Ethan's hand, then Maggie's, and seemed particularly interested to learn Maggie was also a chef.

'And will we be picking pumpkins today, Annie?' he asked, receiving a wide grin in response.

'Excellent.' He turned to Ethan. 'Meat and veg first or pumpkins first?'

Ethan asked Annie, 'What do you say, Annie-Bannie, can we show Maggie the farm first and pick pumpkins afterwards?'

She shrugged but slipped her hand into Maggie's, taking her by surprise.

'Good girl,' Ethan said, as he walked ahead with Gary, leaving Maggie and Annie to follow behind, with Maggie answering more questions from Annie who, it seemed, was quite a little chatterbox.

After a while, as they wandered rows of vegetables waiting to be picked, it stopped feeling peculiar to have a little girl's hand in her own. In fact, it started to feel nice.

Maggie had so few memories of doing nice things with her own parents when she was younger. For all they were married, the fact that they had been forced into it and then trapped by money troubles had meant their relationship was one of hostility, towards each other, and towards Maggie. They could only stand being in the same room as each other if they weren't speaking. Family trips were not something that featured in Maggie's upbringing.

She loved that, despite her broken home, Annie was loved by both parents. She must be because if she weren't, she wouldn't be as happy, as bouncy, as confident as she was.

The farm was a year-round venture, covering vast amounts of space both outdoors and under greenhouse-type shelter with aids to mimic excellent growing conditions year round for a widely varied selection of vegetables.

After walking the vegetable fields, the four of them stood around a counter in a farm shed, where Gary sliced vegetables for Maggie and Ethan to see and sample. They tasted small pieces of all except the potatoes and parsnips – nobody wanted to taste raw starch – which Gary had arranged to be sliced and roasted with a small amount of olive oil, so as to not detract too much from the raw ingredients.

The fries went down a treat with Annie and she was still nattering away about how much she loved fries when they headed over to the cattle pens, Annie's hand back in Maggie's. Maggie was a meat-eater and chef but she was grateful that Annie seemed to make no connection between the cows to whom she was feeding handfuls of grass and the hanging carcasses that Gary proudly displayed in large refrigerators.

When Ethan started to discuss his anticipated order size for when he took over at Jean Sebastien's, Maggie took Annie towards the pumpkin fields. It was the week before Halloween and the fields were packed with pumpkins that had been cut from their roots and laid on a bed of straw.

A lady sat on a chair by a wood bench, with wheelbarrows of various sizes set out in front of her.

'We'll take one adult and one child, please,' Maggie said, handing off the smaller barrow to Annie and following her with an adult barrow to the start of the field.

'I like the big orange, orange ones,' Annie said, bending to pick up the largest pumpkin Maggie had ever seen, straining with its weight but getting nowhere.

'Can I help you, Annie?'

'Yes, please.'

And so they developed a system of Annie pointing and Maggie picking the biggest, brightest pumpkins they could see, until Ethan appeared, thanking Maggie for paying for the barrows. He held a pumpkin from Maggie's wheelbarrow over his face and put on a silly voice as he said 'Hello, I'm Mr. Pumpkin but you can call me Pumpy.'

Hearing Annie's wild belly-chuckle made Maggie laugh too. They spent an easy hour chatting, picking pumpkins and tossing some back when they found better replacements.

At the end, Gary invited them to his farm kitchen, where they each accepted a hot chocolate and a toffee apple.

By the time they dropped Annie back home, she had fallen asleep in the car and Maggie had to admit, the fresh air and tummy full of sugar had made her a little sleepy too.

As Ethan carried Annie away from the car towards home, Annie opened her eyes and called across his shoulder. 'See you next time, Maggie.'

Maggie held up a hand and thought it really would be nice to see Annie again.

'I'd love to have a farm restaurant one day,' Ethan said as they drove back in the direction of New York. 'You know, where you could cook everything from your own land. Maybe have guest cottages, so people could come for cooking classes, and they could stay for a weekend and get a full culinary experience.'

'Like the anti-detox camp?'

He laughed. 'Exactly.'

'Hmm, it sounds idyllic. At least, it does on a day like today, when the sun is shining.'

'Nothing sounds quite as good in the rain.'

'True.'

'What about you? Do you have a dream?'

Maggie had, but everything was different now. 'That's a tricky question.'

'How so?'

'My dreams are more short-lived, I think. And, I don't know, I'm starting to think I might be in a place of reassessment.'

As they crossed the river, open space was replaced by New York's imposing skyline. It was funny how quickly you could move between two completely different places.

'Back when I worked in the cupcake cafe, all I wanted was to prove I could make it in the big bad city, standing on my own two feet. I was mostly driven by proving to my parents that I was… worth the hassle, maybe. Then all I wanted was to do well in chef school, to impress Jean-Sébastien and be a good apprentice to him. Maybe at some point, I thought about earning my own stars. It drove me to work even harder, even longer hours.' She leaned her head back and turned her gaze to watch the passing scenery through the passenger window.

'Then it all went pear-shaped. Jean-Sébastien died, Alexander basically told me I'm no good and hired you, Emily wrote that scathing review. And the only…' She thought about how pathetic she would sound if she continued but Ethan, though his eyes were on the road ahead, was clearly listening to her; she was committed.

She sighed. 'The only person I had to tell was my cat. Sad, right? You don't even have to answer that.' She watched passers-by on the sidewalk, wandering with shopping bags, as the car came to a standstill in traffic.

The car engine cut out as they sat idle and Ethan turned to look at her. 'So where's your head at now?'

'I thought I wanted to just call it a day. Which I wouldn't do but I felt like I'd hit rock bottom, I guess. Then between you shoving a rocket up my butt and meeting Nayomi, I've found a passion for cooking that isn't solely driven by wanting to impress someone else. I'm actually having fun and I love giving back, watching Nayomi's skills grow.' *Enjoying having a friend again*, she thought but didn't say aloud.

'So what do you want next?'

She gave a wry laugh. 'That, I don't know. I have an itch for accolades still. More to prove to myself that I'm capable of being up there with the best. I also don't want to spend the rest of my life alone. Rephrase that, I actually want to *have* a life, outside of work. Maybe, who knows, even a family of my own.'

She thought of Nayomi and her boys, how much love she saw between them, despite their circumstances being less than ideal. She thought of Annie being twirled around by Ethan, of Annie's hand in hers as they walked through the farm. And she thought of her own parents and how, if she did everything exactly the opposite to how they had brought her up, she might have a chance at being a good mom herself one day.

The traffic started to move and Ethan drove them slowly to Maggie's apartment.

'Home sweet home,' he said, pulling up to the kerbside.

'Thanks for today, Ethan. Not just for showing me the farm but… I've had a really nice day. Annie is… she's wonderful. Such a lovely girl. You should be proud.'

He smiled with only one side of his mouth, almost bashfully. 'So maybe I'm not all bad?'

Maggie unbuckled her seatbelt. 'I didn't go that far.'

Ethan grabbed her hand as she reached for the door handle. 'Maggie, I want you to know, I hope you're coming to see, that I'm not the same guy I was back in chef school. I was a dick back then. I was proud and arrogant.'

She raised one eyebrow as she turned to face him. 'And you're not now?'

That half tilt of his lips was back. 'I deserve that. I am arrogant but only insofar as a good chef needs to be. You could do with an injection of self-belief yourself.'

'Aha. You were saying? Something about change?'

He shook his head playfully. 'I'm not the guy who doesn't care about how other people feel any more. That's what I'm saying. I know you think I spend my nights picking up leggy blondes and who can blame you? That's who I was. But as much as I give it the big I am sometimes, that's not who I am any more and it hasn't been for some time.'

She stared at him, silenced by his sincerity and finding herself falling for it… in every respect. *Dangerous*.

'I had a good day today, Ethan, thank you.' For the second time, she made to get out of the car and this time, he didn't stop her. But he did unbuckle his own belt, too.

'Let me carry your bags up for you. All that veg you bought is heavy.'

Maggie chuckled. 'I have no idea what I'm going to do with it all, it just tasted so good. Maybe I'll make some batches of soup and veggie lasagna.'

Ethan took one paper bag from the trunk of the car and tucked a large pumpkin under his free arm. Maggie took a second, lighter bag.

Inside her apartment, Maggie led Ethan to the kitchen, where they set down their bags. Suddenly, she had no idea what to do with a man, Ethan, in her apartment. She scanned the space, as if the answer would come to her.

'It's a nice place,' Ethan said, turning around on the spot, his hands tucked into his pockets and his shoulders high, as if he too was a little lost.

'Would you like me to show you around? I mean, you've seen the kitchen before.' *Oh, God, she was so lame.*

'Sure.'

Oh. And so, she set off on the very brief tour of her very modest apartment, his presence as he followed her seeming closer than he had all day.

'And this is the bedroom,' she announced, opening the door, a little flustered by his proximity as he leaned past her to look inside.

As if a wind had blown in a complete change of weather, the air around them suddenly felt heavy, more humid, more altogether hot.

The skin of her neck ached for his touch. Her lips felt so dry she was compelled to lick them. Her lower abdomen and lower still, felt heavy, wanting.

She touched her own neck with her hand, wishing it was his. Then Ethan stepped back out of the room and he was looking down at her the way he had in the kitchen earlier today, when she had wanted him to kiss her. Except now, she didn't think she would pull away.

Nothing had changed. *Had it?* It was absurd to think anything *could* have changed in half a day. Yet, when he stepped closer to her and her back met the bedroom door, there was only one thing she wanted. One person.

'Maggie, I'm going to kiss you, and I'd really like it if you didn't pull away this time.'

She stared at his mouth, fairly certain she nodded her head.

Then his lips were on hers, soft to touch, gentle against her own skin. But his kiss was firm and when his tongue met hers, all sensible thoughts left her body.

Her hands were on his back and in his hair, roaming and tugging. His hands found the skin of her hips, her stomach, and higher.

There was no going back.

Afterwards, Maggie fell into a sated, contented sleep on Ethan's chest, too exhausted to wonder whether he would still be beneath her when she woke in the morning.

To her surprise, at three a.m. when she woke feeling parched, Ethan was still in her bed. And at seven thirty a.m., she woke to the smell of coffee and toast.

His presence in her apartment was certainly unexpected.

Was this how he ended all of his nights with women, or did it mean something that he had stayed?

Did she want it to mean something? This was Ethan James. The self-obsessed guy who once called her second best. Who had stolen her dream job.

Yet, as she rolled onto her back and stared at the ceiling, she pressed her fingers to her lips, remembering where his mouth had been just hours before. She felt the fluttering of something in her tummy – excitement, or maybe even hope.

Chapter Twenty-Four

Emily

Emily had started running daily for two reasons. The first was that, with all the cooking she had been doing lately, she needed to strike some kind of balance. The second was that it seemed to clear her head, make her breezier, and set her up for a better day.

As she pounded the sidewalk on her way home, relishing the sweat dripping down her face, breathlessly singing along to the music playing in her ears, she thought she might not cancel the dinner reservation she had made with Janey tonight. Maybe she would go. Catch up with her friend. Eat something (hopefully) tasty that she hadn't cooked herself.

And maybe, she would be inspired to write a better critique than the dross she had been turning into her editor recently.

She came to an abrupt stop on her parents' driveway when she saw the front door close behind Maggie as she was beckoned inside by Isabella.

What was she *doing there?*

But rather than feeling fired up to fight, Emily felt exhausted. Less by her run and more by the saga that had become the triangular fall-out between her, her dad and Maggie.

She was tired of playing her hatred over and over in her mind. Tired of the guilt she felt for not having made up with her dad when he was alive. And tired thinking about the inevitable row that awaited her when she stepped inside that house.

She hadn't seen Maggie since her review of the restaurant. There was every chance that the review was the sole reason Maggie was here right now. She was probably in the kitchen, putting on the kettle for Isabella and learning that Emily, the absolute hot mess that she was, no longer had a fiancé or a home of her own and was, once again, living at home with her mom.

Dropping her hands to her hips and dragging in ragged breaths, Emily contemplated running away. If her legs hadn't failed her on her first step forward, perhaps she would have done. After all, running was easier. *Was it?* She had run from her dad and the restaurant. Run from Maggie. Run from being a chef. Run from her old life. Now, she was running from work, running from Oliver and their home.

At some point, she had to stop running. Since she currently had limited feeling in her legs, now seemed as good a time as any.

So, she took a deep breath, put her shoulders back and headed into the house.

'These flowers are beautiful, Maggie, thank you.' Isabella's voice came from the kitchen and for some reason stole Emily's bravery.

Quietly, she closed the front door behind her and slipped her feet out of her running shoes.

'You're more than welcome.' Maggie's voice sounded bright. Not like she was here to harpoon Emily at all, in fact. 'I hope you like the French toast, too. I didn't make it but it's the best I've tasted.'

'My dear Maggie, are you blushing?'

Emily knew without looking that Maggie would be smiling. That sweet smile she had. 'It's very new,' she said. 'I'm not even sure if it will turn into anything really. I mean, I would like... Oh, I don't know. I'm trying not to overthink it.'

She wasn't sure why exactly but Emily quietly moved along the hallway, until she could just see her mom and Maggie sitting at the kitchen table, each with a hot drink.

'Well, you're glowing, darling. If he makes you happy and he treats you well, that's all right by me.'

All right by her? She wasn't Maggie's mom.

And who was this guy anyway? Maggie never had boyfriends, or not in the time she and Emily had been friends, at least.

She could imagine Maggie would be a dream woman to many men – compliant, easily pleased and always pleasant.

Urgh.

'I see you've been cooking,' Maggie said, changing the subject, no doubt uncomfortable, as she always used to be, with guy talk. 'Is that stuffed bread?'

'Oh, it's delicious. Jambon et fromage. Let me cut you some to take away with you.'

Hey!

Emily watched her mom move to the kitchen counter, take a bread knife and move back to the table. 'I'm afraid I can't take credit for it, though. Emily baked it.'

'Emily is cooking?'

Don't sound so surprised. I can cook too, remember.

'It's wonderful. She cooks every day. We're eating very well.'

'Sorry, I'm not following. Is Emily staying here?'

That's none of your business.

'Oh, yes. She and Oliver separated. It's been very helpful, actually. Jean-Sébastien had a lot of business ventures and I have no idea how to manage them or unravel them. Emily has been fantastic.'

'Oh.'

'She's out for a run now, probably back any minute.'

'Oh.' Maggie pushed out her chair. 'I should probably—'

'Please, Maggie, stay.'

Let her go.

'I'm fairly sure Emily doesn't want to see me, Isabella. And, being totally honest, I don't know if I want to see her.'

'Because of the review? I know. I read it and I'm very sorry, Maggie. Emily shouldn't have written those things.'

What? Don't apologise on my behalf!

'Please, stay and finish your tea.'

Maggie retook her seat and as she did, Emily's annoyance rose. It was just like it used to be, her parents sticking up for Maggie.

'I'm not going to lie, the review hurt. I think it hurt because it felt so personal. And just with the timing. Jean-Sébastien dying, Ethan being hired to replace me.'

Yeah, well, my dad died too and maybe ask why *Ethan was hired.* Emily clenched her fists, teetering on the edge of marching into the kitchen and telling Maggie exactly those things. Yet, something stopped her.

'But,' Maggie said, emphasising the word. Then she paused, turning her mug between her fingers as if she was thinking of her next words. 'There was a lot of truth in Emily's words.'

'Oh, Maggie.'

'No, it's okay. There was.'

Emily's fists unclenched and she listened more intently.

'My own parents never loved me the way you and Jean-Sébastien loved – *love* – Emily. If Emily hadn't befriended me in the cupcake cafe, I wouldn't have anything that I have now. I wouldn't have seen what a family home *should* be like. I'll be forever grateful to you all, Emily included.'

Emily's shoulders were no longer pinned back and her chest felt like it was swelling with an old feeling. Love.

'Emily was right, I wanted to please Jean-Sébastien. I wanted to please him because he believed in me, he wanted to teach me things and encourage me to be something or someone. I guess I also wanted Emily to be proud of me, what she had done for me. So I did exactly what Jean-Sébastien told me to do, what he asked of me, and I did that to the very best of my ability.

'But it's time for me to be my own chef, I think. Since Emily's review, I've been trying new things at the restaurant. Still very much French classics but adding twists. It's been fun and, I guess, enlightening. Like, I can really put dishes together and create flavour combinations, without needing Jean-Sébastien to guide me.

'I can't help but worry that I'm going against Jean-Sébastien's way.' She shook her head as she shrugged. 'It's pretty much my first thought of the day most days. But I am enjoying it.'

Isabella smiled softly. 'Darling, all he wanted was for you to be the best you could be and to be happy. He wanted that for you and Emily alike. If you're doing what you love, that's exactly what he would have wished for you.'

'You think so?'

'I know so.'

Emily's heart felt heavy and she rubbed a hand against her tight throat. *Was she doing something that would make her dad happy?*

'Isabella, I don't know if this is appropriate or not, so you can tell me to be quiet at any time, but one of the reasons I came by was to tell you about someone.'

'Not the new man?' Isabella teased, making Emily smile.

For a fleeting moment, she wished she could just step into the kitchen, that everything would be fine, that she could have girl talk with Maggie and ask all about this man, whomever he was. But she had blown that.

Maggie laughed and Emily didn't need to be sitting across the table from her to know there would be a bashful look on her face.

'No, not a man. Actually, a woman. Her name is Nayomi. I hired her as a kitchen porter a couple of months ago. She's a lovely woman. Her husband died and she lives in Queens with two young boys. I'm pretty sure they don't have much at all. It turns out Nayomi is quite the cook. She's Sri Lankan and, Isabella, you wouldn't believe the dishes she can cook. She's taught me some new fusion ideas and I'm showing her the kitchen basics. We actually created a special together and it was a huge hit.'

'That's lovely, Maggie.'

'It is. She's great. And that's why I wanted to ask, or even see if it would be possible, to have your help. Or, Jean-Sébastien's help. I was thinking about chef school, to give Nayomi a real chance in this industry. You know, the way Jean-Sébastien put new chefs through school, through his charity.'

'I see.'

'I don't mean to overstep and I don't even know if the charity is still going, it's just, she deserves someone to have a little faith in her. Tell me to stop talking if this is inappropriate.'

Emily watched her mom reach out for Maggie's hand. 'The charity is one of the things I told Emily that I would like to keep. Nayomi sounds like a perfect candidate. Let me speak to Emily. If I can help, I will.'

'Oh. I didn't realise Emily was, you know—'

'That doesn't mean it's a *no*, Maggie.'

Maggie nodded and in the way her body slumped into itself, Emily knew Maggie had no faith in her doing the right thing.

And with that, she quietly headed upstairs to shower, trying to wash her sadness away. *When had she become a person that even someone as good as Maggie had no faith in?*

Later that day, Emily took the first of many steps she needed to take towards doing the right thing. Some things weren't so easy but speaking to the relevant people and making arrangements for Maggie's chef, Nayomi, to be offered funding to support her through chef school was a good place to start.

Maybe she could be someone Maggie could be proud of one day again, too.

–

Emily and Janey were led to a table for two in Bouquet, a new restaurant from the chef behind an acclaimed sister restaurant, Waterlily, both places offering Asian fusion.

249

Emily had eaten in Waterlily four times over a period of five months last year and had given the setting, the ambience and the food a rave review.

It was hard to not be spotted as an *NYT* critic in restaurants, particularly new restaurants who were eager to be reviewed by the paper. Tonight, she had tucked her real hair into a net and worn a short edgy bob wig, Taylor Swift-style. The lenses in her square-rimmed glasses were clear and Janey had booked the table under the name of Ms. Lyon.

As they followed behind the maître d', Emily was not disappointed by the design and décor of the place. Dark wood and ambient lighting were the backdrop to delicate cherry blossom trees and lush green leaves. The crystal waterfall chandeliers hanging above each dining table were subtly glamorous.

In short, she loved the get-up of the place. She hoped the food could live up to the food served at Waterlily yet be sufficiently different to offer a unique dining experience.

It was nice to be out again. To be wearing her favourite grey silk dress, that happily fit better than ever, or at least felt as if it did. She hadn't worn heels for weeks but enjoyed how much taller she felt, how her body felt straighter, more feminine. Combined with the wig and the glasses, she could believe herself to be an entirely new person and something about that made her feel relaxed.

'You look well,' Janey said, once they had been seated and both ordered the chef's signature tasting menu with paired wine.

'That almost sounds like an accusation,' Emily said, amused.

'I admit, I didn't know what to expect. You've been off the grid and, whether you like to admit it or not, losing your dad, leaving Oliver, moving home, that's a lot for anyone, Emily. Even a tough gal like you.'

Emily cleared her throat. 'You mean, a tough gal like Charlotte Lyon, even in her Taylor Swift "come and get me, world" wig.'

They laughed. It was nice to laugh again and with her friend.

'I'm pleased you didn't cancel on me again,' Janey said.

Emily smiled. 'Me too.'

Just when it felt like they needed glasses to chink, the sommelier presented a glass of four-hundred-dollars-a-bottle champagne to each of them.

'Guess the wig only fooled me,' Emily said.

'Cover blown. I don't know *how* they do that.'

'Still want to be Charlotte and Melanie for the night?'

'Melanie doesn't have kids or a husband at home to run around after, right?' Janey asked.

'Nope.'

'And she has a fancy car and unlimited access to her daddy's credit card, right?'

'Yep.'

'Hell, I'm all in, Charlotte.'

And so, for six delectable courses of yellow fin tuna and seaweed salad, dim sum consommé, deconstructed sushi, roasted duck, Korean pork ribs and a trio of exotic fruit desserts, Emily and Janey were whoever they wanted to be.

They guffawed about scandals at the paper, amongst the staff and in the news. They discussed their best ever dining experiences. They chatted about their best holidays and where they might like to go next.

'I think you should do it,' Janey said, when Emily told her about her dream, to travel around France and write a book. 'Don't look at me like that. I do. I think it would be great for you to get away for a while, take some time out from the paper, and, I don't know, like, reconnect with your ancestors or whatever.'

'And my job?'

Janey leaned her head to one side as if to say, *come on*. 'If you were still as passionate about being a restaurant critic as you were five years ago – hell, even a year ago – I'd understand that reservation. But you've hardly been interested for weeks.'

'I've had a lot going on.'

'Hey, don't get me wrong, I know that. All I'm saying is, I think you know yourself that your heart just isn't in it any more. Plus, you could ask for a sabbatical. Maybe Archer wouldn't hate the idea.'

Emily scoffed. 'Yeah, right. You heard yourself when you just said that, didn't you?'

'Yeah, okay, maybe it's all in or all out but, seriously, you should think about it.'

'Why do you want rid of me so badly?'

'I'm in the market for a promotion.' Janey winked. 'Plus, when else are you going to do it? You're free as a bird right now. Trust me, when you have a husband and kids, it's not easy to leave the house for dinner, let alone take a trip to another country.'

'Suppose for, like, one second, and only because we've had wine, that I was crazy enough to pack up and do it. Who would want a book by me anyway? I'm not a high-flying chef.'

'True. But you did work for years in one of the best kitchens in the world. And you have been top critic at the

New York Times for years. I'd say there couldn't be a better combination.'

Emily stared at her friend. *Were they both crazy? Or drunk?*

But she was sober. She knew that because the talk of her old dreams had transported her from imaginary Charlotte's carefree body, back to her own.

'There are things I need to deal with here,' she said.

'Like what?'

'Dividing up things with Olly. Dealing with dad's estate.'

'How's that going?'

Emily sipped her drink. 'Getting there on both fronts. With dad's estate, we at least understand what's there now, which is a step further forward than where we were previously. Now it's a case of winding down things mom doesn't want to keep and working out how we do that. Then figuring out how to keep the things she does want, like dad's charity.'

'That's good. It must be nice for both of you but especially your mom, knowing that things are in hand. What are the other things?' Janey asked. 'You said dealing with your dad's estate was one thing.'

'Oh. Well, remember when I said my review of Dad's restaurant wasn't personal? Yeah, it was. I stand by some of it but, on reflection, it was... I was... Well, a dick. I shouldn't have attacked Maggie the way I did. I mean, seriously, she's one of the best people I know. Besides Charlotte and Melanie, obviously.' She shook her head and finished her final tasting-sized glass of wine for the evening. 'I just don't know how to fix it.'

'You could ask Archer to publish a retraction.'

'That's what I've been thinking. Do you reckon he'll go for it?'

Janey shrugged. 'He won't like it. You promised him the article wasn't vindictive. To retract it tells him you lied and it doesn't look good for the publication.'

Emily bit down on her lip. 'I know. But I have to try. For Maggie.'

Chapter Twenty-Five

Nayomi

There was a gentle tap on the staff changing room door as Nayomi was switching her ordinary clothes for her uniform, ready to start her shift.

'Just a second,' she called. She pulled on her jacket over her vest. 'Okay, come in.'

Maggie opened the door. 'Hey, Nayomi. I was hoping we could have a quick chat before your shift starts?'

Her heart sank to her stomach as she quickly racked her brains for what she might have done wrong. She couldn't think of anything but Maggie sounded serious.

'Sure,' she said, trying to hide her fear. She loved this job.

'It's nothing bad,' Maggie said, coming to sit on a bench, encouraging Nayomi to sit on the bench on the opposite wall of the small room.

Nayomi tried to relax but her mind couldn't stop racing through worst-case scenarios.

'As you know, I've been really impressed with you in the kitchen and I've enjoyed working with you recently. Not just working but getting to know each other better. I think you've been having fun too?'

'I have. I've been learning so much. And I'd like to think we've become friends.'

Maggie was warmed to the core, thrilled Nayomi also wanted to be friends and not just colleagues. 'Good.' She beamed, while trying not to seem too full-on. 'Well, I'm in a bit of a strange position as the outgoing head chef. I can't really take anyone on to work on a full-time basis and if I did, I couldn't guarantee that Alexander and Ethan wouldn't change things up within weeks or months of me leaving.'

Nayomi listened, unsure where the conversation was headed but curious to find out.

'I also know that you have the boys to think about and another job and I don't want to create a situation that puts you at risk, erm, financially.'

Nayomi felt sorry for Maggie and her awkwardness. She was poor and couldn't hide that fact.

'So, I've been speaking to some people, I hope you don't mind, and I want to put a proposal to you.'

'Okay...'

'Jean-Sébastien used to have a charity, which his wife and daughter intend to keep going, as part of his legacy, I guess. The charity was set up to help people who showed talent in the kitchen to be funded through chef school. I wanted to check out the possibility before I spoke with you about it, but I guess what I'm asking is, would you like to go to chef school? It would be during the day, course paid for and an allowance from the charity to help you cover the cost of a wage. A small one, I should say that.'

Beneath her sheer astonishment, Nayomi could feel excitement building. Maggie truly believed she was good enough to be a chef. *Her*, who had never had a job until her husband died. Who hadn't been educated in some fancy college. *Her*, who had been struggling to make ends meet for years.

'If you want to do it, I'll speak with Ethan too. I think he'd be crazy not to take you on as an apprentice or maybe even a commis chef. Either way, you'd be paid more than your porter salary.'

A job and a place on the course? 'Oh my goodness.'

Maggie took a breath and as Nayomi began to smile, so did she.

'So, what are your thoughts? Where's your head at? You don't have to decide on the spot or anything.'

But Nayomi was too full of emotion to speak. Instead, she pushed off her bench and wrapped her arms around Maggie, saying over and over again, 'Thank you.'

It wasn't about the money or even the prospects, necessarily. She was thanking Maggie for having confidence in her.

'You really think I can do it?' she asked, once she had recovered and resumed her position on the bench opposite Maggie.

'I do. You can already cook. You have a fantastic instinct for flavour combinations and presentation. Chef school will just help you hone your skills and it will give you a helping hand when you're competing for jobs.'

Nayomi covered her mouth with her fingertips and shook her head, willing herself not to squeal in excitement.

'Like I said, have a think about it and let me kn—'

'Maggie, I don't need to think about it. Yes. It's a huge yes.' She didn't squeal but she did explode with giddy laughter.

Maggie stood, grinning. 'Well, all right then. I'll get some more details together and we can sit down together and go through the forms for the charity and the course. I'm going to speak with Ethan as soon as I can, so I'll let you know about the job. At the very least, you would be able to keep your role as a porter but it would be better if you were cooking alongside the course. If not Ethan, I might have a few other avenues to explore.'

Nayomi stood, her legs like jelly beneath her. 'Maggie, I really can't thank you enough.'

Maggie placed a hand on her shoulder. 'It's your hard work, Nayomi. I'm just… admin.'

Later that night, when Ashley walked Nayomi from the staff taxi into the foyer of her apartment block, he was fidgety and unusually uncool.

'Nayomi… I was thinking. I don't want to step on toes and the last thing I want is to upset your… you know… like, mojo with the boys. I'm not sure what I'm saying. You know, it's just that you guys are like the three musketeers, right? And, I know you don't *need* anyone else. I just…'

'Ashley, you're sweating. Are you okay?'

He swiped his forearm across his brow. 'Would you let me take you to dinner? I mean, just us this time. To celebrate your good news.'

Nayomi had wanted him to ask the question just as much as she had hoped he wouldn't recently. She had feelings for him, she couldn't deny it. He was great with the boys, he was handy in the home, but it was more than that. It was… a feeling, like a quickening of her pulse, a lightness of her thoughts when she was around him. He made her feel… nice. Pretty. Cherished.

But she had worked so hard after her husband's death to make the boys feel secure and happy. Sure, they didn't have much, but she knew the boys loved her and they knew how much she loved them. And they were okay.

Especially since she had been working at the restaurant. They were doing more than okay now.

'Ashley, I... I so want to say yes, please know that. I think you're... kind of incredible.'

He smiled in such a goofy way it made her tummy dance.

'Could you just let me speak to the boys and see if they would be okay with it?'

His smile grew and just like he had after he had asked her and the boys to the movies, he started backing out of the building, as if he didn't want to stick around any longer for her to say anything else.

It made Nayomi laugh. 'You know I didn't just say yes, right?'

'Yup.'

'I need to speak to the boys.'

'Yup.' He opened the door to the street. 'But I know the boys have got my back. So you message me once they've cleared it and I'll book us a table somewhere nice. I know just the place.' He was on the steps outside, the door beginning to close behind him. 'My mom can watch the kids.'

Nayomi laughed as she watched him through the glass pane of the door, getting back into the staff car. 'He didn't listen at all,' she said for no one's ears except her own as she made her way home.

—

'You look amazing,' Farah said from her position sitting on Nayomi's bed, where she had been partly supervising Nayomi getting ready and mostly attempting to calm her nerves. 'You're going to knock him dead.'

Nayomi considered herself in the mirror, the way the black knee-length dress hugged her body but not overly so. The way her whole body seemed brighter by her feet being in a mid-height heeled sandal. Her hair hung long and naturally wavy down her back but tamed by Farah's miracle anti-frizz oil.

'Thank you for the dress. And the shoes. And the bag,' Nayomi said, turning to face her friend.

'You'd do the same for me.'

'I would. If I actually had any clothes you would want to wear on a date. Oh my goodness, I'm going on a *date*.'

Farah laughed. 'You act like you've never been to dinner before.'

'I've been to dinner. I've never been on a date before. Unless walking to the local shop with my neighbour when I was fifteen counts?'

'You've *never* been on a date?'

Nayomi shrugged. 'I was seventeen when my husband's family visited our village from America. We spent a small amount of time together before the wedding but then we moved to America and I guess you don't date once you're married.'

Farah stood from the bed and came over to Nayomi, adjusting the pendant of the gold leaf necklace she had loaned her. 'Well, the good news is, he already thinks you're beautiful. You already get along great. And if you're just yourself, he's going to fall in love with you.'

'*Love?* Oh my goodness. I need to sit down.'

Farah snorted. 'He's going to be here any minute. Come on.'

In the lounge, Roshan and Nuwan were constructing Lego together.

'Whoa,' Roshan said on seeing Nayomi, which she hoped was – and decided to interpret as – a positive response to her fancy dress.

'Are you sure about this? I don't have to go if you guys aren't comfortable, okay?'

She wanted them to be happy. This was only a date. It might not go anywhere. In truth, a part of her wanted the boys to beg her not to go. To put an end to the nervous whirring of her stomach that had meant she couldn't eat her Sunday lunch. The rest of her really wanted to be swept off her feet tonight.

'Mom, it's okay. We like Ashley, he's…' Roshan shrugged. 'Cool. Right, Nuwan?'

Nayomi thought that if her heart were ice cream, it would have melted with Roshan's words. It was hard enough feeling like she was going against her own morals in seeking out a new man but to think that she might upset the boys was too much. Now, hearing Roshan accepting, even speaking warmly of Ashley, made her immensely grateful.

Nuwan seemed to contemplate Roshan's question, then folding his arms and pouting, he asked. 'Why can't we come?'

'Because they'll *kiss*,' Roshan replied, holding out his arms to mimic hugging another person and puckering his lips.

'And what would you know about kissing? Have you got a *girl*friend?' Farah teased, putting an end to Roshan's show.

'You'll be okay with Ashley's mom, won't you? If you need me, you can just call,' Nayomi said.

'I'll be right next door, too,' Farah said.

The sound of the buzzer made Nayomi jump and a minute later, Ashley and his mom were in the apartment.

Nayomi couldn't bring herself to look Ashley in the eye. She was nervous, embarrassed and awkward. Completely not how she usually was around Ashley these days. She did notice the effort he had made to dress in checked trousers that hugged his legs just enough to show a nice shape and the smart white shirt he had tucked into them. She also couldn't help but notice how well he smelled – fresh, slightly spiced cologne.

Instead, she focused on Deloris. 'It's so nice to see you out of your cast and off your crutches.'

'Oh, yes, they were an irritant. I'm not right yet, though. Still need Ashley's help with lots of things.'

Now Nayomi did look at Ashley and they shared a knowing smile – Deloris had no intention of moving out of his place any time soon.

'Are you sure you don't mind looking after the boys?'

'We're going to have great fun, aren't we, boys?'

The boys' expressions conveyed that they were dubious about this, their lack of subtlety making Nayomi and Ashley laugh, easing her tension a little.

'Come on, then, make room for an older one,' Deloris said, hobbling her way to the sofa between the boys, who had been perched on the edge building their Lego. 'What are we making?'

'A car,' Nuwan said, excitedly.

'I'm going to take off,' Farah said. 'You guys have fun. Don't do anything I wouldn't do. And, Deloris, if you need anything, I'm right next door.'

Nayomi had a feeling Deloris might take Farah up on the offer… every time she wanted a drink or a snack.

Then there were just Ashley and Nayomi, standing face to face, with no one between them. Ashley looked her up and down. 'You look really nice.'

Nayomi smiled. 'You too.'

'Are you going to *kiss* her?' Nuwan shouted.

'Nuwan!' Nayomi's cheeks felt like someone had taken a match to them. 'Let's go, shall we?'

Ashley was clearly enjoying the cheekiness of her youngest son, chuckling as he held open the door for Nayomi to leave.

'I love you, guys. Be good.'

Ashley had made a reservation at a Mexican restaurant in Williamsburg. It was busy, in a way that pleased Nayomi. There was enough background noise that no one would be able to overhear if she was making terrible conversation – who knew how she would behave on a date? – but not so busy that they wouldn't be able to hear each other comfortably.

The antique-yellow paint, dark wood furnishings and sombreros hanging on the walls transported Nayomi to sunny Mexico, or at least the sunny Mexico she imagined. They were greeted at the door by a flamboyant man, who called them amigos, and swayed his hips as they followed his cactus-print shirt to their table.

Old wine bottles had been turned into candle holders and the orange light flickered over the table for two. She didn't know whether she was supposed to wait for Ashley to pull out her seat or if he would even make the gesture, so she was relieved when the waiter pulled out her seat for her, although she found his style of tucking her back under the table was a tad vigorous.

'Can I get you drinks?' the waiter asked.

'Do you want to see the menu first?' Ashley asked Nayomi.

'Erm, what are you having?'

'I might have a margarita.'

Cocktails. She was bit of a novice when it came to cocktails. Anything Charles had taught her about wine at the restaurant was no use when it came to cocktails. Her inexperience must have showed, as the waiter said, 'Can I recommend a paloma? It's our signature cocktail and as Mexican as can be.'

'What's in a paloma?' she asked.

'Tequila, grapefruit, soda and lime. Delicious.'

'Erm, sure. I'll take one of those.' Hurdle one complete, though she had no idea if she liked tequila.

She looked around for a place to rest the clutch bag Farah had lent her – did she put it on the table, behind her on the chair, on the floor? What was the correct etiquette?

Not wanting to risk damaging someone else's property, she tucked the clutch behind her back and shuffled forward slightly on her chair.

'You don't do this very often, do you?' Ashley asked, although not in a condescending way, more like giving her a chance to get out of jail free.

'Is it that obvious?'

'A little. But, hey, me neither. How about we forget this is a date and we just have dinner together, just Nayomi and Ashley, the same two people who have a laugh in the kitchen together and share a ride home every night?'

Nayomi instantly relaxed. 'I'd like that.'

They were each given large menus with more selection than Nayomi had ever seen in a restaurant – she was more used to eating in places that had a chalkboard with a few options, when she ever did eat out.

'Where do I even start with this?' she asked.

'Everything in here is great, trust me. The guacamole, though, that's a winner. And the seafood chimichangas, yes! The grilled tilapia is sensational. Ah, the rib-eye steak chilli.'

'Okay, okay.' Nayomi laughed. 'I'm not sure how big you think my stomach is but I've got it. Maybe I'll go for a couple of your suggestions tonight and next time I can try something else.'

Ashley's lips drew into a smirk as Nayomi realised her blunder.

'I mean, you know, if there was… if we did…'

'I really hope there's a next time,' Ashley said, just as their cocktails were brought to the table.

She kind of did too.

Ashley held up his drink and said, 'To your spot in chef school.'

'Oh, I have something else to tell you.' Nayomi brought her glass up to meet Ashley's. 'Maggie convinced Ethan to take me on in the kitchen. I'm going to be learning on the job.'

'You realise that's going to call for a second round of margaritas and palomas, right?'

Nayomi sipped her cocktail. 'Oh wow, I have no problem with that.'

Once Ashley had stopped laughing, he looked at her with his deep brown eyes and said something that made her entire body free fall. He said, 'I'm really proud of you, Nayomi.'

Her fears of awkwardness had been entirely unfounded. With the exception of falling quiet to enjoy the scrumptious food, the conversation between them flowed easily. It was exactly like they were in the kitchen and in the staff car, with one exception. Perhaps the product of three tequila cocktails, or the fact Ashley was dressed up, or perhaps the way he subtly settled the bill while Nayomi was in the bathroom, saving her from any uneasiness, whatever the reason, Nayomi really wanted to end the date with a kiss.

She paid for the cab to her house and tried to give Ashley money for rest of the journey from hers to his, once he had collected Deloris, but he wouldn't accept it. Any decision about whether she was supposed to invite him inside or not was taken out of her hands and she was grateful that Deloris had offered to babysit at her house, if only for that reason.

They walked from the cab up to Nayomi's apartment in relative silence. Her hand felt drawn to Ashley's, as if she was fighting against a magnetic pull, but they walked side by side, untouching. It was polite. It was in keeping with every vibe Nayomi had given off in the past and she knew it was sweet that Ashley wasn't pushing her for more.

Except, she *wanted* him to hold her hand. Perhaps he didn't want that. Perhaps the date hadn't been as wonderful for Ashley as it had for her. Maybe she had misread the evening completely.

But when she made to put her key into the door of the apartment, Ashley reached out to stop her. He took hold of her hand in his and looked into her eyes.

Was he asking permission?

She hoped he was and she hoped that he could read from her what she wanted.

Her heart began to race. *Could he hear it? Was his heart racing, too?*

Her feet seemed to move of their own volition as she stepped closer to him.

His hand rose to cup her cheek. 'If I— Would it be okay?'

This was her chance to back out. She took a deep, steadying breath.

'Ashley, I have to tell you something.'

He withdrew his hand from her face and nodded. It was a subtle move, as if he was afraid of what she might say.

'My marriage to Shan was planned. Or, pre-arranged.' She looked up to him, wanting to get out her words but not wanting to stop him finishing what he had started. 'I was brought up to... belong to one man. To Shan, I guess.'

She had started to fiddle with her fingers and looked down to where Ashley took hold of her hands.

'Except, Shan isn't here any more. And I... I really like you, Ashley. I've just been struggling with the idea that I could... that I *want* to turn my back on who I'm supposed to be.'

She shook her head. 'I get if this is too much. I'm just trying to be hon—'

Then his soft lips were on hers, capturing her words, stopping them, telling her that everything was okay. More than okay. Exactly as it was supposed to be.

His touch made her feel like her blood was dancing in her veins, the fine hairs on her skin stood on end with the desire for his kiss.

She knew, in that moment, that if being with Ashley felt so good, it couldn't be wrong.

And once Ashley and Deloris had left her home and the boys were tucked up in bed, Nayomi lay back on her own sheets, waiting.

But she surprised herself by not feeling a surge of guilt for her husband or her boys, for her family.

Instead, she felt… content. Happy.

Chapter Twenty-Six

Maggie

'You look beautiful,' Ethan said, as Maggie stepped out of her apartment building and walked down the steps to the sidewalk where Ethan was waiting, his hands behind his back.

'I'm wearing jeans and a sweater.'

'Can't I think you look beautiful in jeans and a sweater?'

Maggie twisted her lips to stop her girlish grin from appearing. Ethan had stayed over a couple of nights in the two weeks since they first slept together but this was their first official date, out somewhere. It was new and strange, her and Ethan, her and any man, dating, being complimented. All of it.

Was it weird if she told Ethan she liked how he looked in his jeans and sweater too? Would it be like an afterthought? Would it seem like she had no clue how to behave on a date? Because she didn't.

But she did think he looked handsome, nice… sexy.

Instead of making a fool of herself by the second line of their date, she asked, 'Where are we going?'

Ethan looked to her feet and saw her Keds.

'Are these okay?' she asked nervously. 'You said something practical.'

'I was just checking. They're perfect. Come on, we're walking since it's a nice enough day. This is for you.' He brought his hands from behind his back and handed her a take-out coffee. 'Latte okay?'

'Mmm, yes, great, thanks.'

As they set off heading west, Maggie realised that this was her last Monday still employed at Jean-Sébastien's. The first Monday since she had taken over as temporary head chef that she hadn't been in the kitchen working on a plan to be better somehow.

I'd best get used to days off, she thought. But she stopped herself from saying her thoughts aloud because she was walking alongside the reason she would be unemployed come Saturday night and she didn't want to mix business with pleasure. In fact, she had made a conscious decision not to.

Instead, she let herself forget that Ethan was stealing her job, that she was terrified of Jean-Sébastien's legacy being lost in the art of experimental cuisine, and she let herself forget that Ethan had the worst reputation with women. After all, he had changed, *hadn't he*?

She chose to focus on the man, not the chef or the floozy, just the man. The man who had a wonderful daughter, whom he clearly adored, who had been kind and encouraging towards Maggie in the kitchen – in his own way – and who made love to her unexpectedly tenderly.

'So where *are* we going?'

'Canoeing.'

'Canoeing?' she chuckled. 'In Central Park?'

'Yep.'

'Well, well, well, I never had Ethan James down as clichéd.'

'Hey! It's not clichéd, it's romantic. I couldn't cook for you or take you to a restaurant for our first real date. You'd spend the whole time analysing every bite.'

'I wouldn't.'

'You would. As would I. Plus, I've seen the canoe date work in loads of romantic movies. The guy always gets laid right after.'

Maggie gasped before her shock broke into laughter. This wasn't just flirting, it was brazen, crass, and, unfortunately, quite funny.

Her nerves had been unfounded too. As they walked to 72nd Street and Fifth Avenue, they talked about everything from where they grew up to why they wanted to cook. They talked movies and iconic quotes. They even touched on sports and skirted around politics.

She had come to think it over recent weeks in the kitchen but there was definitely more to Ethan than she had given him credit for back in chef school. Or perhaps it was a recent development. Either way, she cautiously liked the man she was walking into Central Park with.

They headed to The Loeb Boathouse where Ethan made arrangements for a canoe. Oars in hands, they set off on a steady row around the lake.

'I love the park,' Maggie said, wistfully, gazing around at the trees, the ripples in the water, friends and loved ones riding in canoes. 'It's my happy place.'

'The kitchen isn't?'

'Sometimes. Lately, it hasn't been so peaceful. There's just been a lot going on.'

'I guess me coming in isn't helping that?'

Her eyebrows rose in a way that said, *what do you think?*

'But it isn't just that. It was losing Jean-Sébastien and so suddenly. He was more than my boss. He was my mentor, a friend and a father figure.'

She closed her eyes and inhaled the soothing, fresh air around them. 'Then there was the shock of Alexander hiring you. I shouldn't have been surprised, Alexander is a pig. And it's not as if I *expected* to become head chef but I'd served my time, I cooked the way I'd been trained by Jean-Sébastien. Inevitably, resignations followed, not that those guys were my best friends or anything but I'd worked with them for years.'

She pulled her oars onto her lap, suddenly tired, and sighed as she watched a small bird skim the surface of the water.

'Then Emily's review was like twisting the knife in a really bad wound. It hurt. I've never fully understood what happened between us and that review was part hateful and, even worse, part truth. So, I was at sea. Then I finally start having fun again, inventing new dishes, enjoying the kitchen. And...' She glanced to Ethan and found him similarly holding his oars still, watching her, listening to her, '...you're making me all... conflicted. On the one hand, you've stolen my job, just when I was in a good place, or getting to one, at least.'

She looked back to the water. *What on earth was she going to do with her life? She was staring down the barrel of unemployment. She had rent to pay. Bills to pay.*

'And on the other?' Ethan asked.

'Hmm?'

'You said, on the one hand, I've stolen your job. And on the other hand...?'

Maggie found fascination in her shoes.

'On the other hand…?' Ethan repeated. When she didn't respond, he shuffled forward in the canoe, making her reach out and grip the sides as the boat rocked on the water.

'What are you doing? I don't want to go in.'

But he was kneeling in front of her, lifting her chin until she looked at him. 'On the other hand, you kind of like me, right?'

Maggie bit her lip, knowing the answer was written all over her face and in the way she looked to his soft lips and into his eyes. The way her body inched closer to him, betraying her.

'I hope so, Maggie, because I've fallen for you big time.'

Her smile grew until her lip broke free of her bite. 'You have?'

He moved closer to her, encouraging her with his fingertips under her chin to meet his lips. He closed his eyes but before she closed hers, she asked, 'Is this just another move to get you laid?'

'Naturally.'

She nudged his shoulders, just as he bent closer to kiss her. Between the opposite actions, he lost his balance.

'Whoa.' He rocked to one side.

Maggie let out an involuntary short yelp as the canoe toppled. Ethan cast his weight to the opposite side of the canoe but it rocked, left, right, left.

'Arghhhh!'

Ethan fell to the side of the boat, then splashed into the water. The boat shifted so hard that Maggie almost toppled out too.

'Oh my goodness!'

But she caught her balance and the canoe rocked back steady as Ethan surfaced from under the lake.

As he coughed and spluttered, Maggie found herself in hysterics.

'Oh you're so smooth, Ethan James.'

He stared at her as he ran a hand through his hair, lifting it from his face, and shook his head, flicking water across her.

'Hey! Don't bring me down to your level. It's beneath you, Ethan.'

'Yeah, it really isn't.'

Before she had time to react, Ethan had reached up and tugged her out of the canoe and into the lake. She screamed right before she went under the cold water.

She surfaced and kicked her legs until she was right in front of him. 'I ought to—'

But his lips absorbed her words as he finally kissed her. She forgot she was in the middle of a lake, in the middle of Central Park, in the middle of autumn, with no change of clothes. And she kissed him back, something like seven or eight years of crush worth of kiss.

'Are you two okay?' someone called, eventually stealing their attention. A member of staff from the boat-house rowed close to them.

'Sorry, sir, we had a little accident,' Ethan said. 'We're good. No one got hurt.'

'Can you get back in?' The man asked.

Ethan held up a hand. 'We'll be fine.'

As Ethan gave Maggie a helping hand into the canoe, the man held the boat steady. Then Ethan hopped back in and when they were alone, facing each other, looking at the cold and sorry drowned sights they were, Maggie asked, 'Seriously, this is what you think gets you laid?'

But as they chuckled together, she knew there was nothing she would rather do than get back to her apartment and get Ethan out of his wet clothes.

A couple of hours later, they had showered together. Under the hot steam, they had kissed and explored each other.

It was hot, heady, and so unlike Maggie. She felt wild and... maybe a little bit sexy too. Okay, she was no Sienna Miller, but Ethan didn't seem to be complaining.

And who knew those shower scenes from movies could actually work in practice? She and Ethan hadn't been all limbs akimbo like she would have expected, they had just seemed to... fit.

She tried not to think about why Ethan seemed extremely well-versed in making a woman happy and instead, let herself be just that; happy, contented, sated. She had no desire to ask those awkward questions like *Have you had many girlfriends?* Thankfully, he didn't seem interested in asking like questions of her. Her responses would have been equally as embarrassing, for the entirely opposite reason to Ethan.

Now, they were sitting cosily together on the sofa with Maggie's heating on, Ethan in just a towel while he waited for his clothes to dry and Maggie a little more modestly dressed in a T-shirt and shorts. On the coffee table was a large meat feast pizza with extra cheese.

'This is so good,' Maggie said after swallowing her third bite.

'She's come up for air. I was getting worried.'

Maggie laughed so hard she snorted. 'I'm a woman with an appetite and this pizza is, frankly, better than your conversation.'

'Oh, burn.'

'Though it pains me to say you were right about something – this really is the best pizza in the city.'

'I'm right about lots of things, Maggie.'

She rolled her eyes. 'And that, my friend, is why it pains me to say it.'

'My self-confidence?'

'Your self-importance.'

Ethan laughed heartily. When he sobered, he said, 'I was right about something else too.'

'Oh yeah?'

'Yeah. Since you've stepped outside your comfort zone in the kitchen, you've been having more fun.'

She tried not to hear *I told you so*, and instead accepted that she was happier. 'Maybe.'

'Maybe?'

'Okay, it's true. Though it wasn't just you. Emily's disaster of a review forced my hand more than your comments.' She picked a piece of pepperoni from her pizza and ate it. 'It's ironic, really, that the two people who have inspired me to try something new are also the two people who have ruined my career.'

Ethan set down the slice of pizza he was midway through on a plate and looked at her. 'You don't really think that's true, do you?'

Maggie swallowed deeply. She didn't *want* to think it was true. But she shrugged.

'Maggie, Alexander came to me with an opportunity. Not just to be chef but to buy in, to truly replace Jean-Sébastien. Would you have turned it down? I mean, other than seeing you in passing at opening parties over the last few years, I'd barely spoken to you since chef school. More to the point, your career isn't over.'

Oh boy. She had brought it on herself but this was the last thing she wanted to be discussing with Ethan on her sofa after they had shared such a great day together.

'Ethan, come Saturday, I don't have a job. Right now, I'm wondering if being a chef anywhere is better than being unemployed, but I have no idea how much reputational damage being a second-rate chef will do long term. After Emily's review, it was clear to me that...'

No one had faith in her. She had lost the one person who did. Now, she wasn't even sure if she believed she could do it herself.

She sighed. 'Let's just drop it. I'm sorry I made a quip. Let's just try to keep business and pleasure separate, shall we?'

Was she even convinced they could? Could she think Ethan was partly to blame for her downfall and not have any animosity towards him in a relationship?

He stared at her, unmoving, as if he was about to say something, most likely something she wouldn't thank him for. Then he gave a subtle nod, reached out to retrieve his pizza slice and the television remote and asked, 'What are we watching?'

Halfway through *Instant Family*, with a full stomach, nestled into Ethan's side with Livvy resting on her feet, Maggie had put her current troubles to the back of her mind and allowed herself to enjoy the company of a man. A man she really quite liked.

Mortifyingly, her contentedness mixed with a busy day must have left her feeling drowsy enough to fall asleep on the sofa.

She woke as Ethan lay her down on her mattress. Her eyes opening caused Ethan to still. Then his lips curved into his familiar half smile and he reached down, gently combing her hair from her temple with his fingertips.

Taking hold of his hand, she kissed his fingertips, then his palm. She encouraged him closer to her and melted when his lips met hers. They made love for the third time that day, something Maggie had never done. And each time was better. Each time left her feeling more desired. Each time made her want more.

When she woke again, it was light outside and the smell of coffee drifted through to the bedroom from the kitchen. Rolling onto her side, she closed her eyes again and smiled. She had now spent multiple mornings waking up to Ethan in her apartment and each one felt like something to treasure.

The door to the bedroom was nudged open and Maggie wasn't sad to see a half-naked Ethan holding two mugs of coffee.

'Good morning,' he said. *It sure was.* 'Coffee?'

'Amazing, thank you.' She sat up and Ethan mirrored her position on what was quickly becoming his side of the bed.

'I'm not sure how long it takes you to come around in the mornings,' he said. 'Are you compos mentis?'

'Hold on.' She took a sip of coffee. 'I am now.'

Ethan chuckled. 'Good because I have a proposition for you. Of the work kind.'

She scowled playfully. 'You're not going to tell me to set up a cupcake stall, are you?'

Ethan almost spat his next gulp of coffee in good humour. 'A bit more upscale than that.'

Maggie set her coffee on the bedside table, now in work mode. 'I'm listening.'

'Well, I'd like you to stay at Jean-Sébastien's.'

Her stomach leapt at the prospect of staying. But… 'What are you saying, exactly? You aren't going to take the job?'

Ethan blushed. An uncommon sight. 'Ah, no, that's not what I meant. I'm taking the job. Maggie, I'm asking if you'll be my number two?'

Maggie's mouth fell open and she closed her eyes, shaking her head. *Was she awake? Perhaps she wasn't and this was a nightmare. That would be the most plausible explanation for her being thrust back in time to chef school and Ethan openly telling everyone that she was second best.* 'Your number two?'

'My sous chef, just like you were to Jean-Sébastien.'

'I would work for you? Under you?' *God, what she had taken to be jokes in the kitchen had been real.*

She got out of bed, quickly pulling on a robe because she couldn't kick someone out of her apartment when she was completely naked.

'It would be great,' Ethan continued, clearly not catching on to her current temperament. 'We would—'

'Is that what this has all been about? Getting me to cook in a different way. Getting to know me better. Has it all been a trial to see if I'm good enough to work in your shadow?'

'Whoa, whoa, whoa, that's not what—'

'Get out.'

She fastened the belt of her robe.

'Come again?'

'I can't do this, Ethan. I thought I could, but I can't.'

'Maggie—'

'I tried to convince myself that we could set work aside but *nothing* has changed, has it? Maybe you don't want to screw every girl in sight any more but you *still* think you're better than me. You still think—'

Her next breath made her nostrils flare and her eyes sting with anger. Anger that threatened tears that she would *not* let Ethan see.

'I said, *get out.*' She pointed to the door, feeling every other muscle in her body tense. 'Now, Ethan. Just go.'

'Maggie. What the hell?'

She hated herself for crying but her tears wouldn't hold, they fell from her eyes and rolled down her cheeks. 'Please... Just leave me alone, Ethan.'

He looked at her with pity, forcing her to turn away from him as he dressed, then left without saying another word to her.

When he had gone, Maggie scooped Livvy onto her lap and continued to cry.

Just another person who didn't believe she was good enough. Why had she dared to think differently, to think that Ethan did respect her and her cooking? Perhaps it was time to accept that she truly wasn't good enough.

It felt like the countdown to the end of days. Tuesday was the first day of the last week that she would ever work at Jean-Sébastien's. She was determined to get over her sadness from the morning after Ethan's bombshell request. She wanted to absorb every sound, every taste and every smell of the kitchen and box up the memories.

She tied her apron tighter around her waist and called out the first check of the evening service, receiving a resounding chorus of 'Yes, Chef'.

It was the end of an era. The restaurant had been her *everything* for so long. She had given herself to it completely, if not forsaking *all* others then giving up a lot for her commitment to the job. She had never had a long-term relationship and could count her friends on her fingers, all of whom were interchangeably work colleagues. She had never taken lengthy time off to go on holidays outside the country.

Jean-Sébastien's had been her life and now, it was coming to an end – and what did she have to show for it?

She enjoyed every second of satisfying the first ten orders of the night. Her specials of spiced Brittany crab soup, duck breast à l'orange with spiced beetroot purée and Nayomi's Sri Lankan-inspired coconut crêpe, were hot sellers, as each dish had been the first time she put them on the menu. She was going out on a high, with her own creations, her own twists on the classics she loved and that Jean-Sébastien had taught her so well.

Happily, Ethan had stayed away from the kitchen. She didn't want to see him and she didn't need him around to ruin her week. After Saturday, he could hire a number two who was *not* her, and he could do as he pleased with the restaurant.

But right now, tonight, it was hers.

Of course, one face she didn't care to see, that she hadn't managed to avoid, was Alexander's. He swanned into the kitchen with his usual air of smug, conceited, chauvinistic jackass about him and leaned over the pass.

'Emily Blanchon is here.'

Maggie had been carefully dripping pea oil dressing onto a dish and paused with her bottle mid-air. 'To see me?'

Alexander's face was like thunder – Maggie had never entirely understood that phrase before now but it seemed appropriate for the way he glowered at her; dark and stormy. 'To eat. To review. To tear you apart again, no doubt.'

Maggie kept her calm, finishing her dish and calling 'Service, please,' before she stood up fully to face Alexander and wiped down her hands on a towel. 'She's only just reviewed us, why would she be here again?'

'How the fuck am I supposed to know, Maggie? Do I look like a mind reader? Why the hell couldn't she wait a week?' He snarled. 'Do not make my restaurant look foolish again. Do you hear me?'

If it hadn't been her last week, she might have tried a diplomatic response. But tonight, she responded in a manner that was wholly unlike her. Tonight, she'd had enough of men and the man in front of her in particular.

'Go screw yourself, Alexander. I'll cook the way I cook. If she doesn't like it, fire me. Oh wait… You already did that.'

She stared at him, her hands braced on her hips, until he huffed and puffed and blew his way back out of her kitchen.

Why was Emily there?

After sending Charles to investigate, it turned out Emily had arrived alone. Though the reservation had been booked by someone called Janey, Emily wasn't trying to hide her presence. It was disconcerting to Maggie. *But really, how much worse could things get anyway?*

When her check came on, Emily had ordered Maggie's specials for each of her three courses, going so far as to place her order for dessert in advance.

Maggie called the check but unlike usual, she asked her sous chef to take the pass and she wandered the floor, checking in on each component element of Emily's starter, the soup base, the fresh crab and coriander to be added just before serving, even the bread selection that was taken to her table.

She waited anxiously for what felt like endless minutes after the soup was served.

Finally, Charles appeared. 'Go on,' she said.

'But for the shells from the crab claw, the bowl is spotlessly clean, she even mopped up with the coconut bread.'

Maggie breathed a sigh of relief as Charles gestured to the waiter who returned to the kitchen with the clear dish.

'Ms. Blanchon sent her compliments to the chef. She said the soup was exquisite, amongst the best she had ever tasted. And… I forget her exact words but she basically loved the sweetness of the crab with the spice combination. Oh, ah, they complemented each other perfectly. Yes, that was it, perfect opposites.'

Maggie bit down on her bottom lip with hopeful anticipation. Equal and opposite; that was what Jean-Sébastien had always taught her.

As she processed Emily's feedback, she realised Ethan had been right, and Isabella had been right; she wasn't going against the way Jean-Sébastien had taught her, she was doing exactly as he had taught her, just in her own way.

She glanced around the kitchen, ready to call out the main course and her eyes found Nayomi's, who grinned and mouthed, *You've got this.*

Oddly, it was exactly what Maggie needed to hear. *She did have this.*

She wasn't sure why Emily had turned up again so soon and there was every chance another scathing review could follow her visit. But it didn't matter because, Maggie realised, she was proud of herself tonight. She didn't need praise from anyone else because somehow, from somewhere, she had found faith in herself.

Chapter Twenty-Seven

Emily

While she waited for her main course, Emily took in the restaurant, already half full for the evening – thankfully, her scathing critique hadn't stopped that.

I was lucky they let me step foot through the door after the last review, Emily thought.

But she had been welcomed back, though she suspected not without suspicion, and her fellow diners were smiling and happy, in love. She remembered how the place used to make her feel that way, too.

Soon it would look different, not like her dad's restaurant but like someone else's. Photographs of the elegant dining room would become memories only.

By midnight, she hoped she would have gone some way towards redeeming herself in her dad's eyes.

Having overheard Maggie in her mom's kitchen, Emily had been desperate to try Maggie's new offerings. More than that, she was desperate for them to be great. If her starter of spiced Brittany crab soup was anything to go by, she was hopeful. Truly and honestly, she wanted to be able to write a rave review of the changes Maggie had made in recent weeks.

Despite having sent back evidence that she had devoured her starter, when her main course of duck à l'orange with a twist of spiced beetroot purée arrived, Emily sensed the waiter's nerves. She hoped that Maggie wasn't in the kitchen suffering with the same nervousness. *After Emily's last review, how could she not be?*

'Enjoy,' the waiter said, nodding subtly, his hands held behind his back.

Before Emily could pick up her knife and fork, a familiar face appeared at the table, as smartly dressed as ever.

'Good evening, Emily,' Charles said.

She had already spotted him, of course, giving his understudy instructions and she had wondered if he would come over. Now, in close proximity to him, Emily felt a pang of embarrassment and guilt in equal measure. 'Hi, Charles. How are you?'

He leaned his head to one side and she half expected him to give her a dressing down, to tell her she wasn't welcome, that he was disappointed in her and her dad would have been too. But after a momentary pause, one so short most people would have missed it but long enough for Emily to read what Charles chose to leave unsaid, he smiled.

'I hope you are here for good reason.'

Emily gave a meek smile and nodded. 'My intentions are good, Charles, I promise.'

'Very good. I see you've ordered the chef's specials. You might just be surprised by your old friend.'

'So far so good, and by the look and smell of this duck, it might only get better,' she said. 'Would you pair the wine for me?'

Charles beamed. 'But of course.' At that point, he brought a bottle of red wine from behind his back and poured a half glass with a wink.

With that simple wink, Emily realised she had missed so much – the restaurant, the kitchen, the banter between the chefs and the ageing charm of Charles.

'How are you, Charles?' she asked.

'Getting older. Sad and tired without my friend. How are you and beautiful Isabella?'

Emily shrugged. Her days of pretending her dad's death hadn't affected her were over. 'Getting older. Sad and tired. Add to that a pinch of bitterness, a teaspoon of regret and a tablespoon of remorse.'

Charles considered her, his frame seeming to sink slightly. 'He loved you very much.'

Emily felt like she mirrored Charles's posture as she told him, 'I know. And I loved him, no matter what happened between us.'

Charles nodded. 'I'm going to leave you with your wine. A ripe, slightly sweet pinot noir, rich enough to complement the duck, sweet enough to cut through the spice and ripe enough to bring out the caramelised sugars of the orange. You'll be impressed with the food and the beverage.'

'Thank you. Oh, and Charles, one more thing before you go. I believe there's a chef working here who's been helping Maggie with fusion ideas, I understand. Nayomi?'

'Ah, yes, a treasure.'

'Would you ask her to come out here? I'd like to meet her. I'd go back there but I'm not sure I'd be top of the guest list.'

As she waited for Nayomi, Emily tucked into her main course, devouring the tender meat forkful by forkful.

Nayomi straightened her apron as she approached Emily's table. The way she fussed was just one giveaway as to who she was – apprentice chefs just didn't exude the same level of confidence as their senior peers.

She was pretty and petite, her chef's hat almost looking too big for her small frame. Emily offered a welcoming expression as Nayomi approached. She pressed her napkin into the corners of her lips. 'Nayomi?'

The chef nodded and interlaced her fingers, letting her hands rest unnaturally at her lower torso. 'Yes.'

'I'm Emily, Emily Blanchon. Please, take a seat.'

Nayomi sat opposite Emily and less than subtly regarded Emily's near finished plate of food. 'Did you enjoy the duck?'

It wasn't the ordinary way of a critic to remark on the food and give the game away, but Emily was breaking the mould with this review in any event. So, she told Nayomi in detail how exquisite the duck dish had presented and tasted, watching as her eyes seemed to light up.

'I understand you've been inspirational in the kitchen recently.'

Nayomi blushed. 'I just offer what I know. I love to cook.'

Emily was pleased with the response. It was exactly what her dad would have wanted to hear. *Skills can be learned*, he used to say, *but passion can't be taught.*

'You might be wondering why I asked to meet you,' Emily said. 'Two reasons, really. I was keen to meet the person Maggie has been raving about and who inspired her to try something new. I also wanted to meet the newest chef to receive a place in chef school through my dad's programme, to say congratulations. And the two dishes I've eaten so far this evening more than justify Maggie's recommendation for the course.'

Nayomi visibly relaxed. 'Thank you. The place on the course means so much to me, truly. I'll try my best not to let anyone down.'

'You only have to try your best, Nayomi. And have fun. Enjoy it. It's surprisingly easy to forget that part.' *Emily had certainly forgotten that at some point and she had fought hard to find pleasure in cooking again.*

Nayomi stood and once again, straightened her apron. 'Well, thank you, Emily.'

Then she started to walk away. No, *It's nice to meet you.* No parting niceties.

As Emily was processing that, Nayomi turned and came back to her table. 'Emily, I don't want to say this. I know I shouldn't, not after everything I've been offered. And I really am grateful but I wouldn't be true to myself if I walked away and didn't say this…'

Emily rested back in her seat, feeling like she knew what was coming. Part of her welcomed it. 'Go ahead.'

'I don't know why you're here tonight. Everyone is wondering. We all read your review, after all.' Nayomi seemed to grow in confidence. As she rolled her shoulders back, Emily no longer saw an apprentice chef but a woman, a strong woman. 'Maggie is my friend. She's a good person and an exceptional chef. She didn't deserve that review. It was hard enough that she lost someone she cared about, then her job. She fights so hard to be the best, constantly battling against people like Alexander, the manager, and you… you tore her apart. I really hope that you're here to put right a wrong tonight.'

Then her confidence was gone, as she looked down to her hands where she was twisting her fingers between each other. 'If my saying that risks my place in chef school, then so be it.'

Emily considered the woman in front of her, oddly happy for her honesty. Happy that she had stood up for Maggie, for doing the right thing.

'You haven't risked your place, Nayomi.' She swallowed a lump in her throat. 'Maggie is lucky to have someone like you looking out for her.' *That used to be her role and she wanted it back.*

Emily watched Nayomi head back to the kitchen, envious of her courage. Knowing she was trying to get back on the good path.

And as she waited for her final plate of the evening, she thought about how much was at stake. Her dad's good opinion of her. Her chance to rekindle a friendship she had thrown away and so desperately wanted back. Her job at *NYT*.

Earlier that day, Emily had put on a work dress and headed to the *New York Times* building.

'If it isn't my AWOL head critic,' her boss had said, leaning back in his desk chair and bouncing the end of his pen against his desk when she entered his office.

She had somehow refrained from rolling her eyes. 'If it isn't my dramatic head of section.' She had taken a seat on the opposite side of his desk. 'You knew where I was, Archer. I was working from home. I've submitted to you on time every week.'

'So, you're back now? Do you have a *new* review for me? One not based on notes that are months old?'

'Actually, I have a favour to ask.'

Archer's expression had been incredulous. 'You've turned up to the office, but I wouldn't say you have favours in the bag. What's do you want?'

'The review I wrote of Jean-Sébastien's a couple of months ago. I want to publish a retraction.'

Archer had scoffed and spun in his chair like a child. 'No.'

'Archer, you didn't even think about it.'

'I don't need to think about it now because I thought about it before that review was published. I asked you if it was a legitimate review and you assured me it was.'

'I know. And I do stand by some of the comments. I just think it was too much. I wasn't in the right headspace.'

'If there's truth in it, semantics don't matter. A retraction is embarrassing for the department. It says we either lied or did a shoddy job. Either way, that's not something I'm going to support. It's a hard no.'

'Archer, we're talking about someone's career here. Someone's life. I didn't appreciate at the time that Maggie was trying to keep a legacy going. She wasn't being boring or unimaginative, she was trying to keep the spirit of Jean-Sébastien's alive.'

Archer had stood from his desk. 'Emily, I've got things to do. The answer is no, and I expect a review in my inbox by midnight for publication. A *new* review.'

A new review. Emily had stood to face Archer. 'How about a compromise? I can give you a new review by midnight.'

'What's the catch?'

'I'll go back to Jean-Sébastien's. I understand the menu has changed, so it's an excuse to review again.'

'Isn't Ethan James taking over from next week?'

'Yes, but I can build in an angle about changes we expect to see.'

'We only published the last review weeks ago.'

'I said it's a compromise. I've given you years of hard work, Archer.'

'And those years will be undermined by a second review. You're bringing emotion to the job.'

Emily had been prepared to go as far as necessary. 'Archer, if you don't let me do this, I'll quit.'

He hid his shock well, but Emily hadn't missed the initial reaction. 'It means *that* much to you?'

'It does.'

Archer sighed. 'I'm making no promises. If you come at it from the right angle and it works, I'll *consider* publishing the review.'

Emily had already known that her re-review would be her final act for the *New York Times* and she was ready. The review meant more to her than the job and when he reflected, Archer would know that too.

Back at her table in the restaurant, Emily was served a coconut crêpe unlike any crêpe she had tasted before. Full of dark honey and coconut, cinnamon, and a crêpe so light she didn't feel too full. The flavours danced in her mouth and she found herself smiling as she hummed in appreciation of the dessert.

What made her happier than any of the food, though, was that she was going to be able to write a stellar review and submit a piece to Archer by midnight that would make Maggie's new creativity shine. No lies, no emotions, just an unbiased critique of a magnificent menu. An unbiased critique that made her incredibly pleased for her old friend.

Perhaps, at least on some level, Maggie would understand that Emily still cared for her. That she was grateful for the way she had stayed in her parents' lives, even though it had taken years for Emily to realise those things herself.

When Emily arrived home from the restaurant, Isabella was still awake on the sofa in the lounge, watching a movie.

'Hello, darling. How did it go?'

Emily smiled. 'It was great, Mom. Maggie is going to be just fine. I've got one more trick up my sleeve for her, if I can pull it off.'

'Oh yes?'

Emily nodded. 'You'll see, hopefully.'

Isabella patted the space on the sofa next to her. 'Why don't you come and watch the end of the movie with me?'

Emily checked her watch. 'I need to write my review and send it to my editor, but I can sit for a few minutes.'

She nestled into her mom's side, feeling... contented. Something she hadn't felt in a very long time.

'Are you still sure you're making the right decision with work?' Isabella asked.

'I'm just going with my gut and my gut is saying I've felt happier since I made the decision.'

'Then it must be the right one, darling. I can't wait to read your book already.'

Closing her eyes, Emily let her mind wander to France. To rolling hills of vines. To driving through the countryside in an open-top car, the sun on her face, the wind in her hair. To eating and cooking the best France has to offer. To seeing long-lost relatives. And to sitting down in Paris to write up her own adventures and recipes.

She eventually prized herself away from the dream, kissed Isabella on the forehead and went upstairs to write her review. As soon as the review was published, Emily would submit her resignation and begin the rest of her life.

Change can be a fine thing.
Emily Blanchon for the New York Times.

With my previous review of Jean-Sébastien's at the Grande Parisienne Hotel having been published only two months ago, it is unconventional that I would review the restaurant again so soon.

Why have I? Well, because I was informed of changes to the menu that sufficiently piqued my interest to draw me back. Rarely are food reviewers welcomed back to a restaurant they have critically reviewed.

Before arriving at Jean-Sébastien's this time around, I admit, I was anxious about how my presence would be received. My nerves were unfounded. I was greeted with the usual grace and high standard of service that diners have come to expect from the three-Michelin star fine-dining restaurant.

In a bid to put rumours to the test, I ordered the chef's special menu. Of course, that had been my intention on arrival but on perusing the dishes, I was salivating at the descriptions alone – crisp roasted canard with caramelised orange segments and Sri Lankan spiced beetroot.

For starter, I enjoyed Brittany crab curry soup, a lightly spiced twist on a French dish. I was immediately struck by the aromas of cardamom, cumin and ginger, then by the sight of the smooth yellow curry soup and a mass of sweet white crab meat, topped with a crab claw and fresh coriander. The first spoonful of soup was a taste explosion in my mouth. The savoury sauce was balanced perfectly by the sweetness of delicate white crab meat, and light enough not to lose the depth of flavour from the brown meat. It had the heart of an autumn dish and the lightness of summer.

The duck main course tasted even better than its description. The skin was flawlessly crisped with deep pink hidden beneath. The contrast of sweet caramelised oranges with spiced beetroot purée can only be described as delectably moreish.

For dessert, I was treated to the lightness of a classic French crêpe with a sweet honey and cinnamon coconut centre. The freshness of the ground coconut was a sponge for the sweet spices.

If the food wasn't enough, the wine was impeccably matched.

The crux is, there has been change at Jean-Sébastien's under the reign of temporary head chef, Maggie Hill. And change has proven to be a fine thing. The chef's talents were on display like a top-dollar exhibition in a gallery of art, her creations masterful.

On reflection, what I had previously misinterpreted as a lack of imagination, it seems, was the intention to uphold the legacy of a great man and a great chef, Jean-Sébastien Blanchon. In fact, the temporary head chef has worked hard to maintain the elegance of the French classics of her predecessor, while adding a wonderfully balanced twist with the exciting exotic flavours of South Asia. She has succeeded in creating a fusion of culinary excellence amongst the finest I have tasted.

Every dish was bursting with flavour and the wow factor of the food at Dillon Kerridge's Waterlily, which readers will know I hold in very high esteem. Yet, there is nothing quite like Maggie Hill's new dishes. They are artistry. Her own flair and stamp on the fine dining scene.

I had previously said that Jean-Sébastien's restaurant would need to be rescued by incoming executive and head chef, household name, Ethan James. Now, I would suggest the celebrity chef will need to be at the very top of his game if he is to match the standard of what is currently being served at Jean-Sébastien's.

And if Jean-Sébastien is looking down from a culinary heaven, he could feel nothing other than proud of the way his legacy has been honoured by Maggie Hill.

Chapter Twenty-Eight

Maggie

As she read the words on her phone screen, Maggie didn't know whether to laugh or cry. She scrolled down the *New York Times* website, her other hand pressed to lips that trembled as certain lines and phrases jumped out at her. She knew the food she served Emily had been good. This was a new version of herself, one that knew she had talent. What brought tears to her eyes was Emily's endorsement that Maggie had honoured Jean-Sébastien's legacy. And what surprised her, was that she now had an answer to the question she had been asking herself since Emily turned up at the restaurant on Tuesday – *was Emily doing this to put the nail in the coffin of Maggie's career, or was she doing it as some kind of redemption?*

After a shower, Maggie dressed quickly, with just minutes to spare before Nayomi and her boys arrived to go for breakfast. Nayomi had said she no longer needed to work two jobs with her grant from Jean-Sébastien's programme, and the boys had the day off school for teacher training. The truth, Maggie suspected, was that Nayomi had made plans so that Maggie wouldn't be alone if Emily's review came out this morning and was bad.

It was rare and welcome to have people and noise in her apartment, though as the boys chased Livvy around the place, Maggie figured the cat would feel less pleased about it.

'Should I stop them?' Nayomi asked.

'Meh, it's good exercise for her. She'll sleep while we're out. Make yourself comfortable in the lounge, I'm just going to grab my handbag and boots.'

But Maggie was stopped in her tracks by the intercom. 'Maggie, it's Emily. Could I come up?'

'It's Emily,' Maggie told Nayomi as she waited for Emily to come up to the apartment.

Nayomi's expression put Maggie at ease. 'I think maybe it's a good thing?'

When Maggie opened the door, Emily looked uncertain. Her voice had no conviction as she said, 'Hi.'

Maggie waved and immediately felt like an idiot. 'Hi.'

'Thank you for letting me in.'

Maggie shrugged, knowing that deep down, she had wanted Emily to come. 'Come in. We're just about to head out but we can spare a few minutes.'

Emily was almost tripped by Livvy as she scooted by in a hurry, breaking the palpable tension in the room. Emily peered around Maggie and held up a hand in greeting to Nayomi.

'I won't take up your time. I just came to say… I just want you to know, that I meant every word of my review, Maggie. Your food was… is… incredible. You blew me away with every course and Dad would have been so proud of you.'

Emily's words caught Maggie off guard, stealing her next breath.

'And I want you to know how sorry I am about the first review. I tried to retract it but the paper wouldn't let me. When I wrote it… God, Maggie, I'm so sorry, I wasn't thinking straight.'

When her shock subsided, Maggie was left relieved, more than that, happy. 'I don't need an apology, Emily. In fact, maybe I should say thank you. For the new review and, believe it or not, the first review being a kick up the ass that I needed.'

'I could have done it more tactfully, I'm sure.'

Maggie twisted her lips, then gave a short laugh. 'Yeah, maybe.' She noticed what looked like flour on Emily's black cardigan and reached out to brush it clean. 'What have you been baking?'

Emily rubbed the dirty spot on her clothes. 'Just a bloomer. I think I was nervous-baking, trying to build up the courage to come over here.'

'I'm really pleased you did.' And Maggie meant it. *Was it too much to think she might be able to get her old friend back? Did the old Emily still exist? She was convinced she did, somewhere.* 'It's great to see you back in the kitchen, where you belong.'

Emily nodded thoughtfully. 'It's funny you should mention that. I gave notice of my resignation to the paper today. Do you remember the trip I always wanted to take, around France?'

Maggie had fond memories of sticking pins in a map to help Emily plan her route. 'And the book?'

'Yup. I'm finally going to do it.'

Maggie smiled, so happy for her old friend to be doing what she had always dreamed of. So thankful to see a glimpse of old Emily. 'He'd be proud of you too, you know?'

'I'm certainly going to try to make him proud.'

'I meant he already would be.'

'I'm not so sure about that but speaking of making amends,' Emily pulled the sleeves of her cardigan lower on her hands, 'Maggie, is there any way that you might even be willing to consider… us being friends again, some day?'

Joy soared through Maggie's body. 'I thought you'd never ask.' She wrapped her arms around Emily and felt Emily embrace her back. 'I missed you.'

'I missed you, too. And me.' They separated and Emily's smile faded. 'Now that I've found you again, I'm going to try to find myself, too.'

'And perhaps a French companion,' Maggie said with a look that said, *I've got your number.*

Emily smirked. 'Couldn't hurt, could it?'

Just like that, it was as if they had travelled back in time, back to a place where they were happy and told each other about every cute guy they saw.

'Erm, Emily, if you're free, you're more than welcome to join us for breakfast,' Nayomi said, coming closer to them. 'My boys are a little over-excited.' She gestured to the kitchen, where they could hear the boys, still teasing the cat. 'But it would be really nice to meet you, properly.'

Emily grinned, swiping a thumb under her eye. 'I would love that.'

On her way home from breakfast, buoyed by having a wonderful time with an old friend, a new friend, and two incredible young boys, Maggie's phone alerted her to a new message.

Maggie stopped in the middle of the sidewalk, staring at the message, receiving expletives from passers-by in the process. Her bright mood was instantly catapulted to sadness.

She wanted Ethan to call. Despite how new their... *thing* was, she missed him, even though she was also pleased not to have seen him. If she saw him, she would want to kiss him. She would want to forget about his offer for her to be his number two, second best. And the facts hadn't changed. He saw her as sub-standard to him. He didn't see her as a head chef of her own kitchen.

How could they ever work if that was the starting point?

Nevertheless, when her phone rang, her heart leapt until she saw that it wasn't Ethan calling her, it was an unknown number in the city.

'Hello. Maggie speaking.'

'Maggie, this is Dillon Kerridge. We've met once before when my restaurant Waterlily opened, you might remember?'

'Oh, ah, yeah, I remember. Hi Dillon.' Her response was stilted but the call was entirely unexpected, if not bizarre. *How did he even have her...?*

'I hope it's okay to call. Emily Blanchon gave me your number.'

Oh.

'I saw Emily's review of your restaurant in the *New York Times* this morning and she called me, raving about your

301

new take on fusion. Anyway, as it happens, I've opened up a new restaurant recently, which is where I'm going to be dedicating my time. The head chef I have in Waterlily is ready to move on and Emily's timing was, I guess, very serendipitous. I don't know if you're a free agent or if you've got your next moved lined up already but I'd love to meet with you. Get you into Waterlily for an interview for head chef, if you're interested?'

Interested?

Inside, she was squealing with delight but she managed to respond calmly. 'I've been considering my options but don't have any firm plans as yet. The opportunity at Waterlily sounds interesting, I'd love to come in to discuss it further with you.'

'Great. How are you fixed this afternoon?'

'I could do four o' clock, between lunch and dinner service?'

'Perfect, see you then. I look forward to it.'

Was today real? Had she actually woken up this morning?

She turned on the spot, grinning like Julia Roberts, looking for someone with whom she could share her good news. But all she received in return were tuts and a 'watch it, lady'.

—

'You guys, thanks so much for this. I really appreciate the send-off.'

Maggie held up her glass of wine but kept her words short. She wasn't one for big shows, certainly not one for public speaking, and, in truth, she was feeling a little overwhelmed and emotional about her last night at Jean-Sébastien's.

The other chefs had cleared with Alexander extra drinks after the Saturday night service, which she had a feeling had been instigated by Nayomi and Charles. They had all changed out of their uniforms and were sitting around tables in the dining room with free access to the bar.

'Now, get drunk, it's free,' she added, receiving a cheer in return. 'Or, rather, it's coming directly out of Alexander's top line.' The second cheer was bigger still.

Maggie took a seat as the others either took seats, stood in conversation or wandered to the bar. From where she was sitting, Maggie noticed the subtle way in which Ashley touched Nayomi's arm while they waited for drinks. A light, tender stroke as they stood very close together. A quiet move that spoke volumes.

'Ma chérie,' Charles said, coming to sit on a chair next to Maggie, with a glass of Sancerre he had chosen for her, and one for himself. Charles was the only member of staff who hadn't changed his clothes because his typical attire both in and out of work was a suit.

'It feels like the end of an era,' Maggie told him.

'That's because it is.' Charles looked around the restaurant. 'I'll be sad to leave. The place feels like a good friend. Lots of memories.'

'You're leaving?'

'Yes. It's not for me, all this change. I liked working here, in the place I knew, with Jean-Sébastien.' He rocked his shoulder gently into Maggie's. 'My Maggie.'

They shared a sombre smile and Maggie brought her head to rest on his familiar shoulder.

'I'm going to retire. It's my last night, too.'

Maggie sat up straight and looked at Charles. 'Tonight? I didn't even know you'd put in your notice.'

He nodded. 'When I knew you were going, I started to think I would go too. So, we are just peas in a pod, as people say.'

'Charles, Dillion Kerridge called me this week. You know, the chef who—'

Charles chuckled. 'I know who Dillon Kerridge is, darling. I have a television.'

Maggie blushed. 'Well, I took an interview with him earlier this week and, subject to ironing out a few details...' She couldn't help herself from smiling as she took a sip of her wine.

'Go on.'

'You're looking at the next head chef of Waterlily.'

'Ma chérie!' Charles set down his glass and held Maggie's face between his hands. 'I knew you could do it, you beautiful, special lady. Oh, Maggie, I am so incredibly happy.'

'Come with me. Come to Waterlily and be my sommelier.'

Charles smiled as he shook his head. 'Thank you, Maggie, for inviting me to be part of your next success. If anyone could keep me from retirement, it would be you.' He kissed her cheek. 'But I'm ready to put my feet up. To spend more time with my family. I would like nothing more than to come to your restaurant and eat your wonderful food and be served wine that I do not have to pour myself.'

'Okay. Okay, Charles. But if you change your mind...'

'You will be the first person I tell, ma chérie.'

'Make sure I am. And I'll make sure every visit to Waterlily is on the house.'

'We brought you another,' Nayomi said, handing Maggie a second glass of wine as Ashley handed the same to Charles.

'Double-parked. This hasn't happened for more than a decade. One outing with Emily and she's already having an influence,' Maggie told her, accepting the drink. 'So, can I check, are you two…?'

Ashley and Nayomi looked at each other like two love-sick teenagers.

'I think that's great. I'm happy for you both,' she said. 'Erm, gents, would you mind giving me a minute with Nayomi, please?'

When Nayomi took a seat, Maggie explained the proposition from Waterlily. That she would take a month off first and travel around South Asia, exploring the local cuisine to bring ideas back to the restaurant.

'And, I want to know if you'll come to work with me. As a commis chef, at first, but with a view to working your way up the ranks? What do you think?'

Nayomi didn't say anything but she held Maggie's gaze and slowly her lips curved up. 'I've spent so long scrimping and scraping. Bringing up the boys alone as best I could.' She exhaled heavily. 'Do you ever have a day when you think, have I woken up yet? So many good things have been happening to me and the boys since you hired me, Maggie. I just don't know how to thank you.'

'Nayomi, your talent and the person you are, they were there already.'

'But no one took a chance on me before you.'

'Should I take that as a "yes"?'

Nayomi's eyes filled with tears and she nodded her head, half-laughing. 'Yes. It's a huge yes.'

As the women hugged, Maggie found herself thinking, not for the first time, just how much she and Nayomi had in common.

She was thrilled for Nayomi to have two wonderful boys, a job she enjoyed and, now, Ashley.

Maggie felt like recently, a lid had been lifted on her need for relationships, friendships, that she couldn't replace. Now, she had Emily back and Nayomi in her life.

But as she had that thought, Maggie's mind drifted to New Jersey. To the farm visit with Ethan and Annie. She drifted to Central Park and the laughter she had shared with Ethan at the lake. Maggie had fought for so long to have the job she wanted. She had that now.

So maybe it was time to work on the other things that might make her life as complete as Nayomi's.

–

'Can I come in?'

Maggie paused with her hand on the intercom. Not because she didn't want to see Ethan. She did. She really did. But because she knew that when she saw him, there was a danger she would sweep everything under the carpet and the fact was, nothing had changed since he asked her to be his number two. Since she came to understand that he would always be the guy who stole her job.

She leaned against the door to her apartment, her finger still braced on the buzzer. But something had changed. Something fundamental had changed.

Maggie wasn't in need of Ethan's praise. She had found belief in herself. It was a seismic shift in the mindset she had had all of her life. A work in progress, she was certain, but a step towards a stronger, better version of herself.

And she could acknowledge that Ethan hadn't stolen her job, or if he had, wasn't she better off in any event? Hadn't her hand been forced? Hadn't she been compelled to find *herself* in her cooking?

Ethan's voice came over the intercom again. 'Maggie? Are you there? Fine, I'll just stand here on the street and tell you how I feel about you. You like PDA, right?'

That would do it. 'That's unfair. You're targeting my weak spot.'

'If you let me inside, I promise to play fair.'

With a deep breath, she buzzed him inside and opened the door, waiting for Ethan to appear.

A minute later, he was coming towards her, walking carefully it seemed, with a large cardboard box in his arms.

In response to Maggie's silent scrutiny of the box, he said, 'You'll see.'

Inside, he headed for the kitchen and set the box on the table. 'Can you give me a minute?'

'Give you a minute?' Maggie asked. 'This is my apartment. I haven't spoken to you all week and you've shown up here unannounced and told me to leave my own kitchen.' She wasn't a person for conflict and, truly, she was more intrigued that annoyed.

Ethan must have sensed this as he twisted that damn gorgeous half smile, half smirk on his lips, gently pressed a fingertip to Maggie's lips and told her, 'I gave you space this week. You needed some time. *We* needed some time. And it took me probably longer than it should have for me to appreciate exactly what and how badly I did wrong. I didn't want to ruin your last week at the restaurant. So, can you just give me one minute? Please? Because words really aren't my forte.'

Maggie did as he asked, a little confused and a whole lot fascinated by whatever was going on in her kitchen as she sat on the sofa and waited.

'Okay, I'm ready.' Ethan appeared in front of her. 'Close your eyes. Trust me.'

She closed her eyes and he took her hands in his, guiding her to the kitchen.

'You can open them.'

When she did, Maggie saw the most incredible sight. It was like Jurassic Park. Herbs and edible flowers covered a large round tray, trailing over the sides and some standing tall. Between them, dry ice bellowed like a tropical storm. As she looked more closely, she saw different colours and shapes of eggs. They looked like...

'Dinosaur eggs?' she asked.

'Yes. Prehistoric. Like me. Or how I must have seemed when I asked you to be my sous chef.'

From somewhere, tropical sounds began to play out into the room, then the sounds of dinosaurs, making Maggie chuckle.

Ethan smiled. 'I get it now. What you heard was that I think I'm better than you. That I thought you were only good enough to be second to me. Like I was stuck in a time where men behaved like dinosaurs.'

She raised one eyebrow. 'Didn't you think those things?'

'No.' He shook his head. 'Take an egg. One of the white ones,' he said, offering Maggie a tiny spoon, smaller than a teaspoon.

She reached out and took an egg, the top lifting off to reveal an orange yolk and a fluffy egg white.

'Try it,' Ethan instructed.

She did. To her surprise, she wasn't hit by a savoury taste but by a rich orange cream, then a vanilla white chocolate mousse that was as light as air. She felt her eyes go wide with surprise and delight.

'This is you. I'm no good with words, so I want to show you how unexpected and incredible you are, Maggie, just like this egg.'

His idiocy was adorable. 'I'm an egg.'

He laughed, short and gentle, then looked into her eyes. 'When I asked you to be my sous chef, I wasn't asking you to be secondary to me. I wanted to show you that I think you're incredible, Maggie. That I'd be privileged to work with you. The way you have taken on the last three months has been nothing short of admirable. The new dishes you've created have been outstanding.'

He raised his arms from his sides, as if in surrender. 'I wanted to help. You didn't have anything lined up for work and I knew that it was only a matter of time before someone else saw your greatness. So, I guess I wanted to buy you time. But more than that, I wanted to use some of your professionalism, your perfectionism and your genius to make my kitchen even better.'

He gave her a weak smile and took the empty egg shell from her hand, placing it on the kitchen table, where the dry ice was still frothing, crawling across the table, making her feel like she was in a dream world. 'I'd also enjoyed my time in the kitchen with you.'

'Even though I couldn't stand you most of the time?'

'Even though.' He reached up to brush her hair back from her temple. 'I wanted to spend more time with you. Asking you to work for me was more of a request for you to work *with* me, Maggie. It couldn't have been further from an attempt to belittle you. In my mind, at least. I appreciate that message didn't translate and I see why.'

Ethan leant over the jungle and picked out a perfectly spherical rose-pink egg with a gold dust sheer.

'I'd also like you to know that my first two hires in the restaurant are women. Not as good as you, obviously, but I heard you, and I won't let my restaurant be a chauvinistic place to work. Decent people will have fair opportunities.'

Maggie nodded. 'That's all we want.'

'Open your mouth.'

Maggie did as instructed. Ethan placed the ball onto her tongue. She closed her eyes as she closed her mouth around the sweet treat and bit down. When she pierced the hard shell, smooth liquid spilled from the centre, rose-hip and champagne trickling into her mouth. She groaned with the sheer delight of the surprise soft centre.

'This is me,' Ethan said. Though her eyes were closed, she could feel his increased proximity, his heat near her body, his breath on her lips. 'On the outside, I try to have this flashy shell, covered in gold. That's the perception people have of me, and the one I've always tried to give. But if you can bring yourself to break through that cocksure shell, you'll find a gooey-eyed guy.'

Maggie opened her eyes and found Ethan's sincere gaze, focused entirely on her.

'The only other person to melt my heart before you was Annie. I don't know how you did it or why you. Why after all these years.'

She opened her eyes, licking the last of the dessert from her lips. 'You're so cheesy.' She laughed and he laughed with her.

Then he sobered, raising his hands to her face, angling her mouth towards him. 'I know. It's the new me and you only have yourself to blame. But, Maggie, I'm sorry. I'm sorry I upset you and this is me, telling you that my gooey centre is all yours.'

'Ethan, I got a job. Head chef at Waterlily.'

He nodded. 'I heard that on the grapevine.'

She took hold of his hands, removing them from her face and holding them between hers. 'Did you hear on the grapevine that I'm leaving for a month to travel around South Asia?'

There was a flicker of disappointment in his eyes that was genuine; she truly believed that. 'No, I didn't.' He leaned his forehead against hers. 'I'll be right here when you get back. Gooey centre and all. I'm in this for the long haul, Maggie, if you'll have me.'

Even if she had tried, she wouldn't have been able to stop the curve of her lips. As the dry ice dream played out around them, Maggie raised *her* hands to *his* face. And she kissed him. Long and slow, giving him her answer with each second they were melded together.

Epilogue

3 months later...

'Check on. One duck salad. Two vegetable crêpe rolls. One chilli langoustine.'

'Yes, Chef.'

Maggie stuck the paper check into the rim of the pass and turned to watch her chefs – a few of them familiar faces who had decided to follow her to Waterlily from Jean-Sébastien's.

The kitchen was busy; reservations to dine had to be booked twelve weeks in advance and her boss and executive chef were happy with how things were going. The standard of food, even she would admit, was worthy of the two Michelin stars the restaurant held.

But what pleased Maggie more than any of that, was how happy the kitchen was. Everyone wanted to work together and they wanted to work for her. She was enjoying drawing on her experiences from her time in India and Sri Lanka to craft new dishes and discover new combinations of ingredients with the freedom Dillon Kerridge allowed her over the menus.

And Maggie was happy. She had proven herself, not just to others but to herself. She believed she was good enough.

As the next components arrived at the pass, she tested the tenderness of the meat to determine how it was cooked, dipped a teaspoon into the jus to confirm it tasted exactly as it should, and pinched the carrots Nayomi handed to her to make sure they were just the softer side of al dente.

'Perfect,' she said, receiving a grin from Nayomi.

When the Saturday night service had finished, she shared drinks with her staff, sampling the newest creations on the cocktail menu. Lychees, passion fruit, coconut and pineapple offered twists on classic recipes.

She felt part of something, truly.

At one a.m. her phone vibrated. She stepped out of the back door to the kitchen to see Ethan waiting on his motorbike.

'Ready?'

She kissed him briefly as she took the helmet he offered to her. 'Ready.'

Hopping onto the back of his bike, she wrapped her arms around his waist. 'How was service?' she asked when they were weaving through Manhattan's traffic.

'Good. And yours?'

'Good.'

Leaning her head against his back, she hugged him tightly, tired and looking forward to crawling into bed next to him for a cosy sleep before their big day with Annie at Coney Island tomorrow.

–

Those lychee cocktails were Nayomi's new favourite thing about Saturdays but boy were they strong. She felt giddy from just two. Then again, she felt giddy a lot these days and it had something to do with having only one job, which she loved, doing well in chef school, which made her feel accomplished, her boys being able to go on school trips without her worrying about how she would pay for them, and something to do with the man sitting next to her in the staff car.

They pulled up outside her apartment and she and Ashley went inside together. They had reached the point that Ashley stayed over most weekends but not during the week, which they agreed would be best for the boys for the time being.

Ashley's mom and Farah mostly split childcare and Nayomi felt better now that she could offer Farah at least some money for her time. Ashley had fixed just about everything that was broken in Nayomi's apartment and maybe… in the future… that would help her sell it. *If* things stayed on track as they were. Because right now, her life felt pretty great.

Inside the apartment, Farah was just finishing watching a romcom, then she said goodnight and left Nayomi and Ashley to it.

Nayomi went quietly to Roshan and Nuwan's bedroom, kissing Roshan on the cheek and pulling the duvet over his exposed shoulders. When she got to Nuwan, he rolled over and opened his eyes.

'Hey,' she whispered.

'Is Ashley here?'

'Yes.'

'Can he say goodnight to me?'

Smiling, Nayomi kissed his brow and stroked his hair. 'I'll send him in.'

With the boys safely tucked up in bed, Nayomi and Ashley showered and got into bed together, her tucked tightly against his chest, his big arm holding her tight.

Life was more than pretty great. It was perfect.

—

'Bonjour, mademoiselle,' Emily said. '*Aimeriez-vous goûter?*'

When the young lady standing in front of her nodded her head in the affirmative, Emily spooned a portion of her shellfish soup into an eco-friendly cup and leaned across the table of her market stall pop-up restaurant to serve.

She was currently in a little village called Samur, where the wine was delectable, the bread to die for and the men, well, they were really quite scrumptious, too.

Emily was truly living out her dream. For almost three months, she had been travelling around France. She had met long-lost relatives, who had all welcomed her with open arms, and for days at a time would show her their highlights of local food.

Since being in Samur, she had met a rather handsome man, with a pert bottom, who wore silk shirts and tight-fighting chinos and slicked his hair back like something out of the movies – all bronzed and Mediterranean-looking. Said man happened to be a chef at a very fancy restaurant, where she had dined by design for a number of nights before he sent a free glass of wine to her table for one and asked that she wait for him to finish service.

His name was Claude and he was as sweet a treat as a raspberry macaron. They had spent days strolling the river, wine-tasting, and picnicking with what Claude said were the finest cheeses France had to offer.

Emily had tried out several of her new recipes on Claude and he had put in a word with a friend at the local market. So, for the last two weeks, Emily had trialled her dishes on the locals. She had even taken on board some suggestions for tweaks.

Slowly but surely, she was building a stack of recipes, travel stories and photographs that would eventually become the travel and food book she had always wanted to write.

She spoke to her mom almost every day and she Face-Timed with Maggie once a week, usually on a Sunday.

Who knew how long she would keep flapping her wings around France? Perhaps until she had enough material for her book. Perhaps until she had covered every inch of the beautiful country, or until the sun went to sleep for winter.

But she was free as a bird. Here, in France, she was whomever she wanted to be, doing whatever she wanted to do. She was still figuring out what those things were and, she had decided, that was okay.

She felt connected to her dad here and soon, she knew she would be able to forgive herself for not having said the things she should have said to him in recent years. Because she knew now that her dad was part of her and she was part of him. That they were perfectly equal and opposite. He would be watching over her from his cloud, scrutinising her recipes, encouraging her to be better. But most of all, he would be happy that she was happy. Because when you love someone, that's all you really you want for them.

Acknowledgements

As with every book, there is a wealth of people who make it possible.

But first, I want to thank my biggest inspiration for this book. On holiday in Sri Lanka, I found out I was pregnant with my first child. It was also the place the idea for *The Kitchen* came to life. From the idea to the end of the detailed edits for this book, I was carrying my baby. The book, like the baby, took 9 months to grow. This book belongs to my son – my inspiration, my light, my love. *The Kitchen* is such a happy book because I was so immensely happy to be carrying you.

Thank you to my husband – my travel buddy, my baby daddy, my best friend and my soulmate. You can be a real tinker when you want to be but there isn't anyone I would rather have by my side in all things, including lockdown and pregnancy.

To my friends and family who offer words of encouragement, who read my books, who listen to my stories before they really make sense. Thank you so much… I adore you.

And to that team I mentioned… thank you to my agent, Tanera Simons, who had eyes on this story earlier than ever before and championed it from the very beginning. Thank you also for keeping everything ticking over whilst I took a step back to be a new mummy.

To my wonderful editor, Emily Bedford, the book wouldn't reach readers (nor would it be as polished by half!) without your time and effort. Thank you also for the confidence you have in me and my writing, which I try my very best to take onboard. To everyone else at Canelo who has worked on this book, from the words to the cover, from marketing to sales; I am incredibly lucky and grateful to have such a talented group of people around me.

Finally but by no means least, to you, Reader, thank you for your time and for giving my work purpose. I am sending you a huge hug from this very page!

Best wishes,

Laura xx